SAVAGE MATES

OMEGA HEAT

ALLIE SANTOS

Savage Mates
Copyright © 2022 by Allie Santos
All rights reserved.
ISBN: 979-8-218-05666-7 (Paperback)

Cover Art by JV Arts.

Proofread by Melissa Tarrington from MT Editing & Proofreading Services.

This book is for my monster peen lovin' girlies and for my fellow Latinas that rarely saw themselves in the books we read—I see you.

Content Warnings

Murder (on page), Rejected Mates, Shifted/Monster Sex,
Emotional and Physical abuse

SAVAGE MATES is a Why-Choose Omega wolf-shifter novel.
There is primal play, breeding elements (no pregnancy), heats,
nesting, ruts, purring, & knotting. The main female character is
mistreated at the beginning of the book and her fated mates are
cold toward her.

There is monster smut contained within. You see the wolfman
on the cover? That's what she gets freaky with, so proceed with
that in mind.

An element of Omegaverse is a "heat" which can be considered
dub-con to some since a 'heat' is an undeniable need she must
satisfy. There is also an age-gap, but the story is set in a mythical
world and ALL characters are consenting adults above the age
of eighteen.

Once the heroine's true mates find out she's theirs, they do not
touch anyone else.

Check my website for spoiler warnings: alliesantos.net

A Note from Allie

You know those pesky rejection type of stories we get stuck on reading as we're scrolling through Facebook? The ones with some cringy—I mean cringy but like in the best way possible—as hell images that we come across on our feed. The ones where you say, 'oh that looks interesting' and you end up downloading some random app to read it lol. There was always something that called to me about the girls that couldn't defend themselves that made my heart hurt.

I always felt like it wasn't a bad thing to be soft. I understood the hopeful side of the heroine at the beginning. They were gentle souls that needed protection and love. To be spoiled. This is my version of the sweet girl that doesn't lose her soft soul, but gains strength in ways other than physical.

LIANA

I WAS A USELESS EXCUSE FOR A WEREWOLF.

"Are you almost done with the dishes, Liana?"

Tipping my chin down in an affirmative, I attempted to smile at Janice.

"What's wrong?"

The knot in my throat thickened. Crap, the tears were about to burst free.

Again.

That was the last move I should make today. Since I was already considered the weakest pack member, it didn't matter that I cried at the drop of a hat since they already saw me as pathetic, but I'd resolved to stop—unsuccessfully.

Plus, once the waterworks started, it was downhill from there, and these dishes needed to get washed. I scrubbed the grease from the pan, scraping the wire sponge across the surface to break away the grime. Finishing sooner meant I could actually spend time talking to her before I had to start dinner. So, no moping. I should be ecstatic that Janice came to visit me, since I seldom saw her.

My teeth sank into my lower lip, hard, and the sting helped me suck some of those tears back. Her concerned glances were nothing new, but I wasn't used to them. We both had it hard here, but her rank was much higher since her mate was a Beta pack enforcer. That meant she had it a pinch easier since she was able to use his position and dominance as a shield. No one wanted to get on the bad side of an enforcer.

Werewolves were primitive, instinctual creatures that thrived under the primal rule of law. All of us contained a wolf within us, separate to our human consciousness, though there were many that had a different relationship with that side of themselves. Those that had harmony between their two halves were the most successful—so I'd overheard, since I had no experience with my wolf, considering I was defective. A werewolf with a wolf so weak that it wasn't able to come out when it was supposed to when I turned eighteen. After that age, there was no use hoping to ever experience a shift.

"Liana, what's wrong?" Janice repeated.

"Feeling sorry for myself," I answered in a raspy tone. Turning my back to her, I shoved my hand in the sink drain to clean out the gunk that had collected. I used my shoulder to wipe the tear that had escaped.

There was a tug on my clothing. "Liana, how many sets of clothing do you own?"

My face heated. Thank the Moon Goddess that my back was to her.

The frayed edges of my black, featureless shirt mocked me. I didn't have to look down, because I saw them every day.

They'd worn out so rapidly because I had to wash them every other day or else I'd feel dirty. I didn't want to answer. I didn't want her to feel bad for not being here for me. Even though Janice and I lived in the same pack, we hardly saw each other more than a handful of times a month. She had bigger and better things to worry about than me.

I winced at the poke in my shoulder. She had barely tapped me, but my entire body hurt when I moved. I'd gotten used to my body aching at every moment.

"What was that?"

"Two," I repeated a little louder. I should have lied, so I didn't worry her. My body was tired, and not only was I exhausted, but it was the worst day of the year for me. Today was another reminder of how much my life sucked.

The ringing silence thickened the shame weighing on my shoulders. When Janice still said nothing, I peeked over.

Janice's eyes were bright with unshed tears, and I forced a smile.

"It's no big deal. I don't mind washing them when they need it," I hurried to assure her. "I go overboard with the scrubbing." Grimacing, I eyed the thin material.

"I should have noticed." She sniffled, and I swiftly washed and dried my hands before approaching her. I wrung the towel between my hands.

"You've been so busy since Clara moved you two years ago. I've hardly gotten to see you." She was the last person that should be blaming herself.

Janice's eyes widened, the white of her eyes showing as she studied my face. Her fingers lifted and grazed my cheekbones over the fading bruise.

This was why I hadn't wanted to face her directly. I stifled my sigh.

"You're skin and bones, Liliana," she whispered. "Did Clara do this to you?"

My shoulders lifted closer to my ears as my heart rate picked up.

Oh, no, no. No one could know how bad it was with Clara. She'd murder me. My pulse thundered in my ears.

"I can speak to the Alpha on your behalf—"

"No, please, Janice." I swallowed hard. "Calling attention to myself has never gone well." It would be bad if I involved Alpha Lore. If people started asking questions, then everything she'd done to me would come out.

I crossed my arms, tucking my hands under my armpits to hide the tremble.

No one was ever down here other than me and Clara. No one wanted this duty, so it wasn't difficult for Clara to keep them clear.

Anyway, the Alpha was always busy with many other things. She-wolves, pack disputes, and business ventures. The last thing he should be dealing with was me.

Janice's eyebrows furrowed, her gaze settling on the cookware I'd just cleaned in preparation for dinner. A frown marred her lips as her eyes flicked to the exit.

"Liliana..." she trailed off. "Have you been down here working by yourself?"

"N-no," the word stumbled out of me, awkward and too quick.

The sound of Janice's teeth clicking made me suck in a breath.

"It's been two years since I was pushed out of here, but I know how it works. Others should have been in and out of this place preparing the dinner schedule." I didn't have to prepare because I always planned all meals a week ahead. Since I had such little time, I'd had to figure a workaround to steal moments for myself. A flush inched its way up my neck. Janice pointed at my face. "I knew it. You're doing the work of ten people, at minimum. Has this been happening for the last two years?"

"O-of course not," I said, eyes dropping to my toes. I hated my inability to lie. I swallowed hard.

"You don't attend any pack meetings or spend any extended time outside except for when you deliver food to the schoolhouse. I thought that was because you just didn't like being outside or around others." Those deliveries were the highlight of my life. That was how I got to see her sporadically. "But it's because you never get a day off—" Her eyes widened. "Even on your birthday."

Her expression crumpled. The reminder made my lower lip tremble. I was often exhausted and overworked, but it wasn't like I had anything else to do or even see. It was a blessing that Janice was able to take a moment to visit me. Something she never did with how busy she was.

"I came to wish you a happy birthday since I didn't see you this morning," Janice rasped. "And I find you like this? You're miserable, Liana. If you don't want to talk to the Alpha about this, you should petition to leave this place." Janice's throat bobbed.

"Leave?" I said so faintly it came out in a whisper. I blinked hard. I hadn't considered leaving since my mom died. The knot in my throat thickened.

"I don't want you to," she said feebly. "But you don't have anything tying you here." I understood what she didn't verbalize. I wasn't tied like her. But leaving... At least I had a roof over my head... and I got to see *their* faces. My eyes dropped to my feet, and I wiped my clammy hands on my jeans.

My one and only shame was the way my stomach fluttered every time I was near the main Beta and the Alpha. It was toxic and so, so stupid.

Maybe I *should* leave. They could never and *would never* be mine. Not that I ever thought they would, but at least being close to them lessened the ache in my chest.

My exhale warbled. "I-I'll think about it."

Janice threw her arms around me.

I was never hugged. It'd been years since my last one. I squeezed my eyes shut as my arms hung limply. Leaving... If I did that, she was the only part I would miss.

"If I'd come to visit sooner, I may have—"

"You should be working."

My spine straightened at the snapped words from behind me. I jumped back, wincing when my side slammed into the lip of the sink.

Scooting to the side, I made sure to step away from Janice. I didn't want her in the crosshairs. Every interaction with Clara was copied and pasted for the most part.

Each step Clara took toward me increased my fear.

I swallowed hard and lowered my head.

Keeping my eyes on the rolled bottoms of her jeans, my skin pricked with anticipation. But not the good kind. Not that I would know what the good kind felt like. Clara was unpredictable and always on edge, and though I knew she always struck, I never knew *when*. Her hand cast a shadow across the cement ground as she lifted it.

So, it would be now. I squeezed my eyelids together tightly.

My face jerked to the side, stinging as blood spurt from my nose.

I bit my tongue so I wouldn't cry from the sting, but trying to hold it back was pointless. I lost the battle with myself and tears spilled from my eyes.

"Clara—"

I rushed to press a hand to Janice's arm. The last thing I wanted was for her to get in trouble because of me. Her mate beat her for what he deemed 'insubordination' and I didn't want her in harm's way.

I'd never let that happen, especially because of me.

Janice was just as mistreated as I was. The only difference was that her mate's position offered him a good cover.

I couldn't do anything for her either, and she was stuck with the abuse. Just as much as I was.

Anyway, Clara's behavior was nothing new. She'd hated me for as long as I could remember and she actively worked to make me suffer.

She removed Janice from the kitchens... as well as any other person that could help me cook, clean, and feed the pack. It began four years ago. At first, it was one person removed because of a mating. Then, month by month, another person disappeared until it was Janice and me. I'd been the sole person in the kitchen for the last two years. It was my little corner of Hell.

It was some sick joke to Clara because she enjoyed watching me struggle. She said exactly that to my face—multiple times.

All this hate was because of one stupid mistake that had everything to do with her mate, Declan.

She wasn't the Luna, but since Alpha Lore didn't have a mate, he allowed his strongest Beta's mate to do all the things his mate would have done. If only the Alpha hadn't trusted her four years ago. She'd used every bit of the power to make me hurt.

Her hand raised again, and I flinched.

"Enough," Janice snapped.

Clara's nose flared, and she growled.

"Watch how you speak to me."

I stepped in front of Clara, getting her attention off Janice. If Clara went to Jan's mate, it would be bad.

"It's my fault."

I knew better than to wipe at the blood dripping off my nose. She liked seeing it.

"You're right."

Her fist flew at me again. The sting radiated out from my eye and I yelped. That would leave a bruise.

"Clara!" Janice helped me straighten from my stagger.

"You need to get back to the schoolhouse." Janice opened her mouth. "Would you like me to speak to your husband about your behavior?"

"Go. Think of Jamie." Her ten-year old son was everything to her and my problems were the last thing she needed.

He was also the reason why she was stuck.

Now that Jamie was old enough to understand the strife between his parents, I would not contribute to the scars of his childhood. For all he knew, his parents were a united front, and Janice worked her ass off to keep him thinking that way.

Clara's eyebrow winged as Janice backed away, hesitantly. I didn't turn to look at my only friend, so she wouldn't see the defeat in my expression.

I'd hate to make her feel guilty for being unable to stop the psycho in front of me.

The door slammed, and I steadily stared at Clara.

"Do you ever not cry?" She sneered. "You're disgustingly

weak. No wonder you never shifted. You're unworthy of a wolf."

That hurt more than anything else she could have said. Werewolves shifted when they were eighteen, and I'd turned twenty today, well past the age I should have turned.

It wasn't fair. How could the Moon Goddess bless someone like her, yet I was not worthy enough to shift?

I *was* damaged.

And it was all because werewolves paired themselves with those that weren't their true mate, which lessened the possibility of their child being able to shift by ninety-five percent. The problem was there hadn't been many *true* mate pairings in too long, which was why many settled down and mated to whoever they wished even if they weren't meant for each other. From what I understood, defective werewolves swept through packs increasingly during this century.

And I was one of the unlucky ones.

Others like me stayed in the pack, while some left to become a part of human society. Since I had nowhere to go, I was the former. Even if I did, I didn't consider it after my mom...

Clara remained still as her words created havoc in my gut. I kept my attention fixed on the ground as my head remained low and I waited with my breath held. She would either send me to do some crazy chore or she'd beat me.

There were only two options, and I was prepared for either.

"Pitiful," she muttered. "Go to Lore's spare room and clean it up. He had an eventful night."

My stomach dropped.

Ugh, I particularly hated that duty.

The closet was to the side of the kitchen door, so it wasn't much of a detour. That was the only blessing of my lodgings. As small as it was, it was private and isolated.

The wooden door creaked, and I had to use my hip to shove the door completely shut. I leaned over my small sink to wash my face and take stock of the damage in the circular mirror hanging above it.

Not the worst it'd been.

I winced when I wiped the dried blood from my split lip. It had already crusted over.

Otherwise, the only other mark was a faint beginning of a bruise blooming at my eye. That would be purple by tomorrow.

I sighed. I was used to my face being a mess. I guessed it was a good thing that I didn't see people often.

I wiped my face with a ragged cloth and neatly folded it before stepping out.

The gravel crunched as I made my way to the side entrance of the pack house. The estate sprawled on Alpha's land, and it was easily the largest building by thousands of square feet.

The kitchens connected to it. It needed to, since everyone who wasn't mated ate in the dining room. There were even some mated couples that didn't want to bother with cooking that sometimes showed up.

I always had to make sure there was enough food, and if there were ever leftovers, I visited pack homes to deliver food trays.

The single rule?

I couldn't touch any of it, which meant the only time I managed to sneak food into my stomach was when I cooked.

I smacked at a mosquito buzzing near my ear. Damn humidity wasn't making it any better. I plucked my shirt and let air billow under the fabric. Cool air brushed my skin when I opened the door. Must be nice to have an air conditioner running twenty-four seven. I softened my steps as I padded to the staircase.

If I was quiet enough, they wouldn't bother me—

"Girl."

I froze with a foot on the staircase, and my heart raced. I could act like I didn't hear him and keep going, but my leg wouldn't move.

"Come here, now."

My shoulders fell at the order and I trudged to the living room. The half-circle of couches faced a large television. Two Beta enforcers lazed on the couch, legs splayed. Their shorts rode up on their thighs, showing too much skin. I evened my expression before he saw my grimace.

"Come here, girl," Daniel said, leering, as he dragged his eyes over my hunched form. There was nothing to see, so I knew he wanted it to make me uncomfortable. Hanging my head, I shuffled to his side. I'd learned the hard way that I shouldn't fight or deny. He thrived on driving up my anxiety and making me uncomfortable.

Daniel palmed my ass as soon as I was close enough.

I swallowed hard.

They lived in the rooms on the second floor as all un-mated shifters did, so I'd had one too many experiences like this.

"Daniel. I need to get to work," I whispered.

"You can spare me a moment, girly. Or do you think you're too good for us?" The palm on my hip flattened and pulled so I fell into his lap.

Jacob grinned and scooted closer to sniff my hair. My face heated. Why did they always sniff and lick my neck? They acted like I was a shifter when I knew I smelled like a human. Daniel's leg bounced, so I lost my balance, and my legs straddled his thigh. I cringed into myself. This would be over soon.

They never failed to get frisky or cop feels, but fortunately, it never went further than this and it was all thanks to the threat posed by—

Daniel's head jerked back, and I followed the harsh grip in his hair to the owner.

"Daniel. Leave her the fuck alone."

Because of him.

Declan jerked his chin, and I scrambled off Daniel's lap. Daniel growled until he saw which Beta manhandled him.

My voice stuck in my throat as I backed away until the wall pressed into my back. Declan had threatened Daniel after he'd almost raped me a year ago, which was why Daniel's 'fun' never turned into more than the perverted gropes.

Declan and Lore had shown up right as my clothes tore from my body. They'd shifted and shredded into Daniel until he was ribbons. It took Daniel a month to recover from how broken his body was.

That was reason number two, why Clara hated my guts. They beat her brother close to death because of me.

"We're playing around," Daniel said, forcing his voice low. It'd been a while since Daniel got frisky. There were always weeks between his advances. As if he waited until enough time passed so he wouldn't be caught by Declan. I didn't know why, though. It wasn't like Declan would kill his mate's brother.

Declan grunted and grabbed the hand Daniel carelessly waved in front of him.

"Seems like you need one last reminder." Declan squeezed and the sudden crunch of bones popping made me suck in a breath. A vein throbbed in Daniel's forehead as his expression strained. "Will you do it again?"

"N-no, I swear, Declan." He wheezed, panting as tears sheened over his eyes. "I'll leave the bitch alone."

Declan shoved Daniel's head forward and Jacob scrambled back. The brothers-in-law were so different. There was a quiet menace that radiated from Declan that never failed to comfort me. My shoulders relaxed, and I exhaled in the face of the violence.

Declan leveled his gaze on me. I couldn't let him see the bruise, so I dipped my head until my hair properly hid me. I licked my lips nervously, fixing my gaze on the bronze tint of his skin attributed to his Hispanic background—something we shared. The only difference between our coloring was my eyes were brown, and his were a rich hazel that popped beautifully with his coloring.

Every time he set those eyes on me, I couldn't help but suck in a breath. It was as if he could stare into my soul. Warmth bloomed in my chest and my mouth dried. He dragged his hand through his dark hair, and I struggled to focus with the rippling muscles of his biceps.

"Get to work."

I jumped at his barked order and scurried to the stairs. There was a pained yip from behind me that made me speed up. I wasn't in the mood to handle any more violence.

Declan was... he was who I wished could protect me. He was an enforcer. Only second in dominance to the Alpha out of the dozen enforcers.

He was always too serious, almost solemn. Yet, his presence settled my heart and when I was near him, my guard lowered enough for me to breathe. If I was being honest, he made me feel *too* safe if there was such a thing.

And *that* was reason number one that Clara hated me with a passion. On a night of weakness, I sank into his comforting embrace. In my defense, I'd just discovered mom had died. She may have not been the best of mothers, but she was still kin.

We'd had to leave our pack when I was eight because of me. My father had died *because of me*. A smokey scent floated to my nose, and I rubbed the back of my hand against it. A familiar pinch in my gut turned my stomach. It was my fault.

Every time I'd asked her what I had done to cause his death, she'd burst into tears until I learned not to ask. Mom and I spent a couple years going from hotel to hotel, but it was a blur —much like the holes in my memory from my prior pack. Then she found the Eastland pack. We'd lived uneventfully, but one day she'd decided we should leave and she'd left to seek out other options for us since she felt it was time for us to live among humans—all *because of me*. How? I wasn't sure, but she said we needed a change.

It'd led to her death.

The base of my neck tightened, and I puffed out my cheeks.

I reached the third floor of the mansion. This floor was all Lore's. He had two bedrooms. One I was never allowed to enter at the end of the hall and the one where he... entertained.

Shuffling foot to foot, I sighed and puffed out my cheeks. I could do this. Whatever mess was behind the door was nothing new, right? Using my toe to nudge it open, I froze, lifting my shoulder to rub against the pricking at my ear.

Just as I expected.

I *really* hated this. I stifled a whimper and rubbed my neck as I took in the damage.

The king-sized bed was a complete mess. Bedsheets were strewn all over the ground. Pillows were half on the floor, half on the bed. There was a huge tear in the middle of the bedsheets wrapped over the mattress. I swallowed hard and rubbed my nose to rid myself of the tingles there. I should be numb to this. My eyes slid closed as I processed the dull ache throbbing through my body. They were the same hollow feelings that flushed through me any time I had to clean his messes after he slept with she-wolves. These messes had unfortunately started two years ago, before that, Alpha wasn't known to be promiscuous. Now, everyone knew about his extracurriculars, it was a huge gossip topic. I was just as curious as everyone else as to why all of the sudden he seemed to have changed so utterly. He used to be polite to me whenever we crossed paths, but when that change came, he stopped looking at me completely, as if a jerk-switch had been turned on in him. The sad, pitiful defective girl was invisible to him.

My lips tightened, and I blinked quickly, shaking myself out of those useless thoughts. Time to get to work.

It took me particularly long to vacuum the feathers from a ripped pillow. As I worked, I collected the trashed stuff in one corner and everything else in another. A half hour later, I groaned, rubbing my neck and stretching my arms up to relieve the pinch. Now to fetch a fresh set of sheets and their matching comforter from the hall closet.

I set them on the settee near the bed and smoothed them on the bed layer by layer. The bed was so huge that I pinched a nerve spreading the sheets on the mattress.

I brushed my forearm across my sweaty forehead. This wouldn't be bad if I didn't have to do this sort of stuff so much. At this point, it was just squandering money. A frown curved my lips. Wasteful.

I spread my fingers up the comforter and trailed my fingers as I smoothed it out. Lore must be a good lover. Had he brought up one or three women last night?

The balloon expanded in my chest, making it difficult to breathe.

My teeth clicked together and if I could breathe fire, I would have set the place ablaze. Why wouldn't my tiny obsession disappear? Most times, I *really* didn't like him, but the attraction wasn't something I'd been able to squash.

I collected the three unharmed pillows I'd tossed on the nightstand and set them on the bed, fluffing them out. A scent that was distinctly Lore, wafted to my nose. I peeked toward the door.

I shouldn't...

Just one inhale.

My nose pressed into the material, and I sucked in a lungful.

While Declan's scent was comfort and safety mixed with

mint. Lore's was excitement and citrusy. There was an alluring aura about him that called to any and all.

That was why all he had to do was crook a finger and women climbed him. His control bordered on psychotic, but the beast inside him peeked through his eyes whenever I saw him—which wasn't much.

As invisible as I was, it was easy to overhear people talking, and Lore was a popular topic of conversation. He executed everything he did with a direct control that only hinted at the wildness he never released according to the pack.

It used to frighten many because denying instincts was asking for trouble since it made wolves volatile and quick to turn rabid. But in regard to Lore, that concern dwindled with his strict control.

That was why I knew the person that made this mess was his lover, or... um, *lovers*. So many lovers.

When he mated, would he continue to take other women? Would he have a true mate or a chosen mate?

Either way, it was extremely rare for there to be cheating between mated couples. Lore wasn't your basic wolf though...

I exhaled. Good thing I wouldn't have to deal with it.

I couldn't wait until I found my true mate. He would smell better than this. My stomach dropped.

Right, that wasn't a possibility for me. Hugging the pillow to my body, I gave it a quick sniff before setting it back.

A sharply inhaled breath made me tense. Whirling, I found a girl at the door. Her face twisted in a scowl.

"I-I—" I cleared my throat.

"You're a fucking creep."

Lore stepped through the doorframe, and my entire body flooded with blood.

Oh, no. *No. No.*

Thank goodness he hadn't seen. Before I could motion to her to keep what she'd seen quiet, she kept going.

"This freak, was smelling your pillow."

I jerked back as if struck and held out my hands. She wasn't necessarily wrong. It was exactly as she said. I was sniffing the Alpha's pillowcase.

Wincing, I dipped my head in shame, unable to deny it.

Crap.

She sneered derisively. "Girl, you're aiming too high with your ugly, scarred face."

My heart pounded in my ears. She might as well have slapped me.

The scar on my face... I turned to the side and shook out my hair, so it partially fell over it.

She wasn't from this pack.

It wasn't surprising. He always went to the bar in town where other packs mingled to get himself a lover.

Her hips swayed seductively as she approached the side of the bed and surveyed the nightstand.

"Did you see a necklace?"

My nod was jerky, and I pulled it out of my pocket. I was going to seal it in an envelope before I left it on the nightstand for Lore. That was what I usually did for anything I found of his lovers. If it wasn't collected, I placed the jewelry in a box in the closet where all the others were.

"You were going to steal it, weren't you fugly?" I met her eyes before looking at my feet. I should give them privacy. I could finish cleaning later.

I took a step toward the door, but her fingers dug into my arm. Yelping from the surprise, I immediately went limp.

"Enough." I looked toward Lore with wide eyes. He was taller than Declan, if not as wide. The blond hair glinted from the light as he crossed his arms. His blue eyes were on the other woman, ice glinting in his eyes. "I won't stand for an outsider abusing my wolves."

Bitterness soured my mouth. Yet, he allowed Clara to mess with me. If only I were strong enough to inform him of that.

I snorted. Did I just...

My eyes widened, and I slapped my hand over my mouth.

Lore's eyebrows hiked up.

"Sorry, Alpha. I sneezed."

Please believe me, please believe me.

I dipped my head and peeked through the curtain of my hair. Was that a slight smirk?

"Leave."

"Yes, Alpha." I shook off the woman's hold and scurried to the door.

"Not you." I froze. His blue eyes settled on the other woman. "You, leave."

"Me? After last night?"

I did not need to be here for this. Rushing from the room, I made sure to leave as much room as I could between Lore and me. As exciting as he may seem, he still scared the moon out of me.

Fortunately, he didn't say anything, and other than shooting me a troubled look, he let me escape. I shut the door quietly and whirled too hastily.

My nose bashed into a hard surface, and I grunted. That wasn't there before. Calloused hands wrapped around my sleeveless arms. The fluttering in my stomach heightened until I was looking into questioning eyes.

I gawked at Declan.

"Sorry," I mumbled and skirted around him, acting like I didn't see his hand reach for me before he dropped it.

This was not my day. Curling up in my blanket sounded good right about now, but I needed to head to the kitchen to get started on dinner. Once I cleaned up after everyone, I would be able to catch my breath.

I scrubbed my face with my palm.

I could have cut through the home to get to the kitchens and it would have cut the trip in half, but I'd rather take the long way.

Who knew when Daniel could pop out at me? He especially loved corralling me into the wall and petting my outer thighs like on the day I discovered my mom died. My stomach churned at the memories. Declan had come to my rescue that day, too. I'd gone limp in Daniel's arms, grief stricken and squeezing my eyes shut as tears trickled down my cheeks.

When Declan had snatched me away, I'd instinctively curled into the safety of his arms.

That was how his mate found us and so spawned her hate. I shivered at the memory and slid through the back door, making sure it latched behind me.

Heat washed over me, suffocatingly. It was almost as hot as *that* day she'd found me hugging her mate.

Mates were held to a high standard in any pack, so I could understand Clara's disgust toward me. It was wrong of me to seek comfort from Declan, but my innocent, pain-riddled mind hadn't thought much of it.

If I'd had a mate and I found him coddling a woman. I wouldn't have been happy either, so I couldn't help but understand.

I'd gone to their house to beg her forgiveness, but she'd beaten me within an inch of my life. Declan had arrived just in time to stop her from breaking my neck.

I palmed the healed scar tissue slashed across the left side of my face. It stretched from the top of my eyebrow and curved down the middle of my cheek.

Clara had made it very clear to me to stay away from her mate. I would be just as possessive of my mate. Especially if it was Declan.

Shaking my head, I gritted my teeth. That was impossible. The pressure in my chest ballooned and tears prickled my eyes. There was no possibility of me having a mate.

My life stretched out in front of me. I'd live here the rest of my life, mateless, and a servant.

Oh, Moon Goddess, no.

Janice was right. I needed to petition to leave the pack. The knot in my throat thickened.

Where would I go?

I'd never stepped foot into the real world, and I'd never considered living among humans until my mom brought it up the year she was murdered.

I'd had time to wrap my head around it when she left to prepare everything. Problem was, she never returned, and I'd had to dog Lore's steps to get him to send someone to look for her.

That was probably the most I'd ever put my foot down. Honestly, I was still surprised he'd done as I asked and sent his second-best tracker. That werewolf had brought back her dead carcass.

Any thought about leaving the pack evaporated from my head after that. My brain had been a mess, which was how I'd been limp when Daniel assaulted me and why I'd fallen apart in Declan's arms after finding out the news.

At sixteen, I was already taking shifts in the kitchens since I had to pull my weight around the grounds. Get a job outside of pack lands and contribute to the pot, or work on them. Those were my two options.

I could have worked in Lore's offices within human society, but after losing my mom, the thought of leaving made my chest squeeze.

There were also some who were allowed to go to college, but that was never on the table for me.

Heavy familiar footsteps pounded through the gravel. *Daniel*. I quickened my pace until I was jogging.

At least the kitchens were a haven from the groping.

LORE

She rushed out of my bedroom like a scared rabbit, leaving behind the sweetest scent I'd ever inhaled.

My nostrils flared, trying to suck in as much of her peach scent as I could. It was because she worked in the kitchens. That was the only reason she smelled good.

Her scent didn't correlate with how long she'd worked in the kitchens.

My molars clicked together.

When I first caught her scent, she was a ten-year-old pigtailed little thing that awoke protective instincts in my wolf. Shy and quiet and as she'd become older, she remained just as sweet.

My lip lifted, and my wolf snarled within my chest. His anxiousness bled into my limbs and I regained my strict control over him.

I was sure she was my mate from my wolf's reaction to her scent, but when she turned eighteen two years ago and she hadn't shifted, it obliterated the hope.

She was defective.

And it was a blessing. Even if she was my mate, I would have turned her away. She could never be the Luna.

She was too... gentle.

Nothing like the Luna should behave. But her not shifting was no surprise, she didn't have the backbone to contain a wolf.

I growled and scratched my neck.

She was an annoyance since her mom brought her to live with the pack. Her presence unnerved me. When she first arrived, there was an instance I'd helped her, but it'd backfired.

After completing the pack land rounds, I'd come upon her sniffling and curled into a ball. It took some coaxing, but I eventually got her to tell me about the kids bullying her.

Safe to say those kids never bothered her again, but the outcome of my one good act had repercussions. She'd fostered a crush and set on trying to cling to me as much as she could.

I'd been enthralled by her too much, and as soon as I recognized that I was beginning to care for the Little One, I put a stop to it. At twenty-three, I'd had better things to do than to have a kid following me around. So, I snapped at her. The memory of her watering eyes was a gut punch to this day.

I may have been too harsh if she still avoided looking at me or being in my presence for longer than a handful of minutes. What helped keep the distance between us was she stayed on the other end of the structure, near the kitchens. The same location the prior Alpha placed her and her mother.

It'd been four years since her mother died. I'd had Declan's mate attempt to switch Liliana's bedroom so she could be more comfortable, but she turned it down. I refused to beg her to move somewhere with insulation if she didn't want it.

That innocent care I had for her slowly morphed as I watched her grow. The more I noticed her, the more I stayed away from her to the point that I went months without laying eyes on her.

The fact that she stuck to the fringes of the pack as she tried blending with the walls didn't hurt. It meant I could dash her existence from my senses.

As if it were that easy.

I groaned and hooked my hands behind my neck.

The gentle way she spoke always made the hair on my body stand. It was soothing, and it calmed the bloodthirstiness of the wolf I always stifled. I did not doubt my wolf would rub his pelt all over her body if I let him out, which was why I hardly let him take control. His odd craving for her was a weakness, and I fucking hated weaknesses.

When she turned eighteen and didn't come into her wolf, it hurt. I felt desolate. Despite my claims, I'd allowed my wolf's obsession to stoke hope and had waited for her to turn. When she didn't it crippled me and I tried to bury that agony through fucking. It was a momentary distraction, even when I was with she-wolves, my mind wandered to her brown eyes and I felt worse than when I started. The dissatisfaction was digging its claws into my wolf, but I was learning to live with it, accepting it as my new way of life.

After all, it was best that I didn't mate since protecting the pack was the only importance. I learned my lesson after the prior Alpha destroyed everything because of his fated mate. Her weakness, and his in choosing to accept her, was what destroyed the pack.

As the Luna, you must be strong—a leader. Because if you have one bitch challenge you for dominance and you fail... it puts the rest of the pack in danger. It was a rusted link in the chain.

The Luna's strength reflected her mate's and Liliana was... weak. She scampered off at the first sign of conflict, like earlier today.

I pinched the bridge of my nose.

Instead of clawing the eyes out of the Silverback Pack bitch, she hid her little face behind her hair and cowered.

"You shouldn't defend the weak ones..."

The bitch was still here?

I rolled my shoulders out and gritted my teeth when my wolf pushed under my skin. He wanted to burst out and drag his nails through her throat.

Now that Liliana left the room, I was restless. On edge. As always. And my wolf's unease didn't help my own.

The bitch continued rambling on and I crossed my arms. She was a cousin of the Silverback Alpha, located a hundred miles north. I almost hadn't fucked her because of that, but I'd been craving—*hungry* and I'd needed to drown the neediness, so I chose the first pussy to open her legs.

If only she was as good as she thought she was, then maybe I could have come. I'd twisted her into so many positions to see if any could bring me to completion, but nothing. My mind wandered as it always did.

I frowned. I blame my wolf for this inadequacy, but at least I left my lovers satisfied.

"...scar." Brenda started going on about the scarred girl, perking my ears.

My teeth clicked together, and I snarled, rounding on her in a few strides.

"Why are you still here?" My fingers dug into the sides of her pale throat and the words vibrated with restrained anger. Brenda shook, spooked, so I uncurled my fingers and she stumbled back, heaving on a choked breath. Her expression crumpled with terror.

"Out," I snarled. She scrambled away, trembling.

Declan waited by the door, expressionless.

My wolf writhed at the sight of him. *His* mate was the cause of the scar.

When I'd seen the damage done to Liliana's face, I'd wanted to tear off Clara's limbs.

That was normal. I was protective because I was the Alpha.

Then why didn't my wolf act like that with others? I ground my teeth.

Fucking subconscious was trying to start shit.

I cut off that line of thought. Irritation prickled my shoulders, but I popped my neck to release the energy.

It was pity that forced me to speak in Little One's defense while she was in my room.

Nothing more.

Declan

"Where are you going now?" Clara snapped, dogging my ass. My knuckles popped from how hard I clenched my fists.

She repeated the question, and I ground my molars. The door creaked when I slammed the bedroom door in her face and made my way to the front room. It didn't stay shut for long and soon she was back to following at my heels.

Fucking Moon Goddess, Clara. Shut the fuck up.

"There's suspicious activity bordering the forest. I'm going to check it out."

"You're always leaving. I'm tired of it." I rubbed the back of my neck, blocking out her voice as she yelled about how neglectful I was. She was female. I couldn't hit her. I was a protector first and foremost, but she pulled out aggression from both my wolf and me. That made it difficult to control myself, so I had to leave before I did something I couldn't take back.

I remained silent. There was nothing I could say to defend myself from her claims.

I was not a good mate, but I offered to fucking separate

from the start of the mistake of our mating. I urged for it—she refused. At least if she was the one that left me, then I could look in my mother's face without guilt.

Then Clara began to get sick.

"You can leave me."

Her lip trembled, but a glint lit in her eye.

"You worthless piece of shit." Clara stepped up to me, her head lowered as she spat her venom at me. "Do you want to kill me? Do you want me to die? Because that will happen if you leave." Madness glinted in her eyes.

I snarled, peeling my lip back. In a few swift steps, I was in her face and she was cowering against the wall near the dining room. Was she bluffing? I scoffed and turned my back on her, making my way to the living room.

Would she truly do it? It would be my fault if she did. What the fuck was I supposed to do? I knew she was losing her mind. Literally. But we didn't have any way to help her on pack lands.

That same metaphorical knife hung over my head since the beginning of our mating. She sensed how discontent I was from the start, and that aided her loss of reality.

The first time she attempted to kill herself could have been a fluke. Even so, I didn't want to rock the boat. I simply... stayed away from her.

I offered her my back and wrapped my hand around the doorknob. It creaked under my grip, but before I could whip it open, her hand settled on my arm, voice lowering pitifully.

"I'm sorry, Declan. I love you. You know I love you. If you wouldn't make me act this way, then we would be okay." Her voice turned watery and she fell to the ground with huge wracking sobs.

Make her act this way? She was truly delusional. Was that her madness talking? She had to know we would never be okay.

I popped my neck; the noose tightened around my throat.

Although the madness was incremental and showed up at times, it had gotten worse in the last four years.

I'd gone to Lore for advice. His answer was to keep her busy. He placed her in charge of the others who worked on pack lands, as well as organizing all meals for wolves. Keeping busy seemed to help her focus on the here and now, but the other perk was she had less time to follow me around. Her overflowing schedule allowed me space, so she wasn't on my ass twenty-four seven.

I didn't have time for her bullshit. I needed to get going so I could run the perimeter. After pulling my shirt over my head, I unbuttoned my pants. Clara's eyes were heavy on my abdomen, and desire flickered in their depths.

My skin crawled under her gaze as if little ants crawled up my insides and spilled over my flesh.

I hated her attention.

My fingers un-looped the button of my jeans, but I left them in place. I'd rather rip through another pair of jeans than have her stare me down. She stepped forward, lifting her hand toward my chest, but I easily avoided it, sneering at her.

"I'm sad." Clara sniffled. "You make me feel better when you fuck me."

My shoulders tensed. I hadn't fucked her in years.

"I have to get to work."

"Fuck me, Declan." She gave up the pity angle. In the first year of our mating, that was how she got me in bed with her as my sex drive dwindled to extinction.

There was something wrong with me.

I'd never heard of a werewolf without a drive to fuck. Yet, mine was nonexistent.

Except when—

She reached toward my cock, but I caught her hand before she pressed it to me.

I'd come to terms with the fact something was wrong with me, but Clara hadn't. She loathed it and she took my lack of desire out on me.

She especially hated that I didn't come the times we *had* had sex so long ago—that I had to stroke my dick to come after we were mated.

Stepping back, I pushed her hand away. "I have to get to work."

I pulled open the door and shifted as she cussed me out.

My body burned as the shift stretched my bones and skin, rearranging them into something that should have been impossible.

My face elongated, all my other senses sharpening. My ear twitched as I absorbed the cacophony of woodland noises coming at me all at once.

The pain was barely a pinch now, but those first few years were hell. Thank the Moon Goddess I had fourteen years of shifting under my belt.

I rounded to the outer edge of the pack house where only the shining moon accompanied me. My instincts prodded me to the left, past the back of the house and near the kitchens. Beside the entrance to the kitchens was a door half the size of what it should be.

I used to try to fight my wolf's curiosity, but why bother? Those private moments inhaling the sweet scent of peaches always settled my restlessness.

Inhaling deeply, I whined and my claws dug into the ground from pleasure.

How did she keep her living space?

I'd never been in there. When her mom and she moved here, my obsession with inhaling her scent began. Anytime I needed peace, I came here for just a moment. The slightest second was enough to get me through.

It was my only guilty pleasure, but otherwise, I avoided the girl.

Especially as she grew older and her scent began exciting me.

Staying away from her was necessary for her well-being and with a pack as large as this one, it was easy to avoid her.

Yet, something about her called to me. At first, it was pity. She grew up without a father and I had too. I recognized the lost look in her eyes. The timidity.

It urged me to protect the submissive girl at the lowest rank in the pack. There was something sweet about her and all I wanted was to soothe her. That need only worsened when she'd cried in my arms a few years ago, after she discovered her mother's death. It was the first time I saw her as more than a hurt girl.

It was also the same instant when Clara found us and jumped to conclusions.

Assumptions she was right about on my end, but Liliana was innocent. There had been nothing malicious about her seeking comfort.

Every time I thought of how alone she was, my ache to be near her increased, but I needed to stay the fuck away.

Inhaling her scent on patrol night was the only thing I allowed of myself. Since she became an adult by wolf standards, I feared what I might do if I was too close.

After witnessing Daniel manhandling her this morning, I ached to rub my entire body on her to rid her of the memory of his touch. I wanted to toss her on the ground and fu—

I shouldn't have these thoughts.

Declan, you're fucking mated. I snuffled and turned my back on the door.

I must not get involved. It wouldn't turn out well for her.

The scar on her face proved it.

Liana

I'd tossed all night with the thought of leaving, teasing my brain. If I went through with it, I would be completely alone.

I could die... or it could be what I need.

I must face the reality that I was defective and there was no place for me here. I would never belong.

Defective werewolves were already looked down on, but toss in 'orphan' and it was as if I didn't exist. Like a shameful exile. My mom was my only relative in this pack, and she'd been gone for so long now. The toughest aspect of joining a pack late in life was that pack members have known each other their entire childhood.

I was the only outlier here.

I had no one.

To add insult to injury, my wolf would forever be dormant. If I even had a wolf, which I doubted despite the elders' assurances. According to them, everyone held a wolf, but some had one too weak to burst free, so it lay dormant in those who were defective.

Mating to someone who wasn't your true mate had its risks, and the cost was those like me. But I guess there weren't many options to find your true mate, considering the dwindling population.

With an exhale, I kicked out my feet, untangling the sheets from my legs.

None of it was fair. I snorted, staring up at the dark ceiling. That was the theme of my life.

What would I even do out there?

Go to school?

I pressed my palms into my eyes.

School was... *eh*, nothing had attracted my attention in that environment. It was difficult to focus and my mind always wandered. I'd done the customary schooling offered in the pack. The equivalent of kindergarten to twelfth grade, but accelerated. I'd been done with school at fifteen, which was fine with me since the pack teachers hadn't paid much mind to me, anyway. Mostly, I'd spent my time in the corner, doodling.

Going to a school in the human world would be different, and I doubted I had the necessary skills to succeed.

Turning on my side, I set my cheek on my hand. My elbow dug into the hard floor. The ragged blankets weren't enough to protect me from the cold radiating from the ground. A shiver crested up my spine, and I readjusted my hip's position to lessen the twinge at my waist.

The insulation in the dank little room was pitiful—blistering hot during summers and excruciatingly cold in the winters.

I wouldn't have to deal with this anymore if I left. I could have my own bed. My chest squeezed.

My own space.

Maybe I'd fall in love. My lips tilted up, and tears welled before slipping out of the corners of my eyes.

Yeah, I liked the sound of that...

A scream rent the air, and I frowned, drowsily slapping my hands over my ears with a groan. The sound assaulted my senses again, this time accompanied by a secondary scream. *That wasn't in my dream.*

I sucked in a deep breath and popped up, scooting back until my spine flattened against the wall.

When Clara didn't come barging into my room, I relaxed. I hated when she entered my room in the middle of the night. Those beatings were the worst—like she was taking something out on me.

The yells ratcheted up from outside, drilling into my eardrums. My heart pounded against my rib cage. *What was going on?*

I nibbled on my lower lip. Should I even look? It could be dangerous. I hugged my torso and huddled deeper into the corner. No, it was best I stayed put.

Another scream echoed through my room, the sound muffled and high-pitched and *familiar*. I shoved to my feet. I knew that scream. *Janice.*

I wrung my hands, heart pounding a mile a minute as I stood near my door. My eyes slid shut, and I took a deep breath, but it didn't help my thundering heart.

The door creaked, as I opened it a sliver and inched out. At a snarl, I flattened against the wall and scooted to the corner so I could get a view of everything. Every muscle in my body froze.

It was chaos. Wolves battled each other with deadly precision. Sharp blood-drenched fangs flashed as they mauled another wolf's form they pinned. The wolf went limp, and the beast threw his head back with a high-pitched howl.

I stumbled back, pressing my hand to my chest. The muscle in my chest pounded against the confines of my skin.

Thud.

Each sound vibrated my entire frame. Janice shouted, the noise filled with fear. I needed to see if I could help.

I needed to stop being a coward.

With my limbs trembling, I peeled myself away from the wall and inched my way around, low and hidden.

Bodies littered the ground. Some in wolf form and others in human. I looked down at the nearest one. Good, no one I knew.

Bits of shredded appendages lay on the ground and blood blanketed the grass. The macabre sight was difficult to wrap my head around.

Violence was nothing new, but this surpassed anything I'd ever seen.

"No," Janice screamed again.

My head whipped in her direction. A wolf stalked her as she stumbled back, huddling Jamie at her back. She was leaving herself wide open.

Air exploded from my lungs. She was too far from me and no one was coming to her aid.

My pulse thundered in my ears, but I didn't waste a second more. I rushed past fighting, bleeding pairs as one tore a furry ear free from the scalp and a sharp cry rent the air. Another group of wolves cornered a singular wolf, and they tore into the blood-matted fur. Flesh sliced and red gushed.

A whimper slipped from my lips and I hunched into myself as I quickened my pace, trying to keep myself to the shadows, but that was my downfall. My toe slammed into a hard form and it sent me careening forward with a shout. I managed to catch myself, but I gasped at the wolf prowling in my direction. Its teeth dripped blood, maw opened in a macabre grin.

Oh, no. I backed up frantically a few steps until I forced my body into stillness. I didn't want to bring it joy in hunting me.

Its heaving, snorting exhales reached my weaker ears as soon as it was a yard away. The ground spun, and I sucked in fear-filled breaths. Its next step forward would put it within biting distance. Right when its hind legs bunched to lunge, a massive blond wolf slammed into it.

Thank moon goodness.

I dipped to grab a rock and ran headlong at the black wolf a hairsbreadth away from Janice.

This was crazy. I was practically human. There was nothing I could do against its strength and fangs.

But Jan... I gritted my teeth and used every increment of strength to hop on its back, bringing down the rock on its muzzle. Yips exploded from the beast.

Fur tickled the sides of my thighs as my lungs seized.

"Run," I cried out as it bucked and sent me flying. I grunted on impact. My teeth clipped my lip, and I scuttled back with a whimper.

The world spun, but through my whirling sight, noted Janice pulling a small form away.

Thank the moon.

A branch snapped, and my shoulders drew tight. The wolf was not happy and my death flashed before my eyes, reflecting in the pools of his maddened eyes.

The wolf pounced and snarled.

I closed my eyelids.

Thumps and growls erupted as a spray speckled my skin, and I peeked through blurred eyes. The blood-drenched blond wolf ripped into the black one, burying its teeth into the throat. With a jerk up, stringy meat from the throat stretched and snapped. The light touches splattered on my skin again.

Blood.

My stomach lurched, and I gagged, surveying the smears on my skin.

The wolf shifted, bones popping and fur receding as limbs stretched. Then a naked male was standing a few feet away from me.

"Lore," I whispered. No, breathed. I dipped my head. I didn't address him appropriately. My face heated, and I fixed my eyes where my hands bunched my shirt.

"What are you doing out here?" he snarled, blood dripping on the ground. I dragged my gaze up, fixing my eyes on anywhere but his. His teeth glinted in the moonlight, his face painted in red. It was all over his naked body. I opened my mouth to respond, but it was no use. Words refused to come. Lore's lip twitched up, his disgust clear to see as he sneered at me with derision. My skin itched at the look directed at me and my lip trembled. "Don't move from this spot."

I nodded frantically.

Curling my arms over my knees, I sank deeper into the foliage at my back. Lore shifted and navigated the strewn bodies. The snarls and growls tapered off and Lore ignored the remaining scuffles. Our pack was winning.

Why had this happened?

All the attacks ended a year into the alpha switch. Lore, Declan, and the rest of the dominant Beta enforcers destroyed any threat swiftly and efficiently.

Lore worked hard to build the strength of his pack since his uncle left behind a shit show. Instead of bending under the pressure, he'd made the pack one of the strongest, with the highest number of wolves.

That wasn't the only accomplishment. His business and leadership acumen were revered and widely known. That was why everyone wanted an alliance with him. I couldn't count how many she-wolves were offered to him from other packs wanting an alliance. I squeezed my eyes shut tightly, and I shook the pinch in my chest away.

Sweeping my gaze across the lawn, I shivered. Such savagery.

I could have died in so many different ways tonight.

A tremble worked up my spine. Nothing like this had happened before, not at this level. I licked my lips. Janice was right. I needed to get out of here.

This wasn't where I belonged.

I ground my teeth and nodded to myself. I'd meet with Lore tomorrow, and I could ask him for a small loan to get me started in the outside world. I wrung my hands. The worst he could do is say no, and it wasn't like he didn't already think I was lower than him.

If worst came to worst, I'd sell the necklace my mom left me and get a job at some diner like my mom had before we found Lore's pack.

A shout brought my attention up and my eyes clashed with Declan's who stood a few feet away.

How long had he been staring at me?

Lore jogged up to the Beta.

"What happened?"

My heart jumped at Lore's shout. Declan's lips turned

down harshly as he offered me his strong blood specked back. Gashes sliced across his skin.

"I was ambushed at the edges of the land." His tone was grim. "I came upon them as they plotted their attack. They were looking for something here, but I couldn't hear what. Before I could come to warn you, four pounced on me and the rest headed this way."

Declan brushed back his hair. My eyes dropped to the firm muscle of his ass and heat stained my cheeks. His movement made his muscles ripple, and I forced my eyes away from his nude body.

Werewolves were unabashed about nudity, but I'd never gotten the opportunity to get used to it—for obvious, non-shifting reasons.

Twisting my head to the side, I forced my eyes away to stop my gawking and squinted at the movement within the brush. At a midnight pelt that practically melted into the darkness.

They continued discussing theories of why we'd been invaded as the wolf prowled closer.

"Lore," I called out, voice weak and raspy.

He ignored me. The wolf's head whirled, and he showed me his teeth before he quickened his speed.

I stood up, frantically scrambling off the ground. "Declan!"

His shoulders rippled, but he didn't turn.

Oh, Moon Goddess, no.

My heart drummed against my rib cage, mimicking my pounding steps. I ran straight at the beast three times my size.

At the wolf's trajectory, he was still going to manage to slice teeth into Declan's throat.

I picked up my stride, running faster than I ever had. Just as the werewolf opened its maw, I threw myself in its path.

It had been aiming for Declan's spine, near his neck. I didn't doubt his goal was to rip the bone out. The muscles in my thighs bunched as I tossed myself in the way, and teeth sliced into my neck.

Gurgling, I scrabbled helplessly as pain ripped through my body.

Shouts and snarls exploded as the world blurred with red and my ears rang. Teeth unhooked from my neck as the beast whimpered, and arms caught me before I slammed into the ground.

Agony crippled my mind and froze my body.

A heart-stuttering howl rang in my ears as my life's blood leaked down my throat and soaked my shirt, plastering it to my skin.

My jagged breaths stuttered, and a gurgling sob slipped from my lips.

I should have petitioned to leave the pack long ago.

What kind of life had I led?

A lonely one.

A pitiful one.

LORE

My chest hurt like a fucking bitch and it was taking everything I had to contain my wolf.

I failed everyone. I failed Liliana.

Her assailant lay at my feet, ripped in two. Since he died in his wolf form, he remained in it after. Guts spilled across the ground, rendering everything red. A useless ache drove me to keep ripping into him long after he stopped moving. The image of Liliana's body jerking was seared into my brain. Nausea crawled up my throat, and I pressed my palms to my temples, trying to get a handle on myself. My wolf was bloodthirsty, and he wanted more death. He wanted to tear into everything in the vicinity.

Declan hunched as he held her cradled in his arms, the tail end of his tortured howl winding to an end.

A snarl ripped free from the recesses of my soul, echoing the sharp stab to my chest.

My shoulders curved forward and my breaths sawed out of me. The wolf, the other half of me, fed off the agony writhing in my gut and shoved against my skin.

My body heaved as I struggled to control the rioting emotions. Controlling him was never this difficult.

I speared my fingers through my hair and focused on Declan who was losing it. Declan had never howled about anyone's death. The naked pain blanketing his expression mirrored the one I was sure was on mine.

Why was he reacting as viscerally as me? I didn't think Liliana was on his radar.

He hung his head as he slid his hand over her cheek, wiping back the blood that stuck her hair to her face.

He dipped his head to sniff her matted hair. A growl rumbled in my chest at the sight of him cuddling close to her.

"Declan!" There was a far-off yell. Clara. Her voice was easily and annoyingly recognizable. Declan growled and anger flashed in his eyes, but his jawline tightened.

"Don't just leave her here."

Wasn't planning on it. Declan climbed to his feet with her gently cradled and in a few strides I'd snatched her from him. Blood leaked from her throat and trickled down her body, drenching her clothing. With the amount of blood, I couldn't tell how bad her wound was, but her shallow breaths told me everything I needed to know.

She hardly weighed a thing. The Little One was as light as a feather, so much so I was surprised she'd never floated away. Blood trickled onto my skin, staining my flesh. There was no way she'd survive.

My wolf raked claws against my chest, demanding release. Failure was never an option for me, but I'd failed and the consequence was bleeding out in my arms.

Why was it agony seeing her like this?

I gritted my teeth and tore my eyes away to meet Declan's

before turning toward the woods. She deserved privacy in the moon to breathe her final breath. She came first.

Branches snapped under my steps as I crept deeper into the woods, trying to find the perfect spot for her. I couldn't stop drinking in the lines of her face and the straining of her cheekbones. Why was she so thin?

This was the longest I'd ever allowed myself to look at her in years, and I was just as riveted as I feared. Her dark brows were smoothed out and her lips slightly parted—beautiful. I tried to swallow past the knot in my throat at the lack of life in her features. The pangs in my chest making it difficult to breathe.

Moonlight beamed on a plush patch of forest and I stopped, dropped to my knees, and lowered her. Her long wavy hair slipped over my arm, the dark strands caressing my skin.

Such a pitiful, lovely little thing.

Her neck...

The flesh on her neck was knitting together.

Liliana jerked, and her back arched, a deep groan escaping her before she settled on the ground.

What was happening?

What was that scent? My mouth watered. It was perfect, heavenly, home, and... *mine.*

My nose flared as I sucked in as much of that smell as I could. Liliana suddenly thrashed, and my grip fell from her body as she released a keening sound. The bones beneath her skin stretched and elongated. Her expression morphed into one of pain. Her cheekbones stretched as they molded into a muzzle, and fur sprouted from her pores. Dark hair lengthened and retracted, popping up in a flurry down her body.

My mouth dried at the sight of the panting curved mass.

She was a beautiful midnight black that shone stark against the grass.

All I could do was blink as my body, wolf, and mind focused on the small bundle.

It became hers. *I became hers.*

A warmth spread through my chest, and my cock hardened painfully.

My wolf thrashed and clawed for release. I fell forward to my hands and knees as my body arched. Gritting my teeth, I fought him back, struggling as I regained my strict control. The scent of my blood slipped into my mouth from where I'd bitten my tongue.

My cock twitched with the need to be inside her and claim her. I burned to tear her pussy apart and show her she was mine in every way.

Liliana's chest heaved, and she whimpered as her fur retracted, her body lengthening and stretching until she lay in her human form.

She was my true mate. *Mine.*

It was something I'd always felt, always at the surface, but without her wolf at the forefront, I was blind.

This was impossible.

Liana

My eyelids fluttered as grass tickled my skin, and I smacked at the sensation.

I was dying, but why was I so energized? The taste of blood coated my tongue, and I coughed at the bitter taste. Death. Blood. Gore. My neck! I cupped it, my trembling fingers patting around the slippery skin at my throat.

It felt... fine?

There was something foreign feeling in my body, elusive and difficult to grasp, but it was a separate entity brimming with instincts and emotion. She seemed both uneasy and excited. The muscles in my shoulders bunched. It was my wolf. She'd healed my torn out neck by surfacing. So what was said was true. If you're close to death, an initial shift could save a werewolf from the brink. That sort of healing would be nice to have at all times. Instead, werewolves had a relatively sped up healing rate, but it took hours and sometimes days as opposed to human healing, which took weeks. I'd been lucky, but it didn't make sense. I was twenty, I *shouldn't* have access to my wolf.

Grass tickled my butt and my eyes popped open. I met Lore's stunned expression. The ground shifted and butterfly wings viciously raked my insides, making me suck in a stunned breath. A sweet scent tickled my nose, and my heart throbbed. I ached to turn toward Lore and cuddle my body close to his, to have him shield me, baby me, and *love me.*

My mate.

Tears pricked my eyes as his turned predatory. A foreign sensation in my chest pushed out. It was all instinct and animalistic need.

It was the missing part of me.

My wolf.

Lore suddenly lunged at me. I squeaked, scrambling my bare ass backwards. I stifled a wince at the scrape of a particularly sharp branch, but as quick as I was, it wasn't enough.

Lore pinched my chin between his thumb and forefinger, forcing my face up, and my neck cramped at the angle. He growled into my face, an inch away from touching my lips. His shadowed eyes bore into mine and the sweet citrusy scent enveloped me comfortingly. My fingernails pierced the grass I sat on as I struggled to not move.

The grip on my chin softened and his palm slid up until he cupped the side of my face, holding my cheek with a feather-like touch. His large body blocked out the moon, casting a shadow over me.

Lore's head dipped, and his hand twitched on my face, shoulders spasming. A beat stretched into two and by this point, we were both panting.

"I can't hold back," he said on a gruff growl and dipped forward, capturing my lips. His mouth covered mine, the warm sensation foreign. My lips parted on a gasp and he thrust his tongue into my mouth, lapping into my depths—tasting.

A shiver crested up my spine, and heat bloomed, spreading to my clit. I groaned and tipped my chin higher, needing him all over me. An undulating heat in my gut constricted and unfurled until I was whimpering into his mouth.

Goddess, he felt so good.

I was pure need, and I never wanted it to stop. I wiggled into the grass as the pressure at my clit throbbed. I needed... I needed pressure there. I wanted him *there*.

His unoccupied hand inched down, caressing until his thumb curved beneath the swell of my breast.

My eyes popped open. *W-what was going on?*

His tongue thrust between my lips, flicking into mine. Kisses—from Lore.

Impossible.

Was I imagining stuff now?

I cracked open my eyes and yanked away, scrambling back a foot. The moon's glow caused his blond hair to appear grayish, and his eyes glinted, reflecting in the darkness. His shoulders rose and fell sharply, and he ate up the space I placed between us as I scooted back.

I licked my lips and flattened on the ground as he loomed over me, hovering and unmoving.

With this angle, I was able to see more of his features and I sucked in a breath at the fire in his gaze.

I whined and rubbed the ache on my nipples. His growl vibrated through my body, enflaming the throb more. An uncomfortable tightness pressed against my skin, trying to escape. It was my wolf side. Her instincts pushed under my skin, thrashing for *something*.

It was as if we were simultaneously separate beings, yet the same all at once. The sensation was foreign, but she wanted what I wanted and right now that was our mate.

Lore's nose grazed my collar bone and trailed downwards until his lips fastened around my nipple, suckling.

"Lore," I moaned loud, back arching as heat swept through my belly. The tingling heightened at my clit and numb pleasure spread. A heavy throb pulsed with my heartbeat at the apex of my thighs and I helplessly undulated. Needily. Lore's teeth grazed the flesh of my breast, gently but warningly, and sparks burst behind my eyelids as his lips returned to my nipple. I'd pined for him and now he was mine. I squeezed my eyes shut tightly and the sounds of the world faded as my toes curled with an orgasm so intense I couldn't think. I desperately curved toward his suckling mouth, moaning helplessly. The waves of release throbbed through my body. Each squeeze of my core ripped the breath from my lungs as my legs trembled.

So that was how that felt.

I couldn't catch my breath before Lore crawled higher, so his mouth hovered over my parted lips. His eyes bore into me, feverish and animalistic, as his hand glided to the sensitive bud between my legs. His warm finger slipped between my folds, rubbing in circular motions as he teased low into my entrance and retreated back to my clit, spreading my wetness. I cried out at his demanding touch, twitching to get away from the overload of sensation.

Lore fitted his other arm over my shoulder and leaves crushed under his flattening palm. His wrist settled as a block, and I wasn't able to wiggle away from the sensitivity at the apex of my thighs. I loved the demanding touch, but my body was no longer connected to my brain. It was his to do with as he wished.

The foreign sensation of his fingers shoved inside me had my mouth opening in a silent cry. It felt so good. I tipped my hips toward his hand, searching out more of that feeling.

"Your pussy is ready for me." The words ended in a growl, more animal than human.

Pussy.

Muscles tensing, I grabbed his hair in my fists and tugged the strands frantically to pull him closer to my body. What was I asking for? I needed... something. What was it?

I licked my lips, craving his taste.

"I want..."

I focused on the golden strands poking between my fingers, loving the look of my fingers wrapped in his hair.

The thought dispersed, and I tugged again until he finally dipped his head to nip the side of my breast. The combination with his fingers in my pussy wrenched a groan free. Lore slowly withdrew his digits from their slow exploration and I whimpered my denial.

A steel-like rod prodded my belly as Lore climbed higher up my body. Our lips were no longer lined up since he was so tall. Lore clasped one of my thighs, spreading me open as my heart struggled to beat.

I needed him... so much. I reached up and gripped his shoulders, struggling to wrap my hands around the stiff muscle.

A prod at my sex made me suck in a breath. Yes. Yes. I've wanted this. I've always wanted Lore. My wolf and I were in harmony about this. She unfold in my chest, waiting, needing the claiming.

The tip of his dick slipped past the folds of my pussy and he slowly fed into my wet heat. I couldn't help the undeniable need to peer down as he seated himself in me. A tremble coasted his body and his eyes flashed in the darkness as fur erupted from his skin, climbing up to cover every inch of him. His jaw popped and expanded and the wolf features became pronounced. Furry ears popped out from his head, the pink shells twitched. Lore's entire body grew from all directions until he was a massive furry body looming over me intimidatingly.

What was this? The member deep inside me twitched, excruciatingly thick. My lungs seized and I struggled to breathe from the fullness between my thighs. I whimpered and raked my eyes down his massive, furred humanoid body to where we were joined. How did *that* fit? Lore was seated all the way in but the fit continued to tighten, the base of his cock expanding—stretching out.

I screamed at the sharp pain, eyes watering as he stilled, waiting for my body to adjust to his thickness. I gawked up at the strange wolf monster five times my size with his muzzle hovering high above my face.

What was going on?

Fangs exploded from his muzzle as he released an ear-splitting roar and withdrew his cock from my sheath. The pressure in my pussy lessened for a split second before he rammed so deeply that the air sucked out of my lungs. I grunted and jerked against him, heat spreading from my clit and making me squeeze him. My head fell to the side as my lips parted.

This was wrong. I was sick. I should stop this, but...

More. I wanted more.

LORE

I FED MY COCK INTO HER SWEET WARM PUSSY, groaning at her heat as I bent to stroke my tongue into her mouth. My face felt odd, but I couldn't think right with my cock in her. She was heaven. I nipped her lower lip. Liliana flinched and whimpered as blood spilled onto my tongue. I lapped my tongue across her mouth, panting. My jaw was elongated, and I ran my long wolf-like tongue across the front of my teeth where sharp fangs poked out. What the fuck?

Crimson painted her plush lips and droplets of her blood trickled down her chin. I dipped again to lap my tongue across her mouth to collect the precious blood, my chest vibrating. I lifted and looked down at her lidded eyes and parted pillowy lips calling to me.

That was a miracle in itself. I never craved kissing and had never repeated the experience after my teenage years.

Now, I understood why. I wanted Liliana to be the only taste on my tongue.

Her pussy fluttered around my cock and I helplessly thrust into her again, unable to give her innocent flesh time to adjust.

As soon as I moved an inch, I lost it, helplessly twisting my hips as I slammed my cock into her again.

I should give her time, but I just couldn't fucking stop my hips from moving. My head dropped as I wheezed for a breath. I needed to look at her pussy...

My nostrils flared at her sweet fucking scent as I gawked at my thick cock. Air whistled from my mouth and I helplessly thrust forward again, seating myself deep in her cunt. I was already fucking big, but this was on another level. And what was this fur coating my skin?

Seed thickened at my base, a heavy pressure drawing me taut.

My cock expanded and distended, thickening in girth, but it didn't stop there. My knot ballooned at the base of my dick, her warm lips enveloping the bulbs and filling her silky pussy. Her head thrashed and her mouth opened on a silent cry.

I seated myself until the tip of my cock curved deep within her lush channel. The knot bulged forcing my frantic thrusts to a halt and locking me in place. It would take an effort if I wanted to dislodge her from my cock, but I didn't want to. I couldn't tear my gaze away from the way she stretched around my dick.

I couldn't think—what was this—

The release was instantaneous.

My fucking eyes crossed as my cock jerked painfully in her core. Each jet squirted a long stream of cum into her depths.

Good.

She was mine. With my eyes tightly squeezed shut, my hands trembled at her hips as I released every drop. My thighs twitched as wave after wave of cum pulsated from my cock, claiming her. I craned my neck toward the moon. This was fucking breathtaking. Better than any pussy I'd ever been inside.

This was home.

My heart squeezed.

Liliana's hips pushed against mine, begging for more, and my dick convulsed. The knot at the base expanded with my rising lust and I growled, pistoning my hips as her slippery pussy ate my dick. My neck strained as a tremble coasted up my spine. Her wet cunt sucked at me as her head thrashed, mewls falling from her lips as her eyelids twitched. She was made for fucking. The pressure at my spine built. She clawed at my forearms, frantically meeting my thrusts. Since she was so wet, I was able to pull the knot out of her pussy and I used it to tease her clit with shallow thrusts.

We moved in tandem. Our movements verged on desperation.

I placed my palm on her chest and held her down. With my other hand, I grasped her leg and hiked it over my hip, curling it so she could balance herself on it.

The motion tipped her hips up and I grunted when my dick was seated deep inside her. I rammed into her; the thud resonating through the woods.

A deep groan wrenched from my mouth as her body spasmed and her leg fastened around my hip, tensing against me.

Her entire body shuddered and her channel sucked my dick into her needily. Grinding my teeth, I was unable to hold back a second release. My breaths were ragged and loud as my cock filled her with cum.

Liliana licked her lips and trembled.

I met her eyes and the recognition of who she was to me made my grip tighten on her. I didn't want to ever let her go.

Tears glittered in her brown eyes. A rumble vibrated in my chest and my fingers flexed. Liliana whimpered and tried freeing herself from my grip, but I held her in place. Why was she struggling to leave me?

I sucked in a breath, looking at my furred hands and the black claws at my nail beds. My shoulders tightened, and I loosened my hold on her, but couldn't let her go.

My wolf didn't feel separated from me. We felt like one, our needs and desires co-mingling at the surface.

"Shhh, Little One," I said in a foreign voice. It verged on a growl, rumbling out of me throatily. It was difficult getting the words out. My muzzle moved differently.

My teeth clicked shut.

"Did I hurt y—" My question cut off on a moan as she twisted her hips. Liliana's sigh reached my dick, and her brown eyes glinted.

Fuck, I need her again.

My soaked cock slipped out of her pussy, blood slicked from her channel. I *was* too big for her. Claws burying into the grass, I lowered my head and lapped the juices at her inner thighs as I cleaned her. Her pussy glinted in the moonlight, and a rumbling moan vibrated through me. I prodded my wet nose against her folds. She arched her back, crying out as she rubbed her wet cunt on my muzzle.

A wolf-like chuff escaped my mouth. Her soft thighs trembled. It was too much for me, and my cock hardened. I bared my teeth, grabbing her hips before twisting her.

Liliana flipped over and pushed onto her knees. The way she shoved her ass back almost made me spill all over her flesh.

Mmm. Not a bad idea, but not today. One day I'd cover her entire body in my cum.

I slid my dick into her, sliding my hand over her ass. That would be mine, too.

Her ass cheeks fit my palms perfectly, and I squeezed them as I stroked into her, the building heaviness in my cock starting to inflate. Her movements were erratic, but I allowed her to claim me from the bottom as I stilled over her.

There was nothing better than her.

The words rounded my head.

Thud after thump made me bare my teeth, and I sniffed her neck. She was sweeter than anything I'd ever smelled. I worked to accommodate her tiny body, especially against my newly massive form.

Little Liliana.

My Little One.

My teeth grazed against her neck again.

"Claim me," she whimpered. Her words were a signal and my dick spasmed in her pussy as she squeezed me with her release. I groaned, the sound deep and resounding as my cock spilled into her with jarring spurts. My sight blurred and my teeth clamped on her neck. Right as I was about to slice my teeth into her precious flesh, I stopped.

Control. I exhaled sharply. I needed to *think*.

If I bit her, it would make her my mate. Luna.

The age-old fear weighed on my shoulder.

I needed *time*.

"Alpha?"

The title snapped me further out of my daze. I pressed my claws on my belly and sliced inward. Blood spurted from my self-inflicted wound and splattered on her. The sharp pain helped me push myself off, panting.

"I can't," I said with a growl, shaking my head jerkily.

Liliana jerked as if struck, backing up as she bent her legs closer to her and stretched her arm over her naked chest. Her lower lip trembled, and she curved into herself.

I growled. I didn't like that. She wasn't to cover herself from me.

"Why?" Her words were so soft and confused.

Nausea crawled up my throat. I hated the frown marring her lips, and her quick blinks as she attempted to rid herself of the tears—I shook my head and a snarl ripped from my throat as fur retreated from my skin, slinking back into my flesh. The fullness in my mouth lessened, and my ears and gums felt normal. My wolf railed at my insides, clawing and thrashing, fighting for control.

Now it was as if he was separate from me.

Liliana blinked at me owlishly, her innocent, *weak* eyes brimming with tears.

"You can't be my mate," I spat, not knowing what else to say or how to articulate my fear of her being so weak. I lurched back, her tears searing through my limbs and I curled my fingers.

On the heels of fear came the bitter realization of what had happened.

I'd knotted, which was impossible. My body had changed and my wolf melted into my skin, merging with me, which was also impossible. There were stories about Omega's mates...

My mouth dried. But Omegas were extinct.

She was impossible.

"Alpha!"

I whirled toward the voice of one of the Betas.

"Stay the fuck back," I roared. The foliage stopped moving. My knuckles popped. Turning back to my Little One, I fisted my hands.

"Don't move from here," I ordered.

She looked down. I didn't fear her disobeying me. She was weak, *and* she was mine.

I turned my back on her after a moment of grappling with my wolf's anger. My pack came first. She sucked in a sharp breath, but I quickened my stride.

Once I handled what I must, I would devote all my time to figuring out what the fuck I was going to do.

LIANA

Rubbing my chest, I hiccupped, wiping the tears drenching my face as I gazed at the moon shadowed by clouds. A shiver wracked my body. I must have been sitting out here in the cold for a while now.

I was so tired of being overlooked. My lips trembled. The vision I presented must be so pitiful; curled up on the forest floor, bawling my eyes out. I was so disgusted with myself.

Sniffling, I climbed to my feet unsteadily. I'd almost forgotten the important development because of my pity fest.

I was a werewolf now, but my excitement was overshadowed by the pain Lore had inflicted on my heart. I wiggled my toes and grimaced at the cold ground as I weaved between the trees, leaves crunching under my toes.

Sex was unlike anything I'd thought it would be, and it wasn't shocking that he was magnificent at it.

Something that had simply been an out-of-my-reach concept was something he practiced often.

My steps stuttered at the knifing in my gut. He rejected me, which meant Lore would continue to be with other women. I wasn't sure I could deal with having to clean that room after another night of sex.

Would I even be able to step into that room without the memories assaulting me?

My lip curled as my heart quivered in my chest.

No, I would not be able to deal with it.

A few tears spilled at the visual of him doing to another woman what he'd done to me.

Lore hadn't cared that I was his true mate. He'd turned up his nose at a gift not many experienced. His body had reacted to me, and he'd treated me as his, but he'd turned his back on me. I didn't understand everything that happened when true mates found each other, but it was a much more, er, *visual* and *physical* change than I'd imagined. That thickening of his dick had almost ripped me in half, but even with the sharp pain, I wanted more of it. I wanted to be owned by him.

Even with his physical wolfish aspects—the long tongue, the ears, the muzzle, the size, the *fur*—I couldn't *not* want him. I'd thought he'd felt the same when his teeth had grazed me, ready to claim me... but he hadn't.

What was worse was he'd hinted what it could be between us, and just as easily, ripped it out from under my feet.

I brushed my forearm across my face and crossed my arms, clutching myself. Right before I stepped out of the tree lining, I stumbled to a stop.

Declan stared at me, and my world shifted under my feet. My heart picked up the pace, thudding against my ribcage, and I ached to walk over to him.

Mate.

What was this?

This was impossible. Two mates were an unheard of blessing.

I stumbled back a step. Was it because Lore had refused me? I shook my head.

The knot in my throat thickened excruciatingly.

Declan's lips parted then shut, eyes flashing with confusion and a ton of emotions I didn't understand. The grass crunched under his foot as he took two abrupt steps forward, lifting his hand toward me.

A ringing pierced my ears, and my chest expanded with pressure. I needed him. If I curled into his arms, he would soothe the pain away, he would protect me.

A growl at my back startled me.

Whirling, I cringed back from Clara. She was too close for comfort. She sniffed in my direction. Her face reddened and her lips set into a snarl. "Omega."

My eyebrows furrowed.

"How are *you* an Omega?"

Omega. I mouthed the word, testing it out. What was that?

She wanted to kill me. Her eyes shouted her intention. I trembled in place as she stepped closer to me.

I was given a second true mate, but Declan already had a mate. My lip trembled.

He was already mated with someone. He could never be mine.

Why, Moon Goddess?

When a werewolf chose a mate that wasn't their *true* mate, they still claimed each other with a bite. The difference was the male didn't grow fangs because only half of the whole was choosing. The wolf side wasn't in agreement but he was along for the ride. However, when it was a true mate, both wolf and human were in harmony. The bond was also stronger for true mates.

So why did I have two?

The grass rustled, and I whirled to study Declan, stifling the ache to run into his arms.

That was why I'd always felt safe with him. He was meant to be mine.

But he would never be.

His emotions were veiled behind his harsh expression. I already sensed the rejection coming.

Then it was decided.

I would not stay in this pack.

My wolf was in agony, but instead of it making her wallow, fury rushed through her as she bashed herself inside me. My muddled brain battled to keep control. So much confusion... but I hurt for my mates.

Declan

SHE WAS MY TRUE MATE. A MASSIVE KNOT SOLIDIFIED in my throat and stomach as a roar deafened my ears. I grappled to still myself.

I took another useless step toward her.

You should have fucking waited for her. You should have opened your eyes to those instincts tugging you toward her.

My nails dug into my palm, and the wolf rammed itself against the bars of my psyche. Each jolt was a shock through my system.

What had Clara meant about an Omega? She smelled so tantalizing because she was my mate or not... The wolf pushed under my skin, begging to explode out and tear out Clara's throat. That was *my* scent to enjoy.

Liliana couldn't be an Omega. They'd been gone a long fucking time, much longer than I'd been alive. Some murdered, some hunted, and many bred until they died. Omegas birthed children who wouldn't be defective, which made them incredibly sought after back then. Some were tracked down through their alluring scent that drove male wolves into a frenzy. Stories of Omegas' heats were still passed down by male wolves ruing that would never experience it. Yet, despite all of this... I was more concerned about keeping her safe and out of the clutches of anyone who may hurt her.

I couldn't tear my gaze from Liliana's naked form. One of her arms crossed over her breasts, while the other slipped down to cover her pussy, fingers spread wide to hide herself.

It was such a human behavior that my chest blistered. She was so innocent and new to all of this. Streaks of blood dried on her neck, flaking on her skin.

I took another useless step forward, and Clara mimicked it, forcing me to freeze.

If I stepped closer, Clara would attack.

Studying every inch of Lily's body, I didn't see open wounds, which was the only reason I was able to rein in my control.

"My mate?" The worry glinting in her brown eyes sent shards through my body, pricking my fingertips as my heart raced in my chest, pounding for release. *She was right.* All around. She. Just. Felt. Right.

Liliana hugged herself tighter, detaching her eyes from mine. I followed her gaze to a tight-faced Clara whose eyes glinted menacingly.

Shit.

Clara was too close to Liliana. She could shift in moments and drag her claws across the beautiful flesh with one swipe. I didn't know if I could shift and get to her in time to stop it. I refused to be late to save Lily again—I couldn't chance it.

My true mate may already have access to her wolf, but she was still vulnerable. She didn't know how to defend herself. She'd thrown herself in the way of claws; to defend me. It was a punch to my soul. The injury must not have been as bad as it had seemed since gaining her wolf healed it, but that wouldn't be the case now. She may be more resilient and able to take more pain before dying but that wasn't necessarily a good thing. Her frail body still felt pain as keenly as any human. She'd just suffer longer.

My heart thundered in my ears and my reason for living stared at me with growing hope as she stumbled forward a step. Coming to me.

Clara snarled.

"No," I snapped.

Inhaling sharply, I stared at Lily. "I reject you." My knees weakened, and I staggered, my body physically rejecting causing pain to my mate. She cried out and fell to her knees, clasping her chest with a choked gag. My skin itched with the need to go to her and my nose burned as a gnawing ache hollowed my gut.

Don't do that, my Lily.

Breaths hissed between my teeth and I focused on them as my wolf railed, closer to the surface than it had ever been. My wolf and I were one, in harmony at all times, but right now he felt foreign. It was as if my body wanted to rip itself in two.

My jaw worked. I needed to get Clara away from her, and then I could beg Lily's forgiveness. It'd hurt her now, but I would soothe her pain.

Thankfully, Clara was already staring at me with glee in her expression. She thought she won. She took a step toward me. One away from Lily.

"I already have a mate," I said, fixing my gaze on Lily's shoulder. I didn't have to look at her to know she flinched as if I'd doled her a physical blow.

I ached to fall at her feet and beg until my nasty lies were erased. Unable to help it, my eyes lifted to her agonized ones. I staggered back, but quickly regained my composure, acting like I'd simply stepped back.

More than my pain, I feared for her safety. Clara would murder, and I wouldn't have enough time to slam between them before the she-wolf meant for me was slaughtered.

Damn fucking Clara. The mate I never wanted, nor loved, which was something I'd expressed various times. She'd always been an obligation, and the only reason I'd mated her was because I'd gotten her pregnant.

I never expected her to miscarry, but by that point, it was too late. I had claimed her. The mating bite cemented the relationship, and it was 'til death do us part.

Even though every particle in my body rejected the idea of moving away from Lily, I still did it. I quickened my stride away from the scene, knowing Clara would follow me.

I'd fucked up my entire life.

Clara's hand dragged up my spine in a possessive move, curdling my skin, and the visceral need to shove her away battled within my chest.

I'd never be able to claim my true mate because I was bonded to another.

A vicious urge to slice my claws through Clara's chest invaded my mind, and I tensed. That wasn't only the wolf... it was what *I* wanted.

I gritted my teeth. I wasn't a monster.

Maybe... maybe I could get Clara away and—

Would Liliana accept me even though I was damaged goods? Even though I'd betrayed her?

Fuck!

I dragged my fingers through my hair. I couldn't shift until I was far enough away from Liliana or else I'd fuck her until she understood she was mine.

"Declan."

I bit back my snarl and allowed Clara to trail me. The further she was from my little Lily, the better for my conscience.

There were instances I'd come across where a werewolf loved the person they chose to mate, and in encountering their true mate, it didn't sway them. I wasn't one of them.

I would have Liliana, but first, I had to deal with Clara.

"Dec," Clara cooed.

Grunting in answer, I stalked toward the home we shared. Clara picked up her pace to catch up to me.

The distance from Lily hurt my chest. I needed to curve my body to hers, to baby her, and be everything to her.

Anger thrashed in my gut. I fisted my hands at the reminder looking at Clara brought. As much as I hated admitting it, she was my mate. A hurdle I'd never anticipated. I would never be able to claim Lily. From a simple bite, I'd intrinsically tied myself to Clara unless...

Unless I killed her.

My fingers twitched with the urge to snap her neck. I clicked my teeth together, grinding them hard as I chased the darkness away. I couldn't do that.

Right?

My teeth should have been ash by now. I couldn't do that to my mother who loved Clara like her own daughter.

There was no other option. Lily would have to live with the fact that she was mine without my bite marking her beautiful skin.

The problem was whether I would be able to handle it without going mad. The claiming bite ensured every other wolf knew she belonged to someone. If I couldn't always have my scent all over her, I wouldn't be able to cling to sanity.

Already my wolf instincts writhed with anger at leaving her. He didn't understand my retreat since he ached for his true mate and he sensed my hunger for her. A growl built in my throat and I gritted my teeth so I wouldn't shift and tear the throat out of the female dogging our steps. He'd always tolerated Clara since we'd mated her, but as far as any affection went, it was nonexistent. For him, as it was for me, it was duty.

Against his will, I'd claimed Clara with my bite. I'd made her and her wolf ours, something he'd fought me on. Now I understood why. He'd been lying in wait.

Stairs creaked as I climbed them, and the front door slammed behind me. I waited for her to pass me.

Now that she was away from my Lily, I could be transparent.

"We're done."

Clara's grin wilted, and her eyes narrowed. "I'd be lying if I said I didn't see this coming. I'm not letting you go." Her eyes blazed and a glazed sheen covered them the same way they did when she had a madness bout.

I studied her, weighing my options. I needed her stalled until I consulted with Lore. Whether I left with Lily or sent Clara off elsewhere, I refused to be stuck with someone I've wanted to escape.

My first mistake was allowing her to back up. The second was her knowing where I hid my weapons, including the tranquilizers. Her hand dipped behind the cabinet and she leveled a barrel at my chest. Fuck, I'd left it loaded.

"Don't."

She bared her teeth, madness glinting. Clara cocked the

gun, and I lunged. There was a discharge and a sharp stabbing pain on my side as I gripped her arm, throwing her at the wall. There was a satisfying crack of her body slamming into the plaster. She cocked the gun she'd miraculously kept hold of and shot me again.

My sight grew fuzzy, and the ground spun as I stumbled after her as she discharged again. Clara panted, lips curved into a snarl.

My heart thudded in my ears as I faltered, falling to my knees. The floor pressed into my cheek. She was going after Lily and I was helpless to stop her.

LIANA

I BENT IN HALF AND VOMITED UNTIL ALL I DID WAS heave. Being rejected twice in a row hurt so badly, and I wanted nothing more than to curl up and die.

Never in a thousand years would I have thought both true mates wouldn't want me. Moon Goddess, I couldn't imagine how difficult that could be. Every cell in my body was weighed down, dragging me into a depression I would never escape.

There were no longer tears. Simply numbness.

I couldn't pry my eyes away from where Declan disappeared with his mate. There wasn't a doubt in my mind they returned to the home they shared amongst many of the other families. A home they'd shared for years.

A howl brought my attention to the manor looming in the distance, seeming so tiny from where I stood. It was deceptive. The place was ginormous and could be considered something similar to a mansion. It was just out of reach, as my mates were. Seeming so small and within my grasp but that was laughable.

This couldn't be my life.

I couldn't stay here.

The kitchen door at the side of the building made the familiar bitterness rise. That would not be my life any longer.

A wolf howled eerily and werewolves scattered throughout the pack lands joined the mournful cries. How many had lost their lives in tonight's attack?

Some packmates inched around limp bodies as others walked around, helping collect the dead or to drag attackers into a pile.

If I left now, no one would notice my absence until it was time for breakfast, and by then I would be long gone.

Pushing to my feet, I made my way to my hovel on trembling legs.

What was it about me that made me so unwanted?

Opening the door, I rushed to my things. Swiftly donning my only other articles of clothing, I finished getting dressed and shoved them on without worrying about wiping myself down. I didn't have time.

The same bag my mother had when we moved the first time hung on the knob, and I yanked it over my shoulder. Stretching it open, I collected the small savings mother managed to accumulate when she'd planned for us to leave.

I peeked out through a sliver and it all seemed the same. No one was looking for me. Something that used to hurt so badly was now something I was grateful for. My cheeks puffed out as I held in air, clasping the straps of the bag with trembling hands. It was fashioned in a way so I could shift with the bag remaining strapped to me. Slipping off my necklace, I placed it in an inner pouch and patted it.

With a sharp exhale, I studied my bedroom one last time before decidedly pushing through the door. Turning in the opposite direction I usually went, I rounded the building. The forest was closer from this side.

Although I'd never stepped out of our small community, I knew the general direction of the road. I just needed to avoid being directly on it and head parallel until I hit the main road to get as far away from here as possible.

The possibilities stretched out in front of me, and I swallowed hard. There was fear—undoubtedly, but also a tinge of excitement racing through my chest.

I moistened my lips as I neared the edge of the forest, casting my eyes over my shoulder. The cleanup was winding down, and it looked like the pack was making their way into the manor. Good, no one would care to pay attention to me. A smile spread on my lips and I picked up my pace.

A crunch of leaves made me pause and look around, but after no movement, I continued. My neck prickled, and a growl built at the back of my throat. My wolf's instincts were going off. Before I could pay more attention to what the urge was in my legs, a body hit me full force.

I grunted and fell onto my back, scrambling to get back to my feet. A heavy weight pinned me, and I met Clara's maddened eyes.

"You bitch. He's mine. *Mine*."

"Clara," I cried as spittle dripped on my face. "Stop, please." Blood burst from my nose and I cried out at the assault on my face. Her fist withdrew and flew toward me. I cringed to the side, trying to avoid her attack, but she angled to follow my retreat. Bone gave under her fists, and my nose burned. The numbness spread over my cheeks.

My heartbeat raced a mile a minute and my wolf thrashed in my chest. I should let her out, I should do *something*—fight, but I remained frozen under her beating and tried curling into myself to protect my head.

A copper taste flooded my mouth and her next aim at my chest made all the air expel from my lungs as I froze up, unable to breathe.

Blood dripped into my eyes, and my face was in agony. I wasn't new to this, but I didn't think she'd stop this time. She would have already stopped by now if that was her plan.

Death was her aim.

I wanted to muster the strength to fight back, but I deserved this. I'd wanted something that wasn't for me.

My teeth clicked shut. No, I didn't.

I didn't do anything wrong.

My wolf pushed at my skin, pissed both at me for cringing and the woman that challenged us.

A shout rang in my ears, and arms curled around Clara, pulling her back. Shivering, I scrambled back, wiping my blurred eyes.

A werewolf Beta my age, fought to contain Clara, his eyes wide as he looked at me.

"Thank you," I whispered, but doubted he heard me since I gurgled out blood from trying to speak.

Finally, giving in to my wolf, I let the shift sting my flesh. Pain wracked my body, pinching my limbs as they stretched. My vision blurred and my sight became hyper-focused and clearer.

The pulsating near my ribs hurt so much, but I couldn't falter now. I needed to get away and then I'd take stock of my wounds.

My muzzle was easy to see, and I opened my maw. Taking a step forward, I stumbled like a colt. I was thinking too much. Relaxing my mind, I let my she-wolf instincts take the reins.

Gathering my footing, I dashed through the break in the forest. It was easier for me to ignore the ache with her at the forefront. She was pure survival and less thinking. We wanted the same thing, but she wasn't bogged down by emotions. Trees slapped my body as I ran like a murderer was on my heels, which wasn't far off. Who knew how long the werewolf would be able to hold her?

Leaves kicked up under my paws, and I wove through the dark woods, my bag staying in place and slapping into my sides. If I was in my human form, I wouldn't have been able to make much out other than shadows, but with my wolf's eyes, there were shapes and hues, making it easy for me to navigate in the darkness.

My chest puffed with exhaustion as I pushed in the direction of a roaring motor. My ears flicked as I remained hyper-focused on my surroundings. Instinct begged me to run in the other direction, but I talked my wolf into going toward it. It was a car and by the sound of it; it was big. When I saw the massive tires and a truck bed, I was glad I had.

I was getting out of here tonight.

Pushing off the ground, I simultaneously jumped, putting everything I had into my legs. My body thumped on the bed of the massive truck. Catching my balance, I swayed as the vehicle bounced, the world spun, and I promptly lost consciousness.

LORE

"PLACE HIM IN THE SHED AND GUARD HIM," I BARKED at Lincoln, one of my Beta enforcers. The prisoner snarled weakly at me, his eyes flashing with pain. Sweat dripped from his face as Lincoln dragged him toward the reinforced building. The excitement of the night dwindled as I worked to get everything back in order.

Where the fuck was Declan?

It should have been easy to clock Declan's unmistakable stature after a quick scan of the area in front of the manor.

I scraped my hand through my hair. I couldn't make an Omega my Luna. As rare as they were. She was still weak. From my understanding, Omega's were to be coddled and taken care of. I needed someone who could stand by my side during battle. Who I didn't need to worry about at times like this because I knew she could take care of herself.

Liliana was not like that, but knowing that, I couldn't bring myself to care. Even now, I wanted to rush to her to ensure her safety.

Omegas had been gone for decades, and hide nor hair had

been seen of one, so I only had stories passed down from elders to go off of. And much of what was claimed was seeped in toxicity.

If what they stated was true, the Alpha mate of an Omega always ended up leaving their pack because they couldn't handle the jealousy of the attraction Omegas caused in un-mated werewolves. That wasn't an option for me. I hadn't worked as hard as I could to pick up the crumbled pieces after my uncle destroyed the pack for a she-wolf.

Especially now that someone saw fit to mess with my pack for the first time in five years.

"Alpha!"

My head whipped toward the young Beta rushing up to me. I quirked a brow at the panting mess Alex presented with blood splattered on his chest.

I inhaled sharply. The familiar sweet scent slid into my nose. My teeth sharpened, and I snarled.

Gripping the front of his shirt, I used it as leverage to toss him. The pup landed with a yelp, whimpering as he scrambled back. In a few swift strides, I grabbed his neck.

"Why do you have her blood on you?"

Fear blanketed the boy's eyes. He went limp in my grip.

"Answer!"

"T-there was a fight!" He panted, eyes moving side to side. "Clara was beating the serving girl half to death. I didn't know what to do."

A red haze filled my vision. His whimper dragged me out of the encroaching shift. Grabbing onto control with all my strength, I loosened my hands, and he fell to the ground.

"What happened, speak quickly."

"The girl was covered in injuries, cowering as she was

beaten. I feared if I didn't pull Clara off her, she would have killed her." My body quaked.

"Where?"

I followed the path that his shaking finger pointed and took off running, shifting mid-run and falling on four paws. Combining the quick shift with running struck agony through my limbs as my skin stretched and bones popped, but I ignored the ache.

My senses sharpened, and I followed my nose to the splatters of blood on the ground. I sniffed the spot filled with sweetness. My mate.

My wolf mentality was at the forefront and he had a single purpose; to get his mate to his side. We were in agreement.

Tongue flicking out, I licked her life's blood. The sweet coppery taste rose the hair on my neck. Where was she? I needed in her slick cunt. Now. A howl crawled up my throat, but a growl escaped.

My head swung in the direction of a raspy cough. I ducked low and growled. Clara.

I gnashed my teeth. What had this bitch done? I pounced.

Looming over her, she bared her neck, trembling.

"Alpha?"

My female's blood was splattered across her face. My maw was half open, ready to rip off her face, when I pulled my wolf back, grappling for control. Shaking my head, I backed up, giving her a weighted look, teeth showing warningly.

Confusion flickered in her expression.

I needed Clara to tell me everything that had happened. My wolf burned to bury his fangs into her neck and rip it out, but I couldn't make rash decisions no matter how much I wanted to. I snarled warningly. She flattened, cinching her eyes closed. Bitch. My claws scraped near her head and I caught a sweet peach scent. My vision blacked out and then I found myself running, desperate to find my Little One. She was injured, and she needed my help.

I knew these woods like the back of my hand, and I quickened my pace, kicking up dirt as I tore off in the direction of her smell. Her scent was raw. Close.

I jumped onto the asphalt, nails scraping into loose gravel, and skid to a stop. Her trail ended here. Turning from side to side, I eyed the main road that too many humans drove down. Where was she? I dropped my nose, but I couldn't catch anything.

Fuck.

Panic clawed my insides, and I took off running, following the road. *Where was she?* The words were chanted in my head, revolving and spurring my panic.

Declan's wolf lunged out of the brush. So he was the rustling I'd heard. In my single-minded focus I hadn't cared to check who approached. He snuffled questioningly, but I ignored him. He slammed into my side, slowing me down.

I whirled and bit his shoulder.

He easily shook it off, and his teeth clicked in my face. *Damn me* for choosing someone as dominant as me to be my second. Even with the title of a Beta he was as dominant as an Alpha, Declan's problem was he didn't want to lead anything, nor did he want to be outside of a pack structure because of his mother.

That made him great backup, but I'd never had to worry about him denying my demands, until now.

Dirt kicked up as I skidded to a stop. He shifted just as

quickly as I did, and I was able to rein in my wolf instinct to rip into his hide for defiance.

"What?" I snarled. His lip curled.

"I've found my true mate."

Shock only lasted for a split second before suspicion set in. I narrowed my eyes.

"I did too." I spat the following words. "Who?"

Declan narrowed his eyes.

"Lily. Liliana."

"Impossible." I set my mouth in a grim line. "She's mine."

Declan growled, showing his teeth.

"You've always pitied her," he said low, and growled.

"You have a mate already." Declan flinched. Good. He was mistaken. Little One was mine. No one had multiple mates.

Except... my nostrils flared. There were stories about how some Omegas were given to multiple mates by the Moon Goddess...

My teeth clicked. She was still mine.

"You've made your search for a strong mate very clear," Declan said, narrowing his eyes.

"I will have her, but I won't claim her." The words ripped out of me forcefully. It was wrong to say them. A sharp stab in my chest made me grit my teeth.

"You can claim her, something I wish I could, and you're throwing it in the Moon Goddess's face?" Declan laughed bitterly, scrubbing his hand through his hair. "Coward. This proves to me she isn't yours. If she could be mine, I would have claimed her the moment I found out."

Unable to hold back my fury, I swung. He easily dodged my fist and threw a punch in return. I grunted at the hit to my stomach. It rolled off as I returned the favor. Blood spurt from his mouth and he snarled.

She was already creating dissent.

Three wolves charged at us, moving between us in synchronization—more pack enforcers. Every strong pack had them. A select amount of werewolves placed themselves in the line of danger to protect the pack. It was a hierarchy, those at the top protected. Lincoln shifted.

"Alpha?" he asked and eyed Declan and me. We were both panting hard, sweat glistening on our naked skin.

I met Declan's eyes. The resolve there reinforced mine and suddenly we were on the same page. We must keep it between us for now. Omegas were coveted when they were around. I doubted that would have changed now.

"Go back. Keep the pack safe."

Lincoln automatically did as ordered and retreated.

When they were finally far enough, I faced my closest friend. "We'll debate all of this another time. We need to find her."

"Agreed," he responded grimly. "She's probably in her room."

"She is not," I said with bitter resolve.

Declan's eyes widened. "What do you mean?" he snapped.

"Your mate attacked her, and she took off running when Alex saved her."

His skin undulated with the urge of the shift.

"Her trace ends here."

Declan's face stiffened, and his nostrils flared.

"I'm going to find her."

My chest burned and the sour taste on my tongue spread. Declan didn't have the responsibilities of an Alpha. I could stop him and demand he stay away from her, but for once, I knew he wouldn't listen or bow his head.

A growl wanted to escape, but I swallowed it because I needed help to find her. After I had her in my grip, I'd decide on killing him or exiling him.

"Let's go." I had to rip the words out of my soul. It was better if I kept an eye on him. My sanity wouldn't handle the thought of him finding her first. Declan grunted in response.

He was done with words, eyes fixed down the road.

"Your mate tried to kill her. Now, I know why."

His lip curled. "I'll deal with her."

"Deal with her now, before Liliana returns. She doesn't need to be attacked by her own pack members."

He growled and stalked away.

With Lincoln, I had nothing to worry about. And all the pack needed to think was I was searching for answers from tonight's attack.

I couldn't muster guilt at going after her. I needed her with me. There was no other option.

I shifted and caught up to Declan.

Tension crackled between us.

This was simply one of the reasons Omegas were extinct—it was said they created too much strife. This was further proof of what I'd heard.

The other reason was the Alpha's put their Omega first, and that wasn't going to happen for me. She would always be second to my pack.

My wolf's instincts were always at the surface when I shifted, and I usually grappled to rein him in, but not today. I wanted my mate by any means possible.

Knox

Exiting my truck, I stretched my neck from side
to side and surveyed the area as instinct demanded. The only
sounds within the miles of forest where my cabin sat were
chirping birds and rustling leaves. I inhaled sharply, trying to
suck in more of the scent that had been haunting me for hours.

What the fuck was that delicious smell?

It had wafted to me the entire drive, making me so hard I
had zipper indents on my dick.

I licked my lips. It was otherworldly, and I wanted more of
it. Yanking my duffle from the back seat, I slammed the door,
and a whimper flitted to my ears. My steps stuttered to a stop,
and I frowned. That sounded close and human. I crouched,
looking under the truck, but there was nothing. A rustle came
from the back and my strides ate up the space.

Someone who smelled like delicious, sweet peaches was in
the bed of my truck. I craned my head and found a shivering
bundle curled in on herself.

Blood sprinkled her all over, and what I could see of her face
was splotchy and swollen. I cursed, grinding my molars. From

the ashen color of her skin, I could tell she needed medical attention. The truck creaked under my grip.

How had she gotten in my truck? I inhaled. She was a werewolf, but unlike any I'd ever scented. The delicious smell was her. My mouth watered, and I hardened more.

Fuck.

What was wrong with me? The girl was on death's door, and I wanted to fuck her. I leaned closer as my neck tingled and the sensation of belonging rushed through my chest. Her eyes popped open, and she cried out, cringing back as she blinked at me with watering eyes.

A rumble vibrated my chest, almost like a purr. She was my mate. My stomach hollowed out, and I struggled to suck in oxygen. I'd never wanted a fucking mate.

The girl scrambled closer to the edge of the truck bed as I devoured her features. Her eyelids fluttered, and she suddenly slumped unconscious.

I'd scared her to unconsciousness.

How young was she?

"Shit."

I dropped my bag, rushed to the other side, and reached down, sliding my arms under her body. She cried out, pain contorting her expression as she curved into herself.

Huddling her close, I marveled at her petite frame, so small against my chest. Her ribs poked out at her torso. My lips flattened. What happened to her?

She whimpered, and that rumble in my chest started up again. The soft purr. With a few long strides, I was at my door, kicking it open.

Damn it, I couldn't pick up dead weight right now. I didn't have time to take care of anyone, especially this unconscious girl against me. Not after securing a meeting with that Beta that had the information I needed.

I struggled to rein in my wolf's purr, but he was relentlessly fighting what my human brain wanted. This was the last thing I needed.

Grabbing my first aid kit, I knelt, maneuvering her on her side so I could see where the blood originated. I sucked in a breath at the scratches slicing down her body and the bruises blooming on her face. I grimaced at the worst of the split skin and my hands shook.

Who had done this to her?

I may not want her, but I refused to stand by as she was hurt. I unwrapped a gauze and a cloth.

She was covered in dirt and blood; the sticky substance was almost completely dry and flaking on her skin.

Bath first.

I pushed to my feet, hurried to the bath, and turned the spout so the water bounced off my hand. When it was the perfect temperature, I collected her and set her in the small tub. Water sloshed over her skin, turning the water pink.

Her nipples pebbled, and I licked my lips, rubbing my palm over my face to detract from the need to take one in my mouth.

Fuck.

I squatted next to the bath and hooked my arm under her back, tugging her up and washing her off with my free hand. Lifting a damp rag to her face, I carefully wiped the crusted shit away, taking care to make my touch as light as could be. Her cheek was cleared first and my shoulders bunched at the sight of a deep scar starting at her left brow and stretching down, the point of it ending near the corner of her soft lips. The unmistakable mark was a different shade on her golden skin.

She'd had this claw mark long before her recent wounds. I swallowed hard. Who would hurt such a lovely creature? I set on cleaning the rest of her and I blinked as I drank her in. Her dark, thick brows furrowed down on her forehead and her eyelid twitched, causing her long eyelashes to flutter. The slight angle to her face was set perfectly to cup in my palms and I was stunned into stillness for a beat. She was beautiful—angelic.

I efficiently scrubbed the rest of her clean, as if I wasn't sporting a hard dick. Even in sleep, she riveted me. Clenching my fist under her breast, I inhaled sharply. Next second, my nose was in her neck, and I was licking the pulse.

The girl moaned and craned her neck to the side, her body wanting more. She sucked in a deep breath and screamed, jerking away from my hold. I forced her still, so she didn't hurt herself, while cursing at myself.

"I'm not going to hurt you," I snapped, a low growl in my words.

She was muttering under her breath about matings. I exhaled sharply, seeking patience before my temper snapped.

"Quiet down." The order came out harsher than I meant. Her lips slapped together as she curled into herself, eyes rounded on me. My stomach soured at her reaction.

I didn't bother saying anything more, and instead, I quickly rinsed her off and pulled the drain.

"This is all I have," I said gruffly, tossing the thin towel at her. It landed over her head, covering her face.

"T-thank you."

I grunted in answer and forced myself to back up. Slamming the door, I leaned against the wall, panting. Fuck. I wanted her.

Rubbing my palm over my dick. I groaned.

I should visit the local town and fuck Sarah, my go-to

whenever I couldn't delay anymore. I usually managed to hold off six months or so before I gave in to the need. It was close to that already since I'd fucked.

The door opened and the newfound bane of my existence strode out wrapped in the small towel. Growling, I took multiple steps away from the girl.

My leg banged into the coffee table.

Why the fuck did I put that there? I scowled at her. She already looked better and the blood no longer crusted her face, unveiling her pretty features: a button nose, soft sensual lips, and smooth tan skin I wanted to lick.

I stalked away before I gave into that. She'd been in my truck for hours; she must be hungry. She needed something in her to gather her strength.

The pantry door smacked into the wall when I opened it harder than I meant. I shoved the canned beans to the side and growled, not finding anything. I stormed to the fridge and pulled out milk. This would have to do.

My nostrils flared. Here I was, scavenging for food, unable to feed my mate a proper meal. She would benefit from a juicy steak and I couldn't even do that.

No, I couldn't claim her. She couldn't be my responsibility.

The quicker she regained her strength, the faster she was out of my hair. Worrying about useless things like what to feed her was not on my list and never would be.

Setting a bowl on the counter, I ignored her curious gaze peeking at me through her damp strands of black hair. I knew she'd followed me, but I was valiantly trying to ignore her.

"You're my mate," she whispered. My shoulders tightened and the box of bland cereal slipped from my fingers.

I glared at the offending carton and dipped to snatch it up.

Ignoring her, I finished serving her and slammed the bowl on the small kitchen table.

"Eat and regain your strength so you can be on your way." My stomach hollowed at my rash words and I lurched back a few steps.

She flinched and her expression tightened as tears built in her brown eyes. I gritted my teeth and turned my back. The counter creaked under my grip. It fucking ached to think that I wouldn't see her.

"Okay." There was that tiny voice again. Doubt crept in and my chest rose sharply, my heart thundering hard.

Fortunately, the clank of the spoon as she picked it up and started eating distracted me from my inner turmoil. I peeked at her and the way she clutched the towel to her chest. My steps rang out in the deafening silence. Combing through my clothes, I snagged a shirt. It would swallow her up, but it was better than nothing.

"Here." I tossed the long-sleeved shirt at her as soon as she turned in my direction. It smacked her face and fell to the ground. Her face pinkened as she scrambled to pluck it off the ground. She should easily catch it, but she seemed sluggish and her coordination was off balance. How weak was she?

She licked a drop of milk off her lower lip and pushed away from the table. It looked like she was debating her life choices as she peered down the hall, then at me, then at the shirt. Resolve tightened her expression—a faux bravery that didn't fool me. She shot me a final glance before edging behind the chair. I turned to the side, keeping her in my line of sight as her towel dropped.

Why was she so fucking skinny?

The hollows didn't detract from the hinting curves

sloping her waist and the full breasts. Her brown nipples were hard and perky. My mouth salivated, and I wanted to suck them into my mouth. I'd never seen anything prettier. The juncture at her thighs was blessed with a tantalizing tuff of hair.

The shirt fell over her body, dropping past her knees and hiding her from me. I narrowed my eyes. I didn't like that. I wanted her flesh bared to me.

Possessiveness gripped me by the balls, and I inhaled her scent mingling with mine. I liked it too much. She needed to leave—soon.

"Where is my bag?"

I wanted to cuddle her close at the panic in her voice.

"It might be in my truck." My words sounded choked. I needed air. Slamming through the door, I hooked my hands at my neck, but the space from her didn't lighten the tightening of my chest.

I turned to the sharply inhaled breath.

She stared up at me with panic splashing her features as she rushed down the steps. I was about to snap at her for following me when I noted her little toes curling into the hard gravel. She followed my gaze.

She stood and looked at me before looking away, discomfort tightening her features. I growled and swept her into my arms, cradling her close to my chest.

Her hands gripped my shoulders, her little nails digging into my skin. *Fuck*. A shiver crested up my spine, and I scowled down at her. She flushed and looked away, squeezing her legs together. The sweet smell of her pussy wafted to my nose, and I growled, quickening my steps.

The bloody, beat down satchel lay on the bed of my truck. I

plucked it and set it on her lap. The press of her body against me was short-circuiting my senses.

Once back in my cabin, I set her on the couch.

"I'm heading out to get food."

A little hand gripped my arm. The touch went straight to my cock.

"Don't leave me!"

Fear seeped from her pores and my stomach dipped as my wolf dug its claws on my insides. Protective instincts rose, and my fingers curled. I didn't *want* to leave her. I studied her strained features. That's why she hadn't dressed in the bathroom and instead chose to huddle behind a chair even though she didn't know me.

I scrubbed the back of my neck.

Fuck.

She struggled to stand. "I'll go with you."

I pressed my hand to her shoulder, keeping her in place.

"You should rest." Frustration made my words harsh, and she flinched back and bent her head. "Fuck." I stepped away, dragging my hands over my face. "Fine, we'll go tomorrow morning."

Relief flashed up at me through her pretty browns and she settled into the couch, energy leaking out of her body. I looked over at my bed, then at her. I shouldn't offer her my bed. Bad fucking idea.

I steeled myself. No, I wasn't claiming her, so there was no need for me to give her expectations.

"What's your name?"

My scowl deepened. I didn't want to tell her; it was a nonissue considering after tomorrow we wouldn't see each other again.

"Knox."

"I'm Liliana." She paused and cleared her throat. "You can call me Liana."

The boards creaked as I retreated to my mattress. Why did my true mate have to be so sweet? I dropped onto my back, setting my forearm across my eyes.

I was too close to crumbling, to crawling to her on my hands and knees to ask forgiveness for my curtness.

Laying on my bed, I reminded myself of all the reasons I didn't have time for this shit. I had a meeting with that Beta that had information. It was a lead I'd been seeking out for years, and finally, I fucking found him.

In two days, I would have the information about who'd slaughtered my pack years ago.

I couldn't get distracted. I owed my family that much.

LIANA

He was scary, but... but I felt safe. My wolf was content wrapped in his scent. She had hope that he would turn to us and mate us. I couldn't say I disagreed with her desire despite his earlier words.

Multiple mates. I'd never heard of that being remotely possible.

There had to be something wrong with me, but I didn't know where to turn for answers. The lack of knowledge put me on edge. How many more mates would pop up for me?

I didn't think I could handle another one. Please, Moon Goddess, let this one accept me. The reminder of his reactions to me mounted dread in my gut, but I couldn't *not* hope. A warm ache pulsed at my clit and I trembled, rubbing my thighs together.

How was this possible? Lore had been in my body hours ago, yet the ache remained prevalent. A hyper-sexual drive always happened amongst mates, but it mind boggled me that I'd recently had my first lover and I wanted more.

Wolves were sexual creatures, but I never thought it would be close to the need trembling through me.

This was my third chance. Maybe the Moon Goddess had known the first two would reject me, so she'd given me multiple options.

Here was my opportunity at happiness. It was decided then. Nerves thickened my throat, but I mustered bravery.

I climbed to my feet and padded over to where he lay. His expression was set into a frown and he had the smoothest skin. I couldn't even see his pores. His nose arch had perfect proportions. No his entire face held perfect proportions. The broad cheekbones and chiseled jawline twitched. From his features, I could determine a mixed Mediterranean background. The corner of his lips dipped. He had to have heard me. His breathing had elevated as soon as I stood.

The bed dipped under my weight.

His growl made me tremble, but I swallowed hard and settled next to him, keeping distance between us.

"Are you mated?" Fear caused the words to rasp from my throat.

I must have surprised him because he pushed to his elbows. His lips parted and his eyes caressed down my body, pausing at my thighs. My nipples pebbled as if he'd touched me, and I cleared my throat.

My teeth sank into my lower lip as my pussy throbbed from the intensity of his deep, almost purple eyes.

I needed him. My swallow was loud in the silence. A beat and then two passed of him staring at me. His eyelids squeezed shut, and he shuddered, baring his teeth. When he opened them, the predatory edge sent a tremble to my hand.

Maybe this was a bad idea. I inched back, but my move seemed to trigger him and he pounced.

Knox's fingers gripped my hips, and he dragged me toward him. The bed bounced under the shuffle, and a weight settled on top of me, pinning me into the bed. I reached up to grip his neck, but he slammed my hands beside my head.

My clit pulsated, need drenching my pussy.

"Are you mated?" I repeated, voice raspy. His jean-clad cock ground into my core. My head fell back and my eyes crossed. Grinding against the rough sensation, I tried jerking away. The question—he hadn't answered.

A small window of reason interfered. "Knox?"

"No, dammit." The growled words made my body clench.

Thank the Moon Goddess.

I bit my lips, craning my neck to look into his eyes. The tension melted away and his brow softened as he stared down at me. His weight moved away, and I bit my lip so I didn't beg him to come back. I exhaled sharply when I noted the wetness soaking the front of his jeans. My face flushed with embarrassment.

"Look at me," he snapped. I followed his order without a second thought. With a step forward, he was at the edge of the mattress, splaying me for him. I sucked in a breath. He was fast. "I like how wet you are." He pressed his palm to the apex of my sex, rubbing against me before lifting his hand to lick his palm. Knox groaned, head tilting back.

That rumbling purr originating at his chest vibrated through me, relaxing my shoulders as heat spread through my body, warming me. My shoulders relaxed and a low throb started at my clit.

Knox straightened and unhooked the buckle, sliding the

leather from its hold. The rasp of him retracting the belt sucked the air from my lungs. I was on the precipice, so close to something intangible I couldn't get a grasp on. He peeled off his shirt and hovered over me.

He peered down contemplatively, then he began sliding up the shirt I wore. The collar tugged at my neck as he exposed me little by little until I was bare to my midriff. Air caressed my breasts before his head came down and he pressed his warm mouth to my breast, suckling. The swirl around my nipple made me jerk off the bed with a cry. The startling shocks to my clit were like electricity.

Then he began nibbling, and I lifted my arms to curl them around his shoulders. Again, he forced them to the mattress.

"I want to touch you." I whimpered. He nipped my breast, and I yelped at the sharp sting. Lifting my hips, I curved my legs at his sides, so they hooked at his back and pushed up, dragging my wet pussy against the flesh of his torso.

His palm flattened on my ass, and he gripped the flesh hard. I jerked against him again, making his skin slippery with my juices. I was working on pure instinct—I didn't know how to verbalize what I wanted.

It just felt so good…

Knox stretched my arms up and clamped onto them with one hand as his now freed hand slid down.

Fingers sank into my folds, wrenching noises from my throat. He shoved an appendage into my channel, twisting with hard jerks that hollowed my stomach with need.

"I ache," I whispered, arching my spine to get closer to him.

"Fuck, baby."

"I need…" I said, ripping the words out. My head thrashed side to side. "I need more." Another finger joined the first and his palm pressed into my clit. The hard pressure combined with the thrusting fingers pushed me over the edge.

Lights burst behind my lids in an explosion of colors. I twitched and my core constricted around his fingers, trying to pull them deeper into me. Each squeeze sent fresh pleasure through my body. His fingers continued working me even after the last jolt, dragging out the spine tightening shivers. The smooth glide of his fingers didn't relent and my molars ground from straining. A slew of noises I'd never made slipped from my mouth, incoherent.

The slippery fingers slid out of my slit, and they fluttered over my pussy, smoothing the moisture.

His cock prodded my entrance, and I wiggled, wanting it deeper, yet he didn't budge as the feel of my pussy lips wrapped around his tip.

I pushed onto my elbows as the tip of Knox's cock slipped into my channel. My attention fastened on the deep red flesh, just barely inside me, my pussy straining around him. Knox froze, his lips parted, and eyes feverish as red bloomed across the top of his cheekbones. The cock twitched when he pushed in a little more, and I cried out, a tremble coasting up my spine. The base of his dick started thickening. The skin stretching around a round swell. I couldn't wait to feel the thick knot pushing past my entrance and ballooning. Moisture leaked from me and dripped down his shaft.

I tried capturing his lips with mine, but he evaded my mouth. Hurt stung my chest.

His brows furrowed, and his jaw was slackened as he stared at his dick. The hand that had been inside me slipped to palm his cock. My wetness glistened on his hand. Why did he seem so stunned?

Knox gripped his cock, and he groaned. He slid down to caress the thickened knot at the base.

"Fucking not possible." Another groan expelled from his lips and he bared his teeth as he squeezed himself.

Wanting the feel of him against me, I reached for him, settling my hand on his chest. Knox met my eyes, and they tightened before he pulled out. My juices dripped from his cock and slicked down my folds, and a profound loss hollowed my stomach. My needy flesh pulsed, and I whimpered. Knox panted, gripping the tip of his dick so hard that it seemed to hurt. He whirled on his heel, storming into the bathroom.

Fear trembled in me. *I didn't want to be alone*. I curled my knees to my chest as I watched the direction he'd disappeared.

Fortunately, exhaustion weighed on my mind as the day caught up to me. My eyes became heavy, and the cabin faded.

DECLAN

THE FOLLOWING DAY, LORE AND I RAZED THE ENTIRE pack and surrounding area. After we'd run ourselves into exhaustion, we'd returned, hoping she'd only been hiding, licking her wounds somewhere.

Liliana was too gentle to try to leave. She would have hidden somewhere until she could come out. It was the only reasoning that I was able to cling to in order to turn back around, but I stood on pack lands and there was still no sign of her. Panic was setting in and it made me erratic.

In my investigation, we'd found out that Lily spoke to only one person—the woman currently standing before Lore, quaking so hard I was surprised she hadn't dislodged her head.

"Where could she have gone?" Lore barked the question. My lips tightened at the fearful flickering of her eyes. Exhaustion weighed on my shoulders. I'd spent the last day searching for any lead to my Lily, but there was nothing. The only explanation was that she'd managed to get on a vehicle.

"Did she have anyone willing to pick her up?"

The woman shook her head quickly.

"Speak, Janice."

Of course, Lore knew her name. He knew everything about the bloody pack.

"No. She had no one except me."

"Had she been planning to leave?"

Frustration simmered in her expression, and she shook her head.

"Speak," her mate, Isac yelled. "Tell them everything you know."

She jumped, a terrified expression crossing her face.

"I can handle the questions."

"Apologies, Alpha."

"She's been miserable, and it has only gotten worse," Janice said, pain filling her voice. "I didn't know how bad it was until recently. I'm surprised she didn't leave sooner. Your mate hurt her a lot in these last years." Bitterness crested the woman's expression as she stared at me.

My heart dropped at the words. What did that mean?

"Hurt her how?"

"You should ask her," she said, tipping her nose up at me. A growl spilled out, and I stepped toward her. She cringed into herself and I pinched my nose, garnering control again. "Last time I was there, she hit her."

Lore tensed and I jerked back. I'd have rather been killed than to hear that about my Lily.

No, it had to be a lie. My fucking mate could not have been beating an innocent girl under my nose.

Clara resented my girl as that scar across her face proved, but that was the only time she'd attacked her. An attack that was another mark against me and one I'd been too late to save her from.

My gut twisted. No.

It sounded like she still targeted her even though I'd stayed away from her. I'd stayed away to an extent where I practically blocked her existence. My skin itched, and I gave in to the need to pace.

"Clara," Lore bellowed. "Get her."

Lincoln sped from the office, and the room fell into silence. My jaw popped with how hard I ground my teeth. Janice fidgeted, clasping and unclasping her hands. Moments later, Lincoln entered with my blonde mate struggling in his arms. He urged her forward, and she froze when she saw my face.

Her head dipped submissively, and she stepped beside Janice with her jaw straining and jerked out of the enforcer's hold.

"What have you been doing to Liliana?" Lore snapped, not wasting time.

"Nothing she doesn't deserve," she answered crisply. He pushed up so fast that his office chair fell back, crashing into the wall. I snarled, lurching forward to grab her around the throat and squeeze it until it popped. Clara cringed back, a scream echoing off the walls in the room as her hands lifted.

Lincoln pressed his palm into my chest, and I kicked his knee. The Beta buckled to the floor with a grunt, but his interjection managed to snap me out of the blind rage.

"What did you do?" I sneered at the bitch.

Her reddened eyes flicked to the ground; her lips pressed together tightly. I knew that expression. We weren't getting shit out of her. Dragging my twitchy hands through my hair, I exhaled sharply. Lincoln eyed me as he climbed to his feet.

I'd never been one to fidget.

"Clara," Lore spat the name out warningly. The color of his

eyes seemed to burn and his lip curled up. I didn't bother telling him she would rather die than speak. I didn't care what he did to her.

Guilt had made me waste time on her, but never again. I was destroying *that house* with everything inside of it. Even her, if she tried to stop me.

There was nothing I wanted from there.

"I think she was beating her," Janice blurted. "She overworked her and made her do all the duties."

My teeth snapped together. "Like what?"

"Cooking for the pack and cleaning the manor."

Food was always prepared and provided. Three meals a day, every day. Lily was in charge of that?

Impossible, it was too much for that waif of a girl to do.

The dark smudges under her eyes flashed in my memory, the ribs poking at her flesh. I never let myself truly look at her, nor did I let myself question anything about her. As soon as I found myself wondering, I'd shoved the thoughts away. 'I wasn't in a position to worry about her', was what I always told myself.

Guilt writhed through me like a poisonous serpent. Lore breathed raggedly, and the surface of his desk cracked under his grip. Clara was my responsibility, and I'd needed to make sure she was in line, yet I'd allowed my true mate to be taken advantage of... and if the beatings were true...

The massive weight in my gut crawled up my diaphragm, expanding painfully. I met Lore's eyes. He'd allowed Clara her power.

Instances flashed forward. The handful of times I'd been home, Clara went directly to the washing machines and tossed her clothes in... the scents... her behavior. I always assumed it was because she was working in the kitchen, not because she was abusing Lily and didn't want me to scent her. I'd never paid much attention because I avoided her.

Clara had calmed after Lore allowed her to help around four years ago. Before then, she would lash out at me, but that had simmered. It wasn't because she was busier; it was because she'd been using Lily's body to target the rage driving her insane.

I allowed my true mate to be treated thusly. Sharp claws sliced at my gut. My wolf wanted out, he wanted to destroy Clara.

My growl vibrated through the room, echoed by Lore's.

"She's banished," Lore said, his tone seeped with fury. "If she's not gone by nightfall. I'll kill her myself."

She hurt Lily. Lily's face flashed in my mind and my wolf shoved forward, overtaking my body. Clara backed up, tripping over her feet.

I ceased control of my human mind and allowed his blood thirstiness to the forefront...

Blood filled my nose, and the taste spread on my tongue as my human consciousness pushed forward. I panted, body quaking as adrenaline worked through each limb.

I had no idea what I'd just done, but based on the blood drenching me, it'd been violent. I shook my head as my wolf made another effort to take control. I groaned and shifted into my human body, finding myself on the second floor of the manor. I couldn't have lost that much time if Clara's screaming echoed in my ears. My teeth clamped together, and I breathed hollowly.

Holding Lily in my arms was the only way I could calm my

restless beast. I needed her. I needed her sweet peach scent engulfing me.

The stairs creaked as someone pounded down the steps.

"Declan."

Whirling, I gripped the collar of Lincoln's shirt, bunching the material. He automatically went limp.

"Burn that fucking house. And that bitch better be long gone before I get back."

"Declan, she needs help—" In an explosion of motion, I socked his face. Blood spurted, and he growled.

This time I didn't pull my swing. Lincoln's head smashed into the wall, denting it. Red dotted his temple, and I buried my boot into his gut. While he was bent in half I angled a hit at his head. It was what he deserved.

Lincoln staggered and dropped to the ground with a wheeze, lowering his head submissively. The stairs creaked as I rushed down them. Fuck you, Lore, for having your office at the highest level.

Daniel stepped in my path, and I snarled at him, shoving him against the front door. My fist slammed into his mouth. Blood sprayed.

Swinging again, I angled for his nose. He'd terrorized Lily. When he'd chased after her. Cornered her. I battered into his body, but with each hit, the ache in my gut didn't fade. There was no assuaging the guilt.

I wish I could bloody myself like this.

What I was doing to him reflected what I wanted to do to myself.

Daniel bashed my temple. I grunted. The pain relieved some of the pressure in my chest. Lifting my head, I grabbed the woodland frame off the wall and shattered it over his face. Glass showered the ground, and I swooped down to grab a large piece. I sliced the sharp shard into his stomach. Blood gushed from the wound as I dragged it up his sternum, opening a gash that he'd have no way of healing.

Daniel sputtered and struggled to tug in oxygen. I watched him, panting, as his eyes glazed over.

Good. He deserved to die.

Slamming open the door, my feet kicked up dirt and gravel. It was easy navigating to her apartment. The place I never allowed myself to enter.

The door creaked when I shouldered through.

No.

I was already shaking my head in horror. The structure of the building had good bones, but the walls weren't the problem.

There wasn't even a mattress on the floor, and my skin pricked from the small space. Dipping, I clutched the rag folded into a neat square. It was so thin I could see through it. Bringing it up to my nose, I inhaled the peaches.

My eyelids squeezed shut as I helplessly imagined her small body shivering during fall and winter.

Never again, little Lily.

You would never feel discomfort.

There was a strangled noise from behind me.

Lore. His scent invaded her room, and my lip lifted into a warning snarl.

The cloth fluttered onto the ground, and I whirled, shifting. I went for Lore's throat, and he shifted mid-jump, fangs flashing.

Blood spilled into my mouth when I clamped down on his shoulder. Lore dragged his claws into my side. My human mindset faded from the forefront as the wolf and instincts completely took over.

When I regained my senses, I laid on my side beside Lore, both of us panting and wounded. I whimpered when I tried to move my broken hind leg. How much time had passed?

Lore coughed, the pelt on his side drenched with blood and an open wound.

The longer I fought with this bastard, the further she got from me. And if we killed each other, no one would look for her. Climbing to my paws, I showed my teeth. We needed a plan. Liliana was out there alone and she needed me. I would take a million more wounds if I could have her with me right now. Nothing hurt more than the absence of her presence.

Knox

I'D STARED AT HER THE ENTIRE NIGHT AND HAD gotten not a wink of sleep. She was alluring. Her midnight lashes rested on the curve of her high cheekbones and her arching brows curved close in slumber. Her soft lips pressed tightly together, and I scowled at her restless tossing. When my chest started up with that low rumbling, she settled with a deep sigh.

She was curled forward, clutching the blankets around her like they were a lifeline, with her dark mass of locks spread around her like a silky halo. The ghost of her touch coasted on my flesh, raising the hair along the back of my neck. She was imprinted on me. The memory of her little pants and the desperate way she gyrated... my nostrils flared as I inhaled sharply.

I'd run away like a little bitch, then rubbed one out in the shower to the promise of ecstasy.

Licking my lips, I couldn't help envisioning her brown eyes full of pleading and need. The way her pupils dilated...

I groaned, rubbing my palm over my cock.

Adjusting my dick, I stretched out my cramped legs. This couch offered no comfort. Damn the girl for taking my bed. Damn me for allowing it, no, wanting it.

I could have easily moved her, but I hadn't been able to bring myself to do it.

She tossed, and the blanket curled around her side, exposing a slim leg. My stomach tightened at the flash of bronze skin, mouthwatering.

Instinct prodded me to claim her and bring relief to the needy scent clinging to her.

I forced my brain elsewhere. Every moment I looked at her, the harder it became to hold on to my will.

She was an Omega, which I'd believed had gone extinct long ago. Wrapping my head around the reality had taken a lot out of me, but there was stranger shit in the world. Omegas were made for breeding, and every fiber they consisted of was made for fucking and temptation. But those weren't the only aspects to them. They had the ability to call forth dormant wolves, making Omegas one of the most coveted, revered, and yet envied.

And one was gifted to me as a mate.

A soft whimper escaped her lips.

Air hissed out from between my teeth. The scratches on her body were in the beginning phase of healing. The process quickened from being a werewolf.

How had she gotten them?

My fingers dug into the couch cushions at the idea of someone hurting her. She'd been terrified when I'd found her.

I debated shaking her awake to ask, but the haunted look in her eyes stayed me. If I questioned it, I would care more than I already did, but more importantly, there was a ball in my gut at the thought of dredging up something that brought her pain.

Trauma and I were well acquainted. After all, my sisters were slaughtered right in front of me.

It was none of my business, anyway. I shouldn't be getting more involved than I was.

She groaned and flopped onto her back, flexing out her limbs. The line of her body arched and my lips parted as her supple limbs curved.

Her long thick lashes fluttered, and the confusion on her face made me want to cuddle her close.

She shot up straight and looked around, panic marring her pretty features. Her eyes bounced and settled on me.

"Oh, right." Grief lined her expression.

"What?" I snapped. "Were you expecting it to be someone else?"

Her shoulders hiked. "I'm used to waking up at a certain time." I stopped myself from asking her to elaborate on her cryptic words. "May I use your restroom?"

My mouth opened and then closed. I just nodded.

She scampered out of the bed, movements less constrained. Every motion she made was marked by the hunch of her spine yesterday, almost like she'd had to push through pain.

Don't go there.

There was a clatter and a little squeal as she shut the bathroom door. She must have dropped something. I couldn't hold back my smile. Good thing she wasn't out here to see.

She took a shorter time than any females I'd ever been around. Snatching my keys and shoving them into my pocket, I stalked to the couch.

"Thank you for the toothbrush," she murmured as she fished a glinting chain from her ragged bag and clasped the crescent-moon necklace around her slim neck.

I grunted and shoved my feet into my boots.

"Where are you going?"

The fear scenting the room made me pause, and I exhaled slowly. *Don't grab her.* I chanted to myself.

I paused at the door. "Aren't you coming?"

Her relief was palpable, and she scurried after me, her soft feet padding over the wooden floor.

The gravel crunched under my boots, and I paused before tipping my head back with a sigh. In a swift motion, I turned and swept her into the crook of my arms.

Her squeal made me laugh, but I cut it off, masking it as a cough. The way her body fit against me, and the way the side of her soft breast pressed into my chest, hardened my dick.

She wiggled in my arms, wrapping her arm over her torso, a blush rising on her cheeks.

She settled into the passenger seat, and I forced myself not to buckle her in.

Soft country music played from the speakers, but other than that there was no noise. I disliked seeing her so silent, and I ached for her perfect voice. The halting way she spoke was endearing and my hand twitched on my thigh with the need to wrap around her cheek. My finger tapped the steering wheel in an effort to release as much of the restlessness gnawing my insides as I could.

I stopped at a convenience store once I reached the small town. Setting the car in park, I shoved out the door. They had some cheap shoes and clothes, but at least it was something.

"Wait here."

She didn't question my demand, but her frown told me she wasn't happy with it. My eyelid twitched at the ding of the store door, and I made my way through the aisles.

Moments later, my arms overflowed with shit.

I would deny with my last breath that I was striding faster than I usually would. The need to return to her was biting my ass.

The cashier rang me up, shoving the feminine things that I collected into the bag. Hopefully, the leggings weren't too large on her. I'd also guessed on the shoes, but I was pretty sure they were big for her. It would have to do.

Hooking the bag on my finger as I stepped out, I automatically sought her out. She peered at me from the truck, her arms crossed on the dash as she leaned forward. The sun glinted off the red paint of the truck and I forced my gaze to fix on a dent in the side instead of the beauty eyeing me curiously.

Clearing my throat, I pulled myself up before tossing the bag into her lap, and she scrambled to catch it.

The girl blinked down at it and then at me.

"I-is this for me?"

I grunted, and her lips parted as she exhaled sharply. "Thank you."

Tears shimmered on the surface of her brown eyes, glittering the orbs. My body tightened, heart beginning to race.

Why was she making a big deal about a few cheap things?

She sniffled and pulled out the leggings, angling them so she could slide her feet through the holes, wiggling her hips enticingly as she tugged them up. Then, she pulled out the bra thing I'd gotten her. It was most likely going to be an uncomfortable fit, but I figured it was better than nothing. She slid under her shirt, pulling her arms into the sleeves, and fiddled under the clothing as she did *whatever* it was to put it on.

Her gaze was heavy on me, and she quirked a brow. Oh, I'd been gawking at her.

I couldn't help it. Her movements were captivating.

She slipped on the sandals, not saying a peep about the odd green color. Her grin mesmerized me. I fisted my hand when she pulled out the shirt I made sure to get a few sizes too big. I couldn't have her showing anything.

She started lifting the shirt, and I growled. Her fingers paused, and she raised a brow.

"There are people around," I snapped gruffly. She frowned and slumped to wiggle the shirt on as I peered around, making sure no one watched. If my windows weren't tinted, I would have forced her to continue wearing my shit.

Yanking my eyes away, I started the vehicle.

"Where are we going now?" Her leg bounced, and she looked around, awed.

"Food."

I slowed for the speed bump and turned onto the main road. The town was small. The way I liked it. In the last decade or so I'd lived here, it had hardly grown.

The convenience store was only one of two stores and the mart down the street had all the food. A small town also meant minimal options for eating out. I pulled into the diner bordering the town exit. The engine went silent when I twisted the key.

She scrambled to unbuckle her belt when I hopped out and headed to the glass door of Shay's Diner. The door slammed in Liliana's face, and I rubbed my neck. The damn girl was making me feel guilty for shit I shouldn't be.

I licked my lips as she pulled open the jingling door.

Leaving her to catch up, I went to my usual spot in the

corner of the diner, where I liked to sit to study who entered. So far, there hadn't been any werewolves that showed up in the last few years. In the past, anytime there were, I easily chased them out. A perk of being dominant.

The town mechanic craned his neck as the Omega sashayed by his table. I gnashed my teeth. Pushing halfway to my feet, I readied to stride over and pluck his eyes out. Then she looked at me and smiled.

It was a punch to the gut.

My ass hit the chair again.

"It smells good here." Her eyes lit up like it was Christmas morning. "This place is so cool."

The awe was there again.

"You'd never been to a place like this?"

"A long time ago," she muttered and eyed the menu distrustfully. I flicked it open. Her eyes bounced around the words. Wringing her hands, she peered up at me as her face reddened.

"Honey!"

She straightened, and her head whirled in the direction of the shout. Dread lined my stomach.

I frowned at Sarah as she approached the table. Fuck. What were these nerves?

Fisting my hands, I fixed my attention on my Omega.

Lore

Too much time was wasted trying to find out more about Little One. And all the knowledge did was make me more anxious. After tearing away from the fight with Declan, I'd gotten a hold of Alaric, one of the best trackers and the second of the pack a state over. It'd taken a lot to get the wily asshole to meet us, but I would have traded everything if he'd asked it of me as long as he found my Little One.

We'd been running all night. My body strained with exhaustion, but I pushed it back as I picked up my pace.

The place we were meeting Alaric was close. Dirt kicked up as we neared. A pinch in my ribs had accompanied my entire run. Damage Declan had inflicted, but I wasn't letting it slow me down. I pushed through the pain, using it as fuel to find my beautiful mate.

On our sharp turn, Declan's hind leg gave out a split second, and he stumbled before righting himself. That was what he got for slicing his claws into my side.

Slowing my pace, my nose twitched as the scent of cigarettes filled it. Beneath a large tree with branches angled down and leaves swaying off it, was the wolf I needed to find my mate.

Alaric waited beside his truck, leaning against it like he'd been waiting since my call.

"I'd never known you to be one to ask for help, Lore."

I snarled and shifted. "Desperate times."

He threw his head back and laughed. I narrowed my eyes at him. I knew this was going to happen when I called for his help, but I wasn't in the mood.

I sucked on my teeth. Irritation prickled my neck, and I reined in my wolf's urge to come out and rip into him.

"I heard you over the phone, and I'll say the same thing." He crossed his arms. "Why should I bother?"

"You're going to fucking help me find her."

Declan didn't bother saying anything as he shifted and strode up to him slowly. Suddenly lunging at him, he drove his fist into Alaric's stomach. I straightened, rubbing my face. He'd done exactly what I wanted to do myself, but Alaric was a stubborn fucker and if I attacked him, I wouldn't have stopped myself from killing him. My wolf was too on edge, *too* at the forefront.

He grunted and swung at Declan who accepted the blow, seeming to revel in the pain.

This was another perk of having a Beta that was as strong as an Alpha. He could beat the fuck out of people, which meant I didn't have to risk losing control since he did my dirty work.

Declan pinned him on his back, hands squeezing his neck as he leaned down to Alaric's ear.

Whatever he said was too low for me to hear, but Alaric tensed and his jaw worked. Declan finally let him go, but not before tightening his hold warningly.

Alaric's nose flared as he rolled to his feet.

"Do I need to bother with any threats?" I said, lifting my brow mockingly.

"No," he responded, brushing his hair back with a smirk. "I am exceptionally curious to find out what type of woman has the Alpha of one of the most powerful packs in knots. Plus, I get a favor from you in doing this."

I snorted and gave him my back. "Enough talking, find her."

Liana

The woman sashayed forward, red hair swishing back and forth with the sway of her movement. I inhaled sharply at the way she stared at my mate.

My lip curled before I knew what I was doing. Pressing my hand to my mouth, I closed my eyelids to collect myself. That reaction wasn't like me.

Peering at Knox, I searched for hints that he'd seen my snarl, but there was nothing but an angry canvas staring back at me.

He was a growly sort. Seemed to be angry at everything, but I don't know, it made me feel warm. Everyone intimidated me, but there was something comforting about Knox.

He's your mate.

No, that wasn't it. Lore was my mate, but he made me feel anxious and scared.

"Sarah," Knox rumbled in his deep voice. The same voice that made me squeeze my thighs together. The rich, deep tones sent shivers up my spine.

Sucking in a shaky breath, I envisioned his hard cock prodding my entrance, and I bit my lip to hold back the whimper. I snapped straight in my seat when she bent toward his face. My eyes widened, but before her red lips settled on his mouth, he moved to the side.

She was a hair's breadth away from smearing red on his cheek—my teeth clenched.

Unable to stuff the emotions, I stared at him accusingly. My eyebrows winged down, lips pursed as my hands trembled. He said he had no mate, but that didn't mean he didn't have *someone*.

He was the same as the others.

My heart thundered in my ears.

"I haven't seen you in—"

"I want the number three."

He exhaled slowly, not moving his eyes from mine. When he settled his hand over my shaking ones, I tensed, shocked.

Lips parted, I searched his purple eyes. Was he choosing me?

My breathing hiccupped, and I blinked a sheen of tears away.

The abrupt way he cut her off made me happier than I wanted to admit. Maybe he wasn't like that. What was he to her? Had he done to her what he'd done to me? I swallowed hard. My eyes flicked from one to the other.

They were staring at me.

Sarah's eyebrow quirked. She'd said something...

"What do you want?" The snapped words made me bend my head.

I blushed furiously.

"Oh, um..." I eyed the strange jumble of words. I knew the letters, but stringing them together was difficult. The first one said something about eggs and potatoes, but the third word that started with *sir*—I couldn't figure it out.

It took me longer than the usual person to grasp anything I read, but I could get it, eventually. Without options to practice the skills after finishing the classes at fifteen, it made it difficult.

"Do you understand me?" The woman drew out her words mockingly. My chest flushed as the rest of my body heated with embarrassment. I fixed my eyes on my clasped hands on the table and jerked them from under Knox's grip. I didn't want him touching me while his—his—whatever she was, spoke to me like this. "Do you not know how to read?" My mouth snapped shut, and I kept my face down-turned.

"Can I get the same thing he is?"

"Talk louder? I didn't hear you." My shoulders curved closer to my ears at the sniped words.

"Enough," Knox spat at her. Her eyes rounded. "Get her the same thing I ordered."

There was a feminine huff and the thud of retreating steps filled my ears. My shoulders didn't relax even then. I avoided his prodding look and picked at my chewed nails.

He cleared his throat, and I peeked at him, only to find him studying me.

"Why were you in the bed of my truck?"

I opened my mouth, then closed it. "I left my pack."

Knox stilled, and his finger tapped the surface of the table near my hand.

"Did they do something to you?"

I smiled wryly. What hadn't been done to me?

"It was just time for me to leave."

"What pack?"

"I'm—" I cleared my throat. "I *was* a part of the Eastland pack."

I knew he'd recognize the name. The pack was the biggest in

the State of New York and in addition to that, Lore founded Eastland Enterprises. The only company that pushed out products that were tailored to werewolves.

"Do you have a pack?" I said to change the subject.

"Not anymore."

"What do you mean—"

"I can tell there was a reason. Why did you leave?"

I shrugged. If he didn't want to share with me, I didn't feel the compulsion to do the same.

The scent of bacon filled my senses, and I tipped my nose up, inhaling the meat. Mouthwatering, I craned to look at the plates approaching our table.

She placed the food in front of Knox with a care that she lacked when slamming the plate in front of me. Bacon fell off my plate, and I frowned, reaching for it.

It was halfway to my mouth when Knox plucked it from my grip. The bacon piece slapped on the table when he tossed it. Then he plucked one off his dish and placed it between my fingers.

My cheeks puffed, and I valiantly held in the waterworks as the pressure in my heart constricted.

The scent of the food wafted to my nose, and my mouth watered.

It was sirloin. Something I was never allowed to touch except for once when I'd gotten the chance to slice off a hunk of fat. It was the most delectable piece of meat I'd ever had. This would top it. I just knew it.

My stomach grumbled, and I picked it off the plate, biting into the edge. A moan crawled up my throat, and I hummed happily. This was delicious. I would sell my soul for more of this meat. Juices dripped onto my fingers and I leaned to lick the back of my hand. Looking up, I found Knox staring at me strangely. Heat flushed my cheeks, creeping down my neck as I slowly set the food down to wipe my hands. That's right. He probably didn't want to see me licking my hands.

I plucked the fork and stabbed the middle of a steak, bringing it up to my lips to nibble on it as I met Knox's eyes sheepishly.

Considering I wasn't allowed to eat with the pack and I rushed to eat as I cooked, I hadn't had much time to use utensils in the last few years. It felt foreign. We continued breakfast in silence and I made sure to slow as I ate. Knox stabbed at his food angrily, his movements edged with restrained violence.

I was right; the taste was much better than it smelled, and it smelled fantastic. He opened his mouth, but a ringing distracted him from what he was going to say.

Knox eyed the caller ID and his eyes sharpened.

"I have to take this." He was already walking away as I stuffed my face. Chewing, I nodded, waving at him as he exited the restaurant.

I continued munching away and didn't restrain myself from scarfing my food. The entrance remained empty, so I reached over to steal another of Knox's bacon and shoved it into my mouth before he returned.

My stomach pinched painfully, and I hugged my arm around my belly at the uncomfortable fullness. I'd never eaten this much. Correction, I'd never been allowed to eat this much.

I dropped the country potato, and my gaze widened on Sarah. She narrowed her eyelids on me and I quickly chewed what was in my mouth.

"Who are you?"

Why did she want my name?

"Um, Liana?"

The response seemed to take her off guard. I didn't know how since I'd answered her question.

"Yes, well, *Liana*. Knox and I have been together for years, so don't get your hopes up."

I had to swallow a few times to get the food down my throat since it felt like sawdust traveling down my esophagus.

Inhaling deeply, I didn't catch the scent of wolf. She was pure human. I couldn't explain to her the connection I had with him. Knox was mine. The Moon Goddess made it so. He was my third chance at happiness.

"Um." I shook my head and chose my words carefully. I fought the angry wolf writhing in my chest and urging me to slash the human's belly open. "He's actually mine."

Her mouth fell open, and a vein popped in her forehead.

I should have seen the attack coming. Maybe a part of me had, but it wasn't new to me. I didn't raise a hand to defend myself when her hand smacked my face. I blinked at her, processing the sting radiating across my cheek. The people at the tables surrounding us gasped, but my lack of reaction seemed to anger her further.

She lunged at me and gripped my hair, pulling me, so I tipped over and onto my back. The chair snapped under me, and I scrabbled in the broken wood.

I just wanted to eat.

Tears built from frustration.

Why was this always happening to me?

A piece of wood dug into my leg, and I whimpered at the sting. I pushed to my knees and froze when I found Knox had returned and his fingers were wrapped around Sarah's throat. If the pinched look and tears streaming down her face were any indication, the grip hurt.

He shoved, releasing her, and she slammed down on her ass. I sniffled and dragged my forearm over my forehead.

Knox crouched beside me, eyes searching my face as he reached and grazed his fingertips on my cheek. His nose flared, and brows furrowed.

Gently slipping an arm under me, he placed the second at my back and lifted me. A huff escaped my mouth, and I instinctively wrapped my arms around his neck to brace as we passed stunned-faced humans.

His heel came down on the door, splintering the board. My eyes widened as humans screamed, but he didn't even twitch.

"Open the car door." I unclasped my arms from around his neck to do as he gruffly ordered, then he gently placed me in the car and buckled me in with jerky movements.

Knox revved the engine a beat later and smacked the radio, shutting off the music. My reflection peered back at me from the windowpane, my brown eyes wide and wet from the leftover shock. I touched the tender red spot on my face and sighed as I turned my attention to the flurry of trees whipping by. They were so tall they seemed to reach the sky at this angle.

"Was she your lover?"

Knox's hands flexed around the wheel. I'd stunned him with my question.

"Yes," he bit out aggressively.

My chest constricted, and nausea soured my stomach. My next exhale shook my shoulders. I wasn't going to be able to hold back from crying. Crap. I dug my nails into my thigh. Now that I was a werewolf, I was better built for dealing with pain, but every blow would hurt as badly as when I was human.

My strength was also a smidge greater than before, but I still felt so weak.

"Why does it smell like blood?" Knox snapped. "Look at me."

I turned my head in the opposite direction. Tears slipped free and trickled down my cheeks.

He pinched my chin and forced me to turn in his direction. After fighting his strength for a second, he overpowered me.

Knox snarled.

"Don't cry." The order made the tears fall quicker. I inhaled sharply and shoved his hand off my face and pressed into the door.

"Fuck," he spat, jolted the vehicle to the side of the deserted road, and exited the car.

I flinched at the slam of the door. I needed to stop. It was what it was. None of my mates wanted me because they had someone better.

The door I was leaning against disappeared and I tilted. My yelp cut off as thick arms circled me and pulled me out of the car. Why was I such an ugly crier?

My ass settled on the hood of the truck. My leggings made me slip down, but his hands anchored me before I fell. "Stop crying."

The order was just as effective as his other demands. His growl made a shiver tremble up my spine, and he gripped the back of my neck, forcing me forward. I arched toward him and his nose touched my neck. The rumble in his chest started up and vibrated through me and it was an automatic relief. My shoulders incrementally relaxed the more he ran his hands over my body and purred at me.

A different type of heat flooded my belly and tingled in my

pussy. I ground my ass into the hard hood of the car, needing the pressure sated. Pulling back, he looked at me. Since his truck was so tall, we were at eye level.

His eyes deepened in color.

My back slammed onto the hood and he gripped the waist of my leggings and arched my ass up so he could slide them off. He tore them the rest of the way until they hung from my foot.

I blinked up at him. Fingers dug into my thighs as I tried to close my legs. He spread them and simply looked at me.

Clearing my throat, I tried to make words come out, but then he dipped his head and suckled on my clit.

I shouted at the sudden sensation.

Wow. Wow.

That was a different type of pleasure.

The warm tongue twisted around my bud with hard flicks, and my lungs stopped working.

Slamming my hands flat, the bang of metal echoed around me. Even with my eyes squeezed tight, my lids turned yellow from the bright morning sun. Someone could drive by and find us like this...

When his tongue traveled to my core and thrust in, all worries evaporated.

His grip spanned my hips, squeezing and massaging. The hands were so big that his fingers curved around my waist and teased my ass cheeks.

The possessive grip kept my restless hips in place.

"You like that, baby?" he murmured before sucking on the nub with alternating swirls. "Good girl, no more crying."

My eyes crossed at the praise, and I arched at the oncoming orgasm. He lifted his head, mouth wet.

"Why are you stopping?" I stuttered, chest heaving.

"Promise me, no more crying." Knox's intense eyes sank deep into my soul. The sincerity there made my breath catch, so I nodded frantically.

The grin he offered made my heart inflate and then he went back to doing everything he had been doing to me. Eating and suckling at my seeping pussy.

I couldn't make sense of the act. I could have never have imagined this was a *thing*. I'd been too sheltered. I jerked my hips up angrily. *I'd been too sheltered.*

Cresting over the hill, my mouth opened on a cry as my channel trembled. Lights blinked behind my lids and when my senses returned I was tugging at his hair angrily.

I quickly released him and looked away sheepishly when I noticed some of his dark strands in my grip.

He licked his lips, eyes dilated as he watched me. I wiggled on the hood and looped my hands around his neck. We were like magnets as we slowly slid closer to each other until my chest was flat against his. A ringing phone invaded the peaceful rustle of leaves and indecision played on his features before he released my ass to fish out the device.

He placed it to his ear, and all he offered was a grunt as his eyes bore into mine. The words buzzed on the other end.

"He's there now?" The corner of Knox's eyes tightened as he studied my face.

The little voice at the other side snapped an affirmative and grim acceptance flashed through Knox's eyes.

LIANA

MY FOOT BOUNCED, AND I FIDDLED WITH THE EDGE of my shirt with the taste of chocolate heavy on my tongue. The treat was the most delicious piece of food I had ever eaten. Thank the Moon Goddess that he'd purchased it for me.

I peeked over at him as he tapped at the steering wheel for the last two hours he'd driven. The entire time he'd been twitchy, shooting me looks from the corner of his eye as he navigated the empty roads.

Knox said we were meeting with a guy that he needed information from, or something like that. He didn't elaborate much.

The tires squealed as he pulled in front of a run-down establishment, and I jostled from side to side as the truck bumped into the uneven lot. The structure reminded me of the diner, but with a marked difference—It swarmed with men leaning on motorcycles. The five bulky guys looked over simultaneously as the truck pulled in front. They did *not* look friendly.

One with a long beard narrowed his eyes at me, and I sank lower into the seat, scooted closer to Knox, and gripped his arm.

Knox's arm stiffened and his jaw moved as he followed my fearful gaze and cursed.

"You can't stay in here."

That was good news. I wasn't a fan of being away from him. He put the car in park and shut off the engine.

"Don't speak. Understand?" I opened my mouth. "*Understand*?" My lips smacked together, and I dipped my head. The intensity he stared at me with made me swallow. Knox didn't seem present in the here and now.

What haunted him so intensely?

The car swayed with the slam of the door, and I rushed after him, pressing into his side. I licked my lips at the frustration on his face, but I was too scared to give him space.

At the entrance, he paused and squeezed my hip. My eyes stung at the smoke that wafted out from inside.

The door closed at my back, and I tried not to be obvious about my gawking. Glasses clanked, and the chattering was low and even. I rubbed my nose with the back of my hand. The scent of alcohol and cigarettes overwhelmed my nose.

Every person in the establishment watched us, not disguising their curiosity. Another interesting aspect was the overpowering smell of wolves. I wouldn't be surprised if every person in here was a werewolf.

My eyes clashed with a woman sitting on a male's lap and she curled her lip at me. I scooted closer to Knox, so close that it was any wonder he could walk.

I licked my lips and my shoulders increasingly tensed up the deeper we stepped into the place.

"Where can I find Johnson?" Knox asked the bartender. The man grunted and jerked his chin toward the door to the side of the establishment as he reached for the remote to raise the music volume.

With a few strides, we were at the door, and Knox gave me another warning look as he pushed it open. My eyes bounced from the group of men gathered around the pool table. Seven of them. I worked to hide my trembles.

The leather-clad man, who was bent over the edge of the table took his turn as Knox spoke. "Johnson."

He straightened and bared his teeth.

"You fucked with my shot."

Knox just grunted. I admired the ease with which he stared at the other man. There was fury simmering at the surface, and the hair on my neck lifted.

I studied the rest of the wolves in the room. They were all intimidating in their own right, and they didn't look very kind. My eyes caught an older man leaning against the nearby wall with his eyes trained on me. I licked my lips.

"Once you give me the information, you'll get back to your game."

Johnson threw his head back with a booming laugh, and I jumped at the abrupt noise. He dropped the pole, and it clattered as it landed.

"Which of the shits outside told you I was here?"

"Tell me what you know, and I'll leave."

Johnson quirked up a brow, a smirk playing on his lips.

"Now, Knox, was it?" He scratched his chin. "You've been trying to set up a meeting with me for the last year. Didn't you take the clue that I wasn't interested in your little endeavor?"

"I'm not leaving until you tell me who was involved."

Johnson didn't look as jovial anymore. His eyes hardened, any light heartedness melting away. "No."

The older gentleman studied me and took a step forward, tipping his head up like he was inhaling deeply. I didn't like the look he was giving me.

"She's an Omega." His eyes were wide and awed.

Johnson's shoulders tightened, and he narrowed in on me. "Not possible."

Another man, this one wiry and with a tooth missing, scoffed. "How would you even know what that smells like? They've been murdered from existence."

I sucked in a breath at the heavy weight of their eyes, and my fingers constricted in Knox's shirt. Knox growled and pulled me behind him.

"She smells like sex and *life*." The old man shook his head. "I've studied on this, Johnson."

Johnson met the older man's gaze, and they conveyed an entire conversation. Seeming to come to a conclusion, Johnson met Knox's eyes. "I'll tell you everything you want to know if you give her to me."

"No."

Relief loosened my shoulders, and I slumped against Knox.

"I know who killed your sisters. I know what pack ordered it and executed it and I know why."

I inhaled sharply. Was this the information he was looking for? He wanted the people that hurt his siblings?

"Give her to me and I'll tell you everything."

My heart raced as I processed the words, and I shook my head frantically. Knox wouldn't. I shouldn't have to pay for something I had nothing to do with. I wanted to help him, yes, more than anything I wanted to help my mate, but I didn't want to be the casualty.

I plead with my eyes for him not to betray me this way.

We'll find another way. I will help you.

I pushed those thoughts at him, hoping he could read them on my face.

Knox met my eyes, indecision playing on his expression before it hardened, and his teeth clicked. "Fine."

The word was so guttural it took me a second to register that he'd agreed.

"No." I gasped and gripped his arm, wrapping my arms around it in a chokehold. "Please, Knox."

Their eyes were not those of nice people. There was darkness and depravity. They would brutalize me, and their twisted lust told me exactly how the Johnson man would use me. My stomach soured, and I started breathing hard, verging on hyperventilating.

I craned my neck and forced Knox to meet my eyes. "I'm your mate. Please don't do this," I said, choked. My world shifted yet again with his next statement.

"I don't want a mate. The last thing I need is to be looking after a pathetic slip of a girl."

I cringed away from him, my body crumbling into itself.

Different arms caught me, a nose buried itself in my neck, and my skin crawled at the sensation.

"She smells so good." A hard dick dug into my ass and I whimpered, meeting Knox's eyes as a sudden need to escape ruled me. I scrambled in the man's grip. He growled, smacking my temple. The ground shifted, and I lost consciousness.

KNOX

As soon as Liliana was out of my grip, I squeezed my fists tightly. The loss burned through every fiber of my body. She was essential to me. I'd find the information I needed another way—not with her as the collateral. Her brown eyes watered as they fixed on me, shock and betrayal all over them.

The fucker slammed his meaty fist across her temple and her too thin body dropped along with my heart.

"Deal's off," I snarled, lunging for Liliana.

A man rammed into my side, and I twisted midair, slamming my fist into his throat. *Squelch.* A sick sucking sound of my fist smashing through cartilage echoed in my ear.

The body dropped to the ground with a thump.

I lifted my head to seek her out, but six fucking men rushed at me, blocking everything behind them. Two got to me first and I buried my heel into one as I socked another one across the chin. Before I could take a moment, another with silver teeth swung his fist.

Blood dripped from my nose, and I staggered.

One of the men rammed into my back and a foul-smelling one slammed his fist into my dick. I grunted, and the shock allowed them to get me on the ground.

I absorbed the beating, gritting my molars.

Liliana.

The tightness in my chest snaked to my throat. I needed to get to her *now*.

My wolf burst forward, and I raked my claws across the one on the ground and buried my teeth into the other, dragging him backward so my flank was against the wall.

I shifted back as her hurt brown eyes flashed in my thoughts and I gritted my teeth, ripping the maws of the wolf open. His skull popped, and I tossed it at the werewolf in human form who reeked of cigarettes coming at me.

The fucking asshole was trying to escape. I gripped the back of his neck and slammed him into the wall a few times.

"Where is she?"

My chest squeezed, the tension spreading through my gut and billowing out.

He groaned and writhed in my grip. Flipping him over, I smashed my fist into his mouth. Teeth embedded into my knuckles and blood gushed onto my skin.

"Where did he take her?" He said nothing.

I slammed him onto the pool table, and it buckled.

My stomach was a clenched mess. I'd refused to look her in the face when agreeing. I'd known just one look at her soft lips, and I'd say fuck it. All I had needed was the information and then I'd have torn his throat out and gotten her back. I hadn't counted on this massive fucking storm of shit going bad.

I brought my foot down on his chest and he jerked, blood dripping from his mouth.

Fuck. I needed him alive and conscious. I swiped the back of my hand across my bloody face to clear the red dripping into my eyes.

This was the last one I needed to kill before hunting my baby down. I sneered at the terrified werewolf at my feet.

I staggered, my wolf at the front wanting to bury teeth into his neck and yank the meat out.

I battled with him, needing to regain control.

Running around with my heart bleeding wasn't going to lead me anywhere. I needed to think. To get it out of this fucker if it was the last fucking thing I did.

The sweet Omega was mine.

Denial was my enemy and no more. I was fooling myself. I didn't know everything about her life, where she was, or why she was so skittish... but I wanted to learn. Protect her.

She'd never have to fear, as soon as I had her with me again.

LIANA

I GROANED AND INHALED SHARPLY. MY TEMPLES throbbed, and my mouth had a cotton taste. My eyelids fluttered open. Light filtered through a slit in the curtains and I grimaced at the mold scent filling my nose. I blinked multiple times to clear my crusted eyes as I studied my surroundings.

Gasping, I scrambled away from the body lying next to me. As I shoved away, I saw that all the girl had on was a thin pair of underwear. The cement rasped my skin, and I slammed into a second person. A feminine voice cursed and shot up.

"Watch it," she groused.

My mouth worked as I tried to make sense of everything. As my brain caught up, the chill in the air registered. A shiver crested over my spine.

"Girl, your eyes are going to pop out of your head if you open them anymore." A girl dressed in shorts and a tank top watched me analytically. Her red hair swayed in the high ponytail. "I'm guessing you're an Omega?"

There was the word again. What was that?

Nerves clogged the question in my throat.

The girl quirked a brow.

"You talk?"

She eyed the scar on my face, but didn't mention it. Appreciation lightened my shoulders.

"Sorry, yes." My head dipped as the moments before I was knocked out flashed in my head. Tears welled, and I inhaled sharply.

Knox. How could you?

"No need to apologize or cry. You're not in trouble." She raised her hands.

I couldn't muster a smile at her lightly said words, since my chest was too heavy. I rubbed the tender spot on my temple.

"Where are we?" My head swiveled in the direction of the door.

"A nasty ass room." She followed my gaze. "Don't bother. They locked and bolted it on the other side."

"What do they want from us?" I licked my lips. "Those men."

"Breed us and fuck us." She sneered. The words weighed on my shoulders and I hugged myself.

The dark-haired girl I'd bumped into whimpered and curled into her body.

"Why is she naked?"

Sadness lined the face of the girl I was speaking to. "She's been here a while."

"What did they do to her?"

"What they will do to *us* once we're in heat."

"Heat?"

"Omega's go into heat... do you not know anything about what you are?"

I shook my head. This was the first I'd heard about heats.

My brain tried to make sense of what she was saying in regard to the nude, abused girl.

"When we go into heat all reason flies out the window. All we want, all we crave, is sex." She paused. "They waited for her to hit her heat before taking advantage of her. When she's mad with desire, they used her. That was as much as she told me. She isn't much of a talker. Understandably."

A shiver wracked the girl.

"Is she okay?" I crouched by her, pressing my fingers into her icy skin. She flinched away.

"She spends most of her time sleeping."

I gripped the bottom of my shirt and lifted it over my head and carefully set it over the shivering girl. Fortunately, Knox had gotten me the basic sports bra that was extra big on me, so it covered a good amount of my skin. I inhaled and my wolf roused in my chest, recognizing the sweet scent. A kindred feeling pressed into me.

When I looked up, I met the other girl's eyes as she studied me.

"Randy," she said, pointing to herself before waving toward me.

"Liliana, but you can call me Liana."

She nodded contemplatively. "How did they catch you?"

"M-my mate traded me for information," I stammered.

She sucked in a sharp breath, and her eyes flashed.

"Asshole."

I nodded in agreement.

"Are you willing to help with the escape?"

I blinked at the sudden change of conversation.

"Escape?" I pushed to my feet. The sports bra was a poor

shield against the chilled room. Wrapping my arms around my body, I surveyed the area.

How exactly was she expecting to escape? There was the window... inching close to it, I peered out and noted the long drop to the ground.

I may survive the fall, but it would hurt, a lot.

"We're on the fourth floor." Randy began pacing, her finger tapping her lower lip. "We need to have a way to get them to take us out of here. It must be life threatening because they need to get us out of this room *and* distracted enough to give us a chance to escape."

The quickest way to clear a room was to get a— "Fire?"

"That's exactly what I was thinking." Randy snapped her fingers and slipped her fingers into her bra. "I stole this from one of the guys that bring us food."

A lighter sat in her palm, inconspicuous yet symbolizing hope.

"We set that ugly ass shit on fire."

I followed in the direction she pointed. It was a rectangular painting half the size of the wall. A woman surrounded by the forest lay on her back, hands cupping her breast with her head thrown back as her mouth opened with ecstasy. A man bent between her legs, doing what Knox had done to me earlier.

The look on her face portrayed exactly how I had felt, too.

My eyes lifted to the wolves peeking between the trees and the silhouette of a man watching the sight. Surprising, since werewolves were such possessive creatures.

"It's really pretty," I said hesitantly and then bit my lip. I didn't want to offend her by disagreeing with her.

"I'd agree, if the sick man-child that had painted it wasn't obsessed with Omegas." She scoffed and her arm grazed mine when she stood beside me.

"So people are obsessed with Omegas because of sex?"

Randy snorted.

"There are too many reasons why we're a hot topic. Some she-wolves get pissed that we smell good to males. It makes them jealous as hell. And it's not just sex and breeding, girl, our sex drive is off the chain." She elbowed me. "I've used up four vibrators during one heat cycle. That's what makes it so nice to have multiple true mates out there. It's the only way we can be fully satisfied. It's the least the Moon Goddess owes us for putting a target on our backs."

"Multiple mates," I parroted, stunned. It wasn't some weird second or third chance. I had three true mates because I was an Omega.

The lack of knowledge tightened the knot in my throat.

"Then there's the other reason so many seek us out." She paused, nose wrinkling. "We're able to call forward the wolf in defectives."

I took a shocked step back, and the sill dug into my spine.

"Fewer defectives, more wolves." I said, almost too low to hear.

"Bingo."

The dwindling wolf population would lower because there would be more true mates finding each other, which would lessen the percentage of defective wolves being born. Even with that life-altering news, I needed to know more about the other part of her comment.

"Have you found your true mates?"

A shadow tightened her eyes. "Nope. Is the one that traded you the only one?"

"No… how many do we end up having?"

She shrugged. "It could be anywhere between two to six. I'm not sure how that works. The stories passed down in my family weren't exactly specific."

"I've found three."

"Three!" Randy faced me, mouth dropped. "How the hell are you not tied up somewhere with them trying like hell to get you to accept their mating bite and then breed you?"

My face heated, and I licked my lips.

"None of them want to be with me."

Her lips tightened, and she shook her head slowly.

"Isn't it funny? We get more chances at true matings, and guys are still such asswipes."

I snorted out a laugh. Pressing my fingers to my mouth, I turned wide eyes to her. That was not a noise I was used to making.

"Don't worry, girly. There are ways to distract yourself in the city."

"The city…"

The idea of any city was foreign to me. Sure, I knew there was so much more outside the pack, but I learned the very basics of it. Werewolves who lived among humans had a different way of life, dramatically different, since they hid their existence. It was the opposite of what I was used to experiencing on pack lands.

There wasn't any other way for me to learn about life outside, since I didn't have a cell phone or a television. It was my mom's fault. She told me stories about the outside world, driving in the fear to enhance my desire to stay among the pack. Everything she said stuck with me. So, I never left, even after she died.

Randy eyed me and narrowed her eyes. "You've been to the city before, right?"

"No, I've stayed on pack lands my entire life."

Her mouth dropped.

"That's so sad." She lifted her hand, and I flinched on reflex; her eyes narrowed as she studied me, but she let a grin slip over her lips before lightly patting my shoulder. "Don't worry. You have me to guide you through getting laid." She winked. "First piece of advice. Always make sure not to fuck anyone during your heat. It gives males ideas about trying to claim you." Her lip curled with disgust.

I shivered at the thought of forcing the biting claim.

It was a good thing a female had to accept the claim.

"What do you mean *getting laid*?"

"How sheltered are you?"

Dipping my head, I pressed my teeth into my lower lip at the incredulous expression.

"This was worse than I assumed. We have to get out of here *now*."

I snorted and watched as she went to the window. It creaked as she pushed it up, and I hurried to help. The wood groaned and snapped. Triumph reflected in her eyes, making me tremble with excited fear.

"It isn't bolted down."

"They think we're so weak. It must be the whole vagina thing we have going on that makes them think we can't rub two brain cells together." She scoffed, disgusted. "We'll have to wait until we're ready to run."

"When are we leaving?"

"Tonight."

My heart thundered in my ears at those words. Finally. I

would begin fresh. I'd thought my new start could be with Knox, but he'd shown me how stupid I was.

A nasty emotion curdled in the pit of my stomach at the image of his angry face as he turned away from me. Unbidden, Lore and Declan were right on the heels. Their rejection watered the existing pain, feeding it with each replay of their rejection and poisoning my soul.

I swallowed repeatedly in attempt to dispel the thickness sitting at the base of my throat and looked out the window.

The forest was bright from the evening sun that shone. It illuminated the span of foliage and the dried grass surrounding the home I was trapped in.

Movement caught my eye, and I found my eyes trained on a bulky male roaming around the home. I quickly averted my gaze, so they didn't get suspicious.

I didn't want to gain any attention.

I just wanted to be left alone.

"Do you have a pack?"

Randy cleared her throat. "I used to. It was a small pack in the South."

Smaller packs were closer-knit, but at the same time, I was grateful that I'd had the protection of a big pack.

"Used to? Are you on your own?"

"Yes." She moved away from the window, mimicking my retreat. "I like living among humans—"

A scream made me jump and turn around. The girl that had been sleeping was panting. The shirt I gave her slid off her form. She met my eyes with wide ones that held pain and shook her head, her terror-filled eyes clearing as she looked down at the shirt in her lap. She palmed it before looking back up at me and holding it out.

"Please keep it." I was dressed in the sports bra Knox had given me, but she was naked.

Her throat worked and indecision flickered in the depths of her eyes. When I continued to calmly look at her, she brought it back to cover her chest. Tears blinded me for a moment before I blinked them away. My heart hurt for her.

I puffed out my cheeks and stifled the waterworks as she slipped her arms through the shirt.

What had they done to her?

Pressing my lips together, I met Randy's eyes. She was grinding her teeth.

"We have our plan of escape, Erin."

Erin nodded, detached, and lay on her side.

That expression on her face made my stomach churn. It was achingly similar to one I'd worn after my mother died.

It echoed how I'd given up.

Declan

My vision blurred, and I shook my head. It was getting difficult to see straight. Lily completely took over my mind, and it was creating havoc. I could usually track anything, but with my emotions involved, it screwed everything up with how unhappy my wolf was. We needed to think together to be able to track, utilizing both advantages, but that wasn't happening with his desperation. His anger overshadowed everything, and the only way it could abate was by having *her* in my arms.

Alaric slowed and tipped his muzzle up, sniffing deeply.

Since we hadn't had anything of Lily's with us, Alaric had sniffed Lore. They'd been close enough that her scent clung to him. I fucking hated that. It was slight, but enough for Alaric to inhale it and catch the trail.

Well, we did have something. I should have had the forethought to grab her blanket for Alaric to use. Now, I was faced with the reality that Lore smelled like her, nor did I miss the fact that Alaric now knew her scent. And what I abhorred the most? I couldn't stop my instinct to sniff Lore so I could breathe in even the slightest of peaches.

The irritation at the thought of Lore was a sliver in comparison to the murderous needs that trembled through me at the thought of Alaric enjoying Lily. At least I was semi-able to talk myself down with Lore, since we'd known each other since we were kids. He was like my brother.

Alaric chuffed and shot off in another direction. Lore grazed against my side as we raced after him. I inhaled deeply. My wolf took hold of my consciousness when I smelled blood and my human side retreated to the back.

When awareness crept back in, I was stepping into a parking lot. Pebbles kicked up at my speed as I shot past a red truck. Other than that vehicle, there were a handful of motorcycles. Blood was heavy in the air. Wolf blood.

The hair on the back of my neck stood.

I would know if it was hers.

Keep telling yourself that, Declan.

Alaric stepped through the propped door, Lore on his heels. Tables were overturned, and blood was smeared everywhere.

I weaved around a broken chair.

A grunt sounded on the heels of a wet thump. Following the sound of violence, I passed the threshold into a room. A man held another by the hair as he pinned him to the pool table in the middle of the room.

"Tell me where you took her." Each seething word accompanied the slam of the male wolf's fist. Dominance seeped off him. He was an Alpha.

My lips peeled back when he rounded us.

His eyes bounced over everyone, but he turned back to the man as if we were of no consequence.

Lore growled.

He didn't like how un-threatened the guy was acting. Following his lead, I shifted.

"Go the fuck away before I kill you."

Who the fuck was this guy?

Lore's head tilted back as he laughed, and I crossed my arms, stepping forward.

Lore edged around the man who'd returned to getting information from his victim. "Alaric, why are we here?"

"She was here." Alaric rubbed his nose. "He smells like her."

I lunged, but Lore stopped my attack as I narrowed my eyes on the fucker. A fucker who was giving me an irritated look like I wasn't going to murder him. He wrapped his hand behind his victim's neck and shoved him to the floor where he lay in a pitiful lump.

"Why do you smell like my mate?" A stillness fell over Lore, and I bit my growl back at his declaration. The man splattered with blood stilled, and the color of his eyes sharpened.

"The only one I smell like is *my* true mate."

It took me only moments to connect the dots. From the tightening of the bloodied wolf's eyes, he understood just as I did.

I eyed him suspiciously. The last thing I wanted was another male sniffing my mate. Damn her for being an Omega.

"Omega," he said bitterly. "She didn't tell me she had already found another true mate." Awareness sparked in his purple eyes and he narrowed them at Lore. "You hurt her."

"What happened to her?" I barked.

"You're one too?" He growled and dragged his hands through his hair.

"I don't envy you assholes," Alaric muttered, leaning

against the wall. "If you are *all* looking for the girl, the last thing you should be doing right now is arguing about her. Find her."

Fuck him for being right.

"This fuck ordered his people to take her while—" the new true mate started grimly. "They crippled me before I could get to her." So that's why there were so many limbs ripped up all over the place. He'd torn them apart when they tried to keep him down.

"Where is she?" Lore angled a kick at the guy on the ground. Crimson exploded from his mouth, and he rolled from the force. Thankfully, near me. In one stride, I was beside him. Grabbing his arm, I snapped the radius. His bone poked up through his skin where the break was.

The new mate's eyes glinted with glee.

"I'll leave all y'all to this." Alaric waved a hand at the scene.

"No, try to sniff her out," Lore snapped, lasered in on the guy on the floor. Frustration tightened Alaric's thin face and he shifted and loped outside.

Lore's hands trembled as he hooked them at his back and nodded at me. Eyeing the crying injured wolf, I studied where I wanted to inflict pain.

The unknown mate stepped to my side, limping slightly. They must have fucked his leg up. He smiled savagely—he would enjoy this.

Licking my lips, I cracked my victim's rib in a swift movement. "Where did your men take Liliana?"

Alaric burst back into the room. "We have company." I didn't look away from the smug smile spreading on the soon-to-be-dead fuck's face. "A pack of at least twelve wolves is coming this way."

LIANA

IT WAS TIME TO ESCAPE. NERVES PRICKLED THE BACK of my neck, making me sweat. Erin was still on her back as she watched Randy pace and fiddle with a lighter.

Stepping next to Randy, I smiled encouragingly.

Her finger rasped against the little cog of the lighter, and a flame sputtered to life.

Her hand shook slightly.

Strength I didn't know I had flooded me. I admired the girl in front of me. She put on such a strong front, but inside she was as scared as me. "We got this."

Randy exhaled and nodded before nearing the flame to the canvas. The painting must have had some sort of chemical because it went up like it was doused in kerosene.

"Shit!"

I yanked Randy back when the flames almost touched her face. We cringed against the corner. Erin watched the flames expressionlessly as they flickered near her. Releasing Randy's arm, we moved in conjunction to grab Erin's arms and dragged her against the wall.

"Where are they?"

The door remained still and my stinging eyes met Randy's. The fire spread and crackled, the noise heightening by the second.

"Help!" Randy yelled, banging on the wall. We needed them to come upstairs before we tried to jump out of the window.

A cough wracked my body. The smoke was too heavy. The thick layer hung over the room. What made everything worse was the window was cracked open. Randy had said the wind would fan the flame, but if we didn't leave it open, then the fire would have exploded out when we'd opened it.

Pressing my hand to my mouth, I kept my breaths shallow.

"Cover your mouth," I yelled over the crackling fire. It moved and slithered like it was alive.

The flames were climbing up the walls, devouring the wood. Embers jumped, and one of them landed on my arm. I hissed and patted it away.

That stung.

"They aren't coming for us..." Randy's words were detached, but the shock in her expression was unmistakable.

It didn't make sense. We were here to be used. They should have come for us.

I caught movement out of the corner of my eye. Wolves ran through the threshold of the woods, *away* from the house.

"Why are they running into the woods?" Dread curdled my stomach.

"Shit, we're on our own." She coughed and pinched her nose.

I looked at the window. "Plan B."

Randy nodded grimly.

"Our bodies can take a beating. Sure, we feel every lick as bad as any human, but we're resilient."

Oh, how well I knew that.

I tipped my head in a nod at Randy's words even though I was pretty sure she was talking herself down from the ledge, but I let her believe I needed the reassurance.

"Even though it's cracked open, the sudden influx of oxygen may cause an explosion. We jump as soon as we open it."

In answer, I rested my leg near the window sill as she did and pressed my hand on the pane.

Randy's lips tightened as she glanced at Erin standing over our shoulder before turning to face me again.

"We push on three," she said, and I nodded frantically.

"Erin." She turned at my call. Her eyes met mine. "Get ready to jump."

Randy began counting down and we threw open the window.

Just as she said, the fire jumped toward us, and I cringed toward freedom, gripping the outside of the sill. Erin held on at the other end and my muscles burned as I tried to keep my balance. Erin was supposed to be between us.

I tugged myself higher to peek inside since the initial burst abated. I cringed at the heat scorching my face.

"Erin."

Her sad eyes met mine, her face was coated in black. It was a miracle she wasn't burned.

"We have to go, Erin, come on," Randy cried over the blazing crackle as her toe scraped the side of the house to find purchase. "Come on, Liana."

With a grunt, she pushed off, and her body sailed through

the air and hit the ground with a jarring thud. She stumbled on her feet and then fell to her knees.

She cringed over her leg.

The heat singed my skin.

"Let's go," I repeated to Erin, fingers starting to slip. She looked back and I could read her intention.

"No. Don't do that." Panic loosened my tight hold, and I dug my fingers into the slat. I balanced from the window sill, my forearms digging into the edge of the wood. I attempted to hoist myself up and onto the ledge, but I was too weak.

"I don't want to live with the memories," she rasped, her hands pressing into my chest.

When she shoved me, my necklace caught on her fingers. The chain tugged on my neck as it snapped.

My arms windmilled as I scrambled for purchase, but it was too late. My stomach dropped as I fell through the air.

My hair whipped around my face, and then my back slammed on the ground. A grunt exploded from my chest and shock made me still for a split second, then the pain set in, and I whimpered.

Randy limped over to me and looked down at me and then back up at the flaming window.

Tears streamed down my face.

"She didn't want to live."

Randy's lips pursed grimly. "Let's get going." She pulled me to my feet, and I bit back a whimper at the pinch in my back.

My teeth sank into my bottom lip at the ache through my body. It hurt so badly to move, but I needed to keep going. With stiff movements, we made our way to one of the vehicles parked at the side of the house.

Randy stepped forward, releasing me. She tried the car door

handle, but it didn't budge. She muttered under her breath and wove to the other side of the vehicle.

I reached for a heavy rock and swung it at the window with all my might. It exploded in a rain of glass and shards nicked my arm. Randy gaped at me.

"Great fucking job." She reached through the window gingerly and pulled it open.

My heart thudded rampant in my chest.

Poor Erin.

How had I ended up here?

Rejected by all three of my mates, then given to creeps, then escaping.

This was surreal. I had such a quiet life cooking for the pack. It was a boring life, but at least I wasn't being traded off like a piece of meat.

This all hurt more than I could even imagine—than I ever thought capable of feeling, but at least... at least I was no longer feeling pitiful about myself.

Hanging around where I was unwanted had damaged me. With the few experiences I'd had recently, I knew that more keenly than ever. It was like I had been in a dream state my entire life and I was finally waking.

I never wanted to experience that again.

Randy's head was under the steering wheel. I craned to see what she was doing. It looked like she was ripping through some wires.

"This fucking piece of shit."

I blushed at the inventive curses.

"Yes!"

I jumped at her exclamation. The car revved as the engine

powered on, and Randy hopped into the driver's seat and looked at me. "Come on, Liana."

I rubbed the back of my hand over my mouth. This would be easy. I only had to hop in.

"Where are we going?"

"The only place we can get lost and hide our scents." She paused. "The city."

Nerves fluttered in my stomach as I climbed into the passenger seat.

The car revved, and she threw it into drive. Looking back, I saw the huge farmhouse emitting smoke as it gradually burned. Poor Erin. How harshly they must have abused her for her to choose this...

I exhaled shakily and faced forward. The car bumped and skid as Randy screeched onto the pavement and then the long stretch of road.

I didn't know what life would bring, but at least I wasn't alone.

Lore

The scent of burning flesh filled my nose. It was thick in the air and I could smell it wafting from the house.

Flames crested over the roof as embers jumped and sparked. The fire had engulfed half the house already.

Liliana was in there.

Shifting, I broke down the door to the burning house. This was where that fucker said she was being held. Only after we'd killed every wolf that came our way had he spoken. Blood trickled down my body, dripping to the floor.

The crimson splashed on the pale tile from me and Liliana's third mate, the gray wolf. It was the blood of the multitudes of wolves we'd slaughtered.

As much as I hated it, Declan, the gray wolf, and I worked well together. We'd torn through throats, slashed at chests, and ripped apart limbs. A frenzy had overcome all of us. There was an understanding working through our unit—we needed to get to Liliana.

Declan stayed behind to deal with the last two wolves,

giving us time to follow the piercing need to my mate. *Our* mate.

My lips lifted in a snarl.

Gray wolf shoved past me and loped up the stairs, still in his wolf form. I followed him.

The higher I got, the more intense the smell of cooked flesh became. A hair-raising howl spurred my stride.

Smoke was heavy in the air, and my eyes stung. I pushed through the singed door, tearing the rest of it off the broken hinges.

Gray wolf's muzzle nudged a burnt corpse, and he tugged the crisp material off an unrecognizable blackened lump.

Skull shone through seared flesh.

Dread made my movements lag.

I crouched and predatory eyes looked back at me. When I stepped closer to Gray, his teeth flashed, and I showed my human teeth and reached down.

He chuffed and whimpered, the fear in his eyes turning skittish. He was full on wolf, there was nothing human in his eyes. Releasing the cloth, he keened and raked his paws over his ears repeatedly—Manically. His movement sliced open his flesh and his blood scented the room.

Dread soured my stomach as I lifted the piece of a shirt to my nose. The room spun.

Beneath the coiling stench was her sweet smell.

I gagged and hunched over. No. This couldn't be my Little One. A glint caught my eye, and I cupped the shiny object.

The simmering fire glinted off the crescent moon.

It was hers...

"Let's go. It's going down." Alaric's voice echoed through

the room. I was automatically in a crouch in front of the charred body.

Alaric held up his hands, bowing his head.

I clasped my head.

He is not the enemy. I chanted over and over again.

Losing sense of time, I stumbled as I was shoved. The last I heard before Alaric pushed me through the door was the cracking of wood snapping onto the ground. With my next blink, I was standing outside of the burning house.

She was dead.

A fist punched through my chest.

She was dead.

I had to control myself... be stro—

I fell to my knees.

My wolf took over.

Liana

Two Years Later

The tickle of the faux fur caressed my arms and legs. I squeezed my thighs tightly together as if to contain the throb between my legs. The low pulsating spread heat at my core, and I wiggled my hips to find some release from the strain.

I'd dreamt of them again.

Of them claiming me.

My hand dragged down my side, and I curved my palm over my mound, pressing hard. My fingers fluttered over my clit. I bit my lip to hold in my needy whimper. Curving my digit, I rolled the bud over the thin material of my panties. My lips parted. Oh, that felt wonderful.

A shiver trembled up my legs, and I continued the gentle touches.

Their eyes flashed in my memory, deepening the need. I wanted them to touch me. I hurt for it. I pressed harder and the teasing caresses weren't enough. Sliding my hand under my panties, I found my lips drenched. With a moan, I slipped my finger between the slit, massaging my wet folds and dragging the moisture to my clit.

My legs trembled as I mercilessly touched myself as my mates would have. Goosebumps lifted on my arms, and I arched off the bed as I was drawn up as tight as a bowstring. The release was instantaneous, and I cried out, toes curling. My body curved as the flood swept me into a lulling tide of release.

I licked my lips, basking in bliss as I caught my breath.

What could they be doing?

How were they living? The thoughts were my constant companions meant to torture me.

My mates were fine.

A massive weight settled over my body, and I squeezed my eyelids tightly as pictures of things I'd conjured flashed in my mind. Lore was surely doing the same as he'd always done and bedding a multitude of women.

The weight compounded.

Declan was with his unhinged mate...

It was becoming difficult to breathe.

And Knox got his revenge—as he'd wanted.

I hoped they were happy with themselves. The bitter, sarcastic thought wasn't like me, but I couldn't help it when it came to them.

My fingers curled into my blanket.

No, no more torturing myself. I had the entire day ahead of me and I had to focus on all the good in my life.

I stretched in bed, cuddling deeper into the fluffy blankets. Groaning, I rubbed my cheek into the plush pillow and opened my eyes. The cream accent of my room brought me pleasure every time I saw it.

It had already been two years, and I didn't take anything I had for granted. It was such a contrast to everything I had grown up with. Or the lack of stuff I had grown up with. My life in the pack was terrible—all of it was a smorgasbord of depression that I'd accepted since I hadn't known any better.

Though I worked to move on from the memories—for the most part—there were times self-pity got the best of me and I bought a huge tub of ice cream. Those bouts where I fell apart and cried into food lasted hours. I refused to let today be another one of those days. They weren't my finer moments, but they would have been worse without Randy.

The Moon Goddess had been looking down on me to send her to me when she had. Randy had seen and known much more than me. She'd already been a shifted Omega for two years when she'd been taken, so she'd been my guide. Not only on the topic of Omegas, but so much more.

Boy, I'd been sheltered to an ignorant level.

I stared up at the ceiling fan. The room wasn't as big as some of the places I'd seen since I'd left my past life, but at least it was nicer than what I used to have.

How had I survived all that time? I shivered. I'd been a kid. I'd known no better, and I'd internalized the blame for things that weren't my fault.

That was something I'd had to work through. Randy had given me no option.

My fingertips trailed over my scar.

Clara shouldn't have blamed me for hugging Declan. Nothing sexual had happened between us. He'd been comforting me after my mom had died. And for goddess' sake, I'd been fifteen.

But in my hormonal teenage mind, I'd thought that since I had lustful thoughts about him, then that meant it was on me.

Acting on desire was different from thought, though. I

would have never crossed that line. And what had I gotten for my young mind's fantasies? This scar.

When I told Randy about it, she'd been livid. Seeing her reaction fired me up as well and more resentment had built.

But turned out Clara was right to be suspicious of me. Declan was my true mate.

My breath hiccupped on my inhale as bitterness flushed through my system. So, despite my best efforts it was going to be one of those days, then.

I exhaled and my eyes slid shut.

These days sucked.

I spread my fingers on the soft tufts of the blanket, as I stretched out and rubbed my arms outwards like I was doing a snow angel.

When I was in heat, I loved rubbing my naked body against soft surfaces. It made my entire body clench with pleasure.

Randy taught me about the nesting and heat aspects of being an Omega. Well, she'd taught me a hell of a lot more in regard to my new sex drive.

It had taken me a while to wrap my head around what it meant, but I'd finally come to terms with all of it. Maybe because I had a slew of ways to get through the phases.

My first heat was intense, to say the least.

I licked my lips at the blur of sensitivity during that time. There had been many a dildo used in this house, and it didn't help that Randy and I were synced.

Puffing out my cheeks, I held air in them before pushing off the bed and slipping on my fluffy slippers.

The ledge of the window dug into my hip as I leaned to scoot open the sheer curtain and unlatch the lock.

Clear, crisp air caressed my face, and I inhaled greedily.

Leaning forward, the petal of my rose bush tickled my cheek. I was proud of the little flower for surviving so long since usually, my rose pot had a huge turnover rate. A yellow leaf detached from a maple tree and floated to the ground in a cradling motion.

Fall was the best.

My gaze clashed with the eyes of the man who lived below me. His legs were splayed on the platform of the fire escape attached to the side of our building.

My face heated, and I waved. Clay was actually pretty decent; he was also the *only* werewolf that lived in the building.

That was the main reason Randy chose this apartment. I guess it had taken her forever to find one. She'd searched up and down for a human building, so she wouldn't have to deal with being found out as an Omega, but it was tough to find one without at least one lone werewolf.

Clay thought we were simply low level Beta werewolves. That had to do with the scent droplets we took daily. The homemade, herb and plant infused scent suppressant Randy had created.

She was a genius that way.

It must have been nice to have an Omega as a great grandmother. She'd been able to pass on such fantastic nuggets of information and advice. After testing it, we learned it lasted around a week, but to be safe, we took it daily. Insofar, there were no adverse effects, and it made me feel safer.

Clay's nose flared, and I could see him swallow even with the distance between us. My wolf paced unhappily.

There was a downside to living in the city, which had to do with my wolf's restlessness. She didn't like it, and I could only put off her frustration for so long before Randy and I headed on a 'hiking' trip to relieve the tension. But even those have been minimal since it was too dangerous.

"Good morning," I said softly.

He straightened like my words jolted him out of a dream. He did that a lot. Just stared at me. I'd gotten used to it since he'd never bothered me.

The only instance we'd had a close call was when he'd come knocking on our door during one of our heat cycles. Randy and I had theorized it was the heavy scent of sex seeping through our apartment.

I'd spoken to him through the little speaker we installed on the door and told him Randy had company over. Per her request, it wasn't a lie. She'd brought a human that heat cycle. The poor guy had hobbled out of the room after three days, a love-stricken expression on his face. He had no idea he'd bedded a sex-crazed Omega.

I still fielded calls from him, but I reached the point where I just said Randy had a boyfriend.

Did that deter him? Nope.

After that, Randy stopped bringing humans over. Her experience before that was just as bad, but she'd chalked it up to an anomaly, and she was wrong.

Thank the Moon Goddess we only had heats every ninety days. If it was a monthly occurrence, I would have gone crazier than I was already going.

Clay cleared his throat. "Mornin'."

"You're up early."

"My brother is visiting, so I'm getting some space from him."

Nodding, I hummed in understanding. He and his brother must not get along.

"Oh, well, good luck."

"Wait! Liana."

I poked my head back out.

"Do you want to get dinner sometime?" He scratched his neck. When I first moved into the building, he'd asked me out. Thinking back, I flushed at the violent way 'no' burst from me.

I'd apologized quickly after, but I couldn't exactly explain to him that I was done with getting hurt.

My mouth opened, the rejection ready on my lips, but I paused.

What was the harm?

He'd already proven he could keep boundaries. Randy's emotional words one night we got drunk repeated in my head.

Why do you punish yourself for your mates rejecting you? You should be living your life instead of tossing everyone out.

I'd cried so hard during that talk.

Shaking the memory off, I came back to the present. "Okay."

As soon as the word was out, my stomach clenched, a sour taste spreading in my mouth. I wanted to take back the acceptance, but I forced the negativity away. It wasn't like my mates were remaining chaste for me. My nose wrinkled at the needle-like spikes striking my flesh.

His reddish-brown brows flew up. I'd surprised myself too.

"O-oh." He cleared his throat. "Are you free tonight?" That was sooner than I thought, less time to prepare, but also less time to talk myself out of it. I nodded slowly, and he continued, "I'll come pick you up around seven?"

"See you then." A little smile slipped over my lips as nerves and excitement mingled.

Straightening, I buried my hands through my hair and tucked the long strands behind my ears.

The pale orange light of the morning sky was brightening to yellow.

I needed to get a pot of coffee going if I didn't want Randy to be in a grouchy mood.

My silky shorts grazed my thighs as I slipped out of my room.

The run-down kitchen was small, but it had everything we needed. Making coffee was instinct at this point. Randy was not a morning person, nor was I, but I needed to get my day started bright and early to prepare myself mentally for work.

Customers were a trip, and I needed to be properly equipped to deal with the chaos of the mall.

The machine hissed, and droplets splashed against the glass.

Once that was set up, I poured myself some water and tipped a few drops of the scent potion into it before chugging it.

In a world where Omegas were supposed to be extinct, I doubted we would be received well. After all, someone had already tried to kidnap us once, so we chose to stay hidden.

The store I worked in had a variety of sections, from clothes to perfume and makeup. My area was shoes. It was perfect. There was not too much reading required and there was a good amount of running back and forth. A need for my wolf, since it sated her need to pace.

Pulling the uniform of a pencil skirt and a white blouse on, I quickly got dressed. I slipped on one of the many pairs of shoes I'd collected through my time working there. It brought together the professional look.

Running the brush through my hair, the dark strands

smoothed out of its hectic nest. The waves settled around my shoulders and I sprayed it with some smoothing oil to tame the craziness.

My heels clicked as I made my way back to the kitchen and pulled two mugs out.

The dark coffee splashed into the clear cups, and I reached for the sweetener. Randy was crazy about the stuff.

Leveling some into her cup, I mixed it, then cupped mine and made my way to her door on the other side of the apartment.

The loveseat was the only piece of furniture in our living room and it sat between the kitchen and both our rooms.

My fist came down on the door.

A groan sounded, and I pulled the door open.

"Coffee's ready," I sang. "It's waiting for you in the kitchen."

Tempting her was one of the easiest ways to get her out of bed. She moaned and tossed beneath the pile of blankets.

Light seared into the dark room when I pushed open the thick light-blocking curtains. I leaned against the wall as she grumbled.

The room was bland in comparison to mine. If I had left the décor to how she'd had it, there would be nothing but dull brown colors.

Not my vibe.

The splashes of brightly colored pillows added a happy element to the space. Something Randy needed.

She denied it, but I knew she loved it.

"I agreed to go on a date with Clay."

She popped out of bed so fast I worried she sprained her back. My lips twitched as she rubbed her face.

"Hold on." Brushing her dyed hair down, she cleared her throat. "What did you just say? Did my ears deceive me?"

"I'll answer all questions once you're up and aware." I exited her room, barely evading the pillow thrown my way.

"Who are you, you evil nymph spirit?"

I grinned and pushed myself on the kitchen counter as I waited for her. It took less than a minute for her to speed out of the room with her hair pulled into a ponytail and her face washed.

"Spill," she snapped and snatched the coffee that was waiting for her. I did exactly that, telling her frame by frame what had happened. "No way. I knew he fucking wanted your peaches, but after you rejected his furry ass, I doubted he'd have the balls to ask you again." She cackled.

My lips tilted up at her mouthy-ness. I'd gotten used to it so much so that it spilled into my own vocabulary sometimes.

It was worse when I was drunk, which didn't happen often after the last time I'd been revved to march back to the Eastland pack and toss dirt into Lore and Declan's eyes. Yeah, I didn't know why *that* was what I was determined to do.

My phone dinged, signaling I needed to start making my way to work. I pushed off the counter and unhooked my purse from the hook.

"Do you want me to drop you off?"

Considering it, I paused.

The bus stop was half a mile from the apartment, but the walk was always refreshing, especially in the morning.

"I need to walk a bit." She automatically understood it, since she lived with the same angstiness from her wolf.

"Remember to text the check in." I nodded. It was a necessary thing to be checking in with each other at all times. I had the door half open when she slapped her hands together. "I almost forgot to give you an update. I think I finally got the mixture to make candles." Candles that we could light when we were in heat, so the hormones weren't so thickly entrenched in the air.

Anything to not call attention to ourselves.

"I'll help you buy the stuff to decorate them. We can go to the store tomorrow after work."

Randy rolled her eyes. She knew my obsession with making things pretty.

"Lils." I turned back at Randy's call. "I'm glad you're moving forward."

Her comment stabbed at my heart, and I sucked in a breath. Taking a moment, I worked to calm my rapid heartbeat.

I licked my lips. "Me too."

I smoothed the sides of my baby pink hip-hugging dress as I looked in the floor-length mirror. Leaning close, I rubbed off the smudge of mascara beneath my eye. The shit was waterproof, so I had to rub like my life depended on it.

Good thing I'd put on light foundation since my under eye was red from the rubbing.

Pulling out the gloss, I patted the little brush on my lips and it made the plumpness of my lips stand out. I nodded at my reflection, stepped back, and admired the heels of the day—five-inch *Jimmies*. The studded strap wrapped around my foot, wrapping up my ankles.

My most expensive ones and the ones I'd saved for months to buy. Even with my store discount, they had been crazy expensive.

I frowned at my reflection, liking what I saw, but my stomach cramped. I pressed my lips together, rubbing my damp palms on my hips. Lifting my trembling hand to my face, it trembled over my scar. Maybe I should back out.

Randy peeked in and whistled.

"You're hot."

My hand dropped from where it was hovering near the scar. Nerves cramped my stomach, and my reflection showed me how wide my eyes had gotten.

"Yes, hot with the scar and all."

I huffed at her straightforwardness.

A knock on the door echoed through the apartment, and I startled. I needed to stop being so jumpy, but I couldn't help it. I'd never been able to shake the looming sense of doom, dogging me everywhere I went.

Randy called it trauma.

"I was going to ask you if you were mentally prepared, but looks like you have no choice now. This guy is *prompt*."

I snorted a laugh and followed her to the front door, the heel of my babies rasping across the carpet. Randy stopped me with a hand on the thin strap on my shoulder.

"I'll be gone later; I have to work." She lowered her voice. "Be careful."

"I will." I squeezed her arm and pecked her cheek.

She gave me a thumbs up when I nibbled on my lower lip nervously. My wolf was freaking out. She wanted to run and run hard.

My anxiety was making her act up.

Exhaling sharply, I opened the door as Randy retreated to huddle behind the door.

Clay stuffed his hands in his pockets, and he pressed his lips together. When his gaze settled on me, it widened and he smiled as his eyes dragged down my body.

Don't hunch.

I chanted repeatedly. In my head.

I shoved past my tendency to curve into myself to hide and

lifted my chin even as my cheeks flushed. I couldn't help feeling shy as he drank in my body sheathed in the strappy pink silk dress. In the last few years, my curves had finally filled out nicely due to finally having proper nourishment and regular heats.

Randy mentioned Omegas tended to be curvier, but dear Moon Goddess, it sucked finding good fitting jeans.

"You... wow." The reddish hue creeping up his neck trailed to his face. Would my mates have reacted the same way if they'd picked me up for a date?

I wanted to groan at the intrusive thought and metaphorically shoved all thoughts of them away.

"Thanks," I said and stepped beside him, shutting the door. But not before I mouthed to Randy to stop her silent laughter. If Clay's wolf was at the forefront, he would have heard her with his above-human hearing.

Clay waved me forward and when I stepped in front of him, he inhaled sharply.

Had he just moaned?

I peeked over my shoulder and he was blushing harder. It was a good thing I'd taken a secondary dose of the droplets before getting dressed. I'd never taken two in one day and I wasn't sure how much longer that would extend the ability to hide my scent.

"I'm taking you to one of my favorite restaurants," he said quickly. I didn't bring attention to the little sniff he did as he leaned close to my neck.

Smiling, I was going to comment on his nice outfit when a loud ringtone bounced off the walls.

He fished out his phone as we stepped into the lift and pressed the button down. "Excuse me a second."

I waved him to do his thing, glad that I got a moment to collect myself.

"I'm busy... no... I'll talk to you later." Clay shoved his phone into his pocket. "Sorry about that. It's the brother I told you was staying with me."

"You guys don't get along?"

"Not really. Our interests, no, our morals are on different stratospheres." He snorted. "He's couch surfing while he figures shit out."

"Can't choose your family," I offered. My mom loved me, I know she did, but she was... difficult to say the least.

"Exactly," he breathed.

His jaw clenched and frustration fluttered over his face as we stepped out of the elevator on the first floor.

"What are you doing?" Clay snapped.

"I had to check out the bitch you were all but salivating at the idea of going out with."

I whirled to find a guy leaning against the side of the elevator, waiting for us. He straightened when I met his eyes.

There was something familiar about him... A long beard graced his face and he was lanky and tall. Where had I seen him?

My heart picked up pace, and my hands trembled. I fisted them and inhaled sharply. It was simply his resemblance to Clay. That was the familiarity.

No one was after me, but... he could know I was an Omega. The knot in my throat thickened.

No, not possible. They would have grabbed us as soon as they could. Plus, no one knew we were Omegas. Our scents were well masked.

The brother smoothed his expression, and a smarmy smile spread over his lips.

"Hey, cutie. You want to ditch this loser and come with me?" A silver tooth glinted when he grinned wolfishly.

I tipped my nose up at him.

He tensed and narrowed his eyes as I swept my hair over my shoulder. Clay pulled me into him with a growl.

I pressed into Clay's side, swallowing hard. He was safe. I knew he was. The only problem was he wasn't terribly dominant. Clay's eyebrows furrowed, and he set his hand on my waist, pulling me to his side as the elevator doors slid shut with his brother on the other side.

"Sorry about him—again." He rubbed his face.

"You are night and day."

He squeezed my hip again.

"Let's get you distracted. I'm sure you'll love the place I chose."

DECLAN

"SHE ISN'T DEAD," I GRITTED FROM BETWEEN MY clenched teeth.

"I'm busy." The heavy smell of alcohol permeated the room. The smell stung my nose and my lip lifted in a snarl. How dare he give up like this?

Even the gray wolf that'd followed us back to the Eastland pack was more human in his reaction, and *he'd* retreated deep into his wolf since Lily disappeared. Sure, his humanity was gone, but his grief had rendered him useless and close to rabid.

Giving over consciousness was a relief. The first few months after the fire, I'd done the same. Snapping and growling at anything that neared me. Then it changed. I'd gained purpose during a sane moment.

Lily was alive. There was no other option.

I held onto that truth with my soul.

"Someone has her," I bellowed, the urge to turn pressing on me. Lore refused to listen to me. I'd been telling him for months and I'd been searching for just as long. But I couldn't do it alone as much as I tried. To track with my nose, I needed the wolf at the surface, and that didn't go well. Every time I allowed him to the surface, his single-minded determination to find his mate blinded him. I'd found myself in a peach orchard, for fuck's sake. He followed everything and anything close to resembling sweet peaches.

"She's. Dead." Lore growled back, his eyes flickering with hate. The words were staccato. His clawed hands set on the desk, furred shoulders bunching. Lore was stuck in his wolfman form.

That was the first time he'd said those words. My breaths sawed out between my teeth. I began pacing, as restless as my animal. The scratch of nails burrowing into the desk echoed in the room. Lore added more to the collection of gouges on the desk.

"She's out there!" I hissed again. Dragging my hands through my hair, I kicked the chair in my way. It careened toward the wall, shattering. "I'm looking for her." Bitterness poisoned my words. "What are you doing?"

Lore slammed his palm on the desk, chest heaving. The wooden desk cracked and papers fluttered to the ground. Lore leaned forward threateningly. It was a good thing the desk was between us, or we would have been tearing into each other's flesh—again. It didn't go well the last time for me since he had the advantage with this form.

"Killing her murderers." A fine tremble worked through his body. His words were a mix of snarls and grunts. The words coming disjointed from his muzzle. "Burning body." His eyes flickered, pupils expanding. "You didn't scent the mix of her sweetness with death."

They were lashes to my chest, but I was already shaking my head, scoffing. I was done. I'd already spent a lot of time away from the pack, searching for her this last year, but I returned to formally withdraw. Being a lone wolf was my only option. I couldn't do this pack life, and I refused to put anything over finding Lily. My mother understood and she would remain here and contact me if she needed anything.

Lore's phone rang. He ignored it as we stared each other down. He'd been my brother, we'd always been on the same side, and this conflict was a new dynamic we couldn't work through.

I couldn't help but resent that he internalized his pain and destroyed everything in his general vicinity instead of channeling his anger and rage into helping me find her. He used to put the pack before everything, but now he was driving it into the ground according to Lincoln. Everyone feared his temper, and it was increasingly worse. There wasn't much I could do since I wasn't here.

Attacks had been coming from all directions because of Lore's instability, but I didn't care. My singular goal was to find Liliana.

At this rate, it wouldn't be long before Lore was dead. He didn't care about anything anymore, like me, but I wasn't convinced she was dead. I didn't see her body. I refused to believe it. Lore and the gray wolf must have seen wrong.

My mate couldn't be gone. She wasn't gone. I ground my teeth as the ball expanded in my gut, suffocating me from the inside, and my skin itched with the need to release this pent-up anger. I wanted it lashed from my skin.

I needed another fight.

Lore's phone rang again, the trill annoyingly high. Lore slammed his heavy paw on the phone.

"What?" he roared.

"Someone is crossing the pack land border," Lincoln's voice filled the room.

"Stop them." Lore grunted, the sound animalistic. Clarity sparked in his maddened eyes.

A howl echoed from outside, and I shoved open the window. Moonlight lit up my arm as I surveyed the area. That sounded like the gray wolf that oftentimes slept in the woods. My Omega's third mate.

He was usually quiet. Living out his life in the room he'd claimed as his own. *Her* old place. No one dwelled near that fucker unless they wanted to have their throat torn out. I'd learned it the hard way when I tried convincing him to help me find her, but it was too late for him. He was so deeply entrenched in his grief that his wolf wouldn't release him.

Liana

My lashes felt like they weighed a ton. I groaned and wiggled into my blankets. Why did it feel like leather under my cheek?

The material smelled like smoke and dirt. Nothing like my bed. My eyes popped open to find ripped leather seats as the car bumped, jostling my body.

Memories rushed back, and I sucked in a breath. Clay dropped me off at my door after dinner. We'd planned our next date, said our goodbyes, and then I'd locked the door behind me.

I hadn't even turned on the light before a hand pressed into my mouth.

That was why my fingers hurt. I'd dug them into my assailant's arms, scratching and tearing.

But I'd been unable to escape or shift before passing out.

I wiggled until I was on my side. Panting, I sucked breaths into needy lungs. Smoke filled them. Someone had a cigarette.

Tugging at the restraints on my wrists, I mentally cursed

whoever put them on me. And why did they have to put them behind my back?

That was discomfort I didn't need. My wrists and arms would ache from being in this position.

I craved rubbing them.

Randy.

Panic clawed my chest.

She wasn't in here with me. Please Moon Goddess, please let her be safe.

She hadn't been home, she'd left to work, so she couldn't have been home when whoever had broken in had arrived.

A cell rang, and there was a beep.

The man driving grunted. "Yes, I swear it's her, man." Excitement seeped through his voice. The voice was familiar…

"If we give those psycho fucks the bitch, they'll stop hunting us down. We can get back to our life."

He went quiet as someone on the other end responded.

I was the bitch? Why? Who was I being taken to?

Wait a minute, it was Clay's brother. The way he said 'bitch' made that clear. There was a certain emphasis he placed on the second half that gave me the same irritation as the first time he said it.

This guy was nuts. They had the wrong girl. No one was looking for me other than those people trying to use Omegas.

My lungs constricted. That's who this was.

"I have no other option. I'm tired of running. It's been two years. We're the last two, man. Everyone else in the unit is gone," he finished harshly. "My guys and I took the job because we wanted to fuck Omegas. We shouldn't have gotten involved with that fucking backwards pack. Now the Eastland Alpha is killing everyone that was there that day because he thinks this bitch is dead."

I gritted my teeth. That cleared it up. He was confused. No one had ever killed for me or cared if I were dead. Wait a second. *Eastland...*

"You have the wrong person," I informed him evenly, and he slammed on the brake, jerking the wheel to the side and causing me to smack into the side door with a grunt. That hurt. A sting radiated down my entire side and I winced when I wiggled my shoulder.

I breathed through the pain, but tears still pricked. The car careened in the other direction and I straightened with an exasperated huff.

The guy should retake some driving courses.

I swallowed hard. I'd been enjoying my date and then this? Clay...

Oh no, was he a part of this? Had he set me up? My stomach churned, and I wiggled until I was sitting.

"Where is Clay?"

"Shut up, bitch." There was that word again. I frowned and opened my mouth and then closed it. Before I could say anything, his hand reached to cup my face, and he shoved me down.

I hit the seats, and my dress rode up my body.

A flash of a shadow was all I caught through the window as I went down. There was a loud pop, and a screech scraped against concrete. He swerved again, jolting unsteadily and rubber scraped on cement as we skidded to a stop.

"Piece of shit," he screamed, and the latch clicked. He shoved open my door, gripped my hair in his fist, and dragged me out.

My foot caught as I slipped out, falling to the ground, and with my hands tied, I couldn't catch myself.

Cement scraped across my cheek and arm, burning. Red dripped onto the ground and the side I'd landed on stung. It'd been so long since I'd had this sort of pain, and it seemed especially painful.

He gripped the back of my dress and pulled me up as I blinked the dizziness from my eyes.

This was not something I missed.

A branch cracked, and I trembled. Someone was coming. My stomach was in knots and nausea crawled up my throat. I followed the rustling, and the world spun, making me lose my balance until I was leaning on the asshole holding me.

Lore strode through the fog, and his eyes went directly to me, his wolfish face angled in my direction. He was in his wolfman form and his teeth were on display in a sneer. Air exploded from my lungs and it hurt to breathe as pressure mounted in my chest. I had the oddest need to cry and run to him. He was so tense that he seemed to be made of ice.

My muscles twitched to crawl to him, but I gritted my teeth and averted my eyes, digging my nails into my palm so hard that they became slick with blood. I rolled my shoulders. The binds weren't helping my discomfort.

This was the last place I wanted to be. Clay's brother had the wrong girl. Lore wasn't looking for me.

"I brought her, Alpha." Clay's brother simpered, fear making his voice tremble. "In exchange for you to leave me in peace."

My tongue felt heavy, and I swallowed with effort. This wasn't making any sense. Why would he search for me? He didn't want me. "No harm, no foul, right?"

Lore's head tipped back, and his fangs flashed with his laugh. Coming from his muzzle, it sounded rough and broken. Scary.

"No harm?" He snarled.

A wide set of shoulders accompanied the next man that emerged behind Lore, and a shiver crested up my spine. Seeing them for the first time in years sucked the breath out of me. It was an unimaginable pain that swept through me.

I cringed closer to the asshole guy with the beard.

Declan growled, lowering his head as his eyes reflected from the headlights. He stepped forward, eyes trained directly on me. I could hear my pulse in my ears. No. I didn't want him close. They seemed so angry.

I scrambled back, but Declan's growl froze my frantic move, and I trembled. Was I in trouble for running away? I was supposed to petition the Alpha before leaving, but after their rejection, I hadn't been about to wait. Were they going to hurt me because I broke pack law? I sucked in a lungful of air and his scent crept up my nose and my shoulders started to relax. The familiar calm settled my heart. It was deceptive. He would just hurt me.

My wolf paced and scratched to escape, but I gritted my teeth to remain controlled. I refused to let her out, but the closer he got, the dizzier I became, and the hold on her was more tumultuous.

I gasped at the sudden lurch in my body as I struggled to keep my instincts to rub up to him at bay. Falling to my knees, I looked up, panting.

From the prick on my knees, they were going to be as shredded as my leg. Lore approached as I huffed from the exertion not to shift. He was narrowed in on the smug man that had manhandled me. Lore's claw grazed my cheek. His gaze sharpened from anger. When his furred hand lifted, blood stained it. His pupils undulated, and he brought it to his mouth and licked it clean.

Swallowing hard, I pressed my thighs together.

In the same movement, he turned toward the kidnapper at my side.

My mouth dropped when Lore reached out and gripped his neck. Fear glinted in the man's eyes and then Lore started squeezing, digging his nails into the soft flesh.

Clay's brother clutched Lore's wrists and softened his posture submissively. "I swear, I'll stay away. I just want to live a normal—"

I jerked when blood oozed. He made a gurgling noise.

My chest pumped, and I looked away with a wince. It was hard to breathe.

That wasn't like the Lore I'd grown up watching. He always allowed people to speak their part. He was always fair and never emotional... but he hadn't even let the man finish his sentence.

The body thumped on the ground and I was able to see the punctures of Lore's claws.

My stomach lurched and I curved forward, breathing in hollow breaths.

"You smell wrong," Lore said gutturally.

I blinked at him from my spot on the ground. He'd murdered someone so easily and by the excitement in his eyes, he'd enjoyed it.

I licked my lips, and opened my mouth but then closed it. I didn't need to explain anything to anyone.

The droplets worked wonders. Randy deserved a medal.

Lore tilted his head as he looked down at me with piercing eyes, and I shivered.

"Lily." The way Declan rasped the name... it was so agonized that it was a slam against my heart. Declan reached for me and I sucked in a breath, scrambling back. He froze, clenching his hands, and instead crouched, meeting eyes at my level.

There was a scrape and a rustle of the brush. The whine behind me lifted the hair on my neck.

"Let's go inside to get you warm, Liliana," Lore said.

I shook my head frantically.

"I'll be on my way. I have to get back home. Don't worry about me, I'll take the, uh, guy's car." I was most definitely babbling, but I didn't know what to do, so playing it off seemed like my best bet. I didn't like the look in their eyes. It felt like walls were closing in on me.

Declan stepped forward, and I scrambled back. My back pressed into a stiff warm body and a *wet* nose prodded my neck.

I screamed and jerked away, but only found myself close to Declan again.

Craning my neck, I found a gray wolf in my face. He loomed over me. Beneath the earthy scent was a familiar one that tightened my throat, and I squeezed my eyes tightly. It brought to mind cabins and hope.

"Knox."

My eyes popped open, and I was already shaking my head.

Even as I stared at him, there was a wildness to his eyes, a lack of humanity. Nothing of the irritated, angry man that had helped me when I most needed to escape. He whimpered again and his wet tongue lashed across my cheek, licking up the blood with frantic swipes. I sputtered and scooted as best I could, scraping my legs as I moved away. This damn rope...

Why were they so touchy?

They were wreaking havoc on my mind. I didn't sense any anger directed at me, and the way they behaved... as if they had a right to...

I needed to get out of here.

My shoulders curved inward as I wiggled the tight bindings at my wrists and turned away from the large dark gray wolf.

Knox took that as permission to rub against me as he whined.

Declan inched closer.

"Please. Leave me alone." I just wanted to go home. I bit back a whimper.

Declan's expression tightened, but his hand flashed out and the tension at my wrists tightened before releasing.

Bringing my hands to my lap, I rubbed one of my wrists. Declan licked his lips as he looked down at me, while Knox continued rubbing up on me. His fur tickled my naked arms. My poor outfit was going to have a dirt patch on the butt area. And my shoes were all scraped up. I lifted my trembling hand to the strap of my dress, righting it.

Everything was too much.

My heart fluttered painfully. My instincts writhed under the surface of my skin, fighting for purchase.

Declan's hand stretched toward my face. A wet tongue lashed across my sore wrist. No, no. They couldn't do this. I didn't want them and they were acting like they'd never rejected me or betrayed me.

My wolf pushed to the surface.

Why was I fighting it?

I shifted, and my skin stretched, turning my groan into a howl. I showed my teeth to Declan and shoved past him. A shiver worked through my body, and my wolf snapped at him when his fingertips grazed my flank.

She was angry at them. So, so, angry.

The emotions I hadn't worked through ravaged my body. Pain, betrayal, excitement, happiness, hope. The mix of feelings was a combination of both of us and they battled with each other, swirling and twining until I couldn't set them apart. All I wanted was to be near them, to rub my face against theirs, to be held. My breath hissed from between my teeth.

They had no right to those positive emotions. The relief.

Taking off at a breakneck speed. I panted as the thrill of being chased excited my wolf.

Breaths sawed from my lungs. The hair stood on the back of my neck and the encroaching thumping of paws made me put more strength into my hind legs.

Inhaling, I recognized Knox's woodsy scent, and I fought with my instinct to roll onto my back. The need pulsing through me worsened when Declan and Lore surrounded me.

Holding on to the need to escape, I pushed myself harder. But no matter how hard I ran, they followed.

No, they corralled me.

Every time I took a sharp turn north, one of them would cut me off in the other direction.

They were making sure that I wasn't going anywhere.

Savage rage swept through my gut, and I charged after the dark color of Declan's wolf, launching my body. Sinking my teeth into his shoulder, he grunted and froze under my fangs as I shook. Blood exploded into my mouth and I tore at his shoulder.

I hated him. Declan had a mate, and he'd chosen her in front of me. He hadn't protected me when I'd truly needed it. My jaw clamped down harder.

Jerking my head from side to side, fur splayed everywhere as he stumbled to the side, still not fighting me back.

No! He needed to show me what a jerk he was.

A body pressed into my side and Lore growled deep, shaking my wolf. I fought her urge to whine and lift my tail in the air for him like my wolf wanted.

I hated *them*. All of Lore's lovers flaunted in front of me and the abuse I suffered right under his nose. The press of Lore's teeth into my throat was firm. My muzzle curled back as I growled.

Knox snarled, pacing by my head, and dipped his head as his ears flicked back. Behaving as if he hadn't given me away in exchange for information.

While Lore was distracted by Knox, I dragged my nails on the underbelly of Lore's beast, pinning me. He grunted, and I was able to wiggle to the side and take off like a bullet. If they refused to fight me. I would run until I couldn't anymore.

A body barreled into my side, and I went flying. The tree rushed to my snout, but before I hit the bark, Knox's wolf appeared and I slammed into him, so he took the brunt of the pain.

I flopped onto the ground, panting. Declan's wolf suddenly loomed over me. My hind paws kicked up as he maneuvered me to my back and settled his weight over me. The fact that he was trying to be gentle didn't help his cause.

I'd take advantage of that.

Knox loped over, growling, and opened his maw around my neck, grazing his teeth on my throat. I froze. Knox was all wolf, right now. And the way wolves dealt with things was through force, and I didn't want to get hurt. I automatically went limp as Declan licked the fur at my chest. The hair on my back lifted and my heart picked up the pace, pounding against my ribcage like a trapped bird.

Knox stiffened, his teeth prodding at my throat as an aggressive and warning growl vibrated against me as Declan neared my neck.

If they fought, it would provide the chance to escape, but Lore, in human form, wrapped his hand around my muzzle and the hope evaporated.

Knox's teeth tightened around me, and I whimpered. I didn't fear for my life, but I worried I'd become the casualty. Knox's wolf didn't snap or attack Lore or Declan, but he showed his teeth, making his displeasure clear.

"She needs to rest," Lore snapped, but his voice sounded wrong, like his mouth was stuffed with cotton. Declan inched off me, dragging his wet nose across my ear as he snuffled. "I'm hanging on by a fucking thread. We all are."

Knox snarled and Declan whirled and clicked his teeth at him.

My sight blurred with how much I shook, and Lore's palm flattened into my fur.

"It's okay Little One, I'll take care of you," he cooed in that odd growl. I was sure it was meant to be comforting, but dear Moon Goddess it sounded frightening.

Claws raked at my insides, prodding for release, but I pushed down on my wolf's instincts. There was no way I could let her take over. Sure, she ached to rake her claws into them and bury her teeth into their necks, but eventually, they'd wear her down in whatever way, and then my freaking dumbass wolf would roll over and offer herself.

No way would that happen. Not after every rejection.

I scratched Lore's chest, burrowing my nails deep into his skin as my sides heaved raggedly and my ears rang.

Lore shook his head, and a growl slipped free. "Stop."

I ignored the order. I shook my head to release his grip, but he didn't budge, so I forced my wolf form back, and my cracking bones settled back into my human body. Without being able to go outside much, I didn't get to shift, which meant the forceful stretch of my limbs and skin hurt so badly. I cried out and tears leaked out of my eyes.

Lore adjusted his grip on me, cradling my shifting form to his rumbling chest.

The way he held me as a wolf was dramatically off in my human body so it didn't take much to shove away and fall on my side. A dull pain radiated out from my rib as I scrambled to get away. His fingers dug into my calf, but I kicked back, hitting something soft.

Not losing any time, I buried my fingers in the dirt and dragged myself away in a quick move.

"Liliana." His roar turned into a howl and a collection of angry yips. I didn't waste any time looking back.

Declan

LORE'S BODY STRETCHED AND POPPED, ELONGATING back into the wolfman form. When he'd grabbed Lily in his human form, I'd been stunned since it was the first time he'd managed not to be more beast than man. His jaw broadened with his face morphing into some disjointed wolf features. Fangs exploded from his gums and his entire body bulked three times its size, widening from all sides.

His fingers sprouted sharp and dangerous seven-inch claws the same color as his wolf's.

I rolled my aching shoulder where the punctures leaked blood. She'd gotten me good, but they weren't as bad as they looked. Regardless, I would have taken worse from her. She was back, and she was *alive*. I'd missed her. Everything about her—I'd pined for my lovely mate. Her scent, her shy glances. And the little smile she used to give me in passing. My heart clamored within my body, the thumps deafening. I was alive again. *She* was my life.

I couldn't help but seek out my Omega as she attempted to escape. I snarled at her desperation to leave me. The throb in my chest radiated through my stomach, making my ears flick. She would never escape. I wouldn't let her. Grass crunched under quick steps.

Liliana sprinted at breakneck speed, running so desperately that she smashed into a low-hanging branch that there would have been no way for her to see with her human eyes. Her head ricochet off, and my stomach dropped just as hard as she fell to the ground. My paws flexed into the leaves under me.

By the sound of the snarls, Lore was pissed, too.

Shit.

Lore was all instinct as he burst forward. He gripped Lily's limp foot and dragged her toward him. His massive form made her seem inconsequential next to him. Lore gripped her thighs with his claws, grazing her skin as he leaned over and snuffled her neck.

His hard cock jutted toward her, and I connected the dots.

He's snapped—completely. He was all instinct, and the beast wanted to claim his mate.

Jerking out of my trance, I tore in his direction. She wouldn't like it if Lore fucked her while she was unconscious.

The thud of running echoed mine, and Knox and I slammed into Lore's massive form. It was a good thing Knox had the same instinct as me or else I wouldn't have been able to take Lore down while he was in this form.

I raked my claws down Lore's side and blood quickly matted the blond fur. Lore tossed his head back and roared, swiping at Knox and me. I managed to avoid his claws and his head lowered, lip pulling up. Knox dashed to the side, chomped on his overgrown thigh, and backed off, taunting him.

He was trying to get his attention away from Lily, but he wouldn't hold him off for long with Lore like that.

My nose tipped up, and I inhaled. Lincoln was near.

I quickly shifted.

"Lincoln, bring the tranquilizer and inject Lore," I shouted.

Wolves bayed, and four forms sped out of the foliage and rounded Lore, joining Knox. Lore tossed his head back, roaring. He crouched, lunging at Alex, one of the wolves, but he managed to scramble back with only a slice through his hide.

He was going to kill one of them if Lincoln didn't hurry. Alex let out a series of yips and kicked up dirt as he sped away.

I turned on my heel, making my way to my unconscious mate as Lincoln cocked a gun. Two years ago, he'd discovered we'd found our mate and that we'd spiraled into madness. Each dealing with the loss in a different way. Lore was fixated on his single-minded vendetta, so I knew Lincoln had the tranquilizer ready. I was the one who advised him to have it ready since I was gone most of the time, and Lore's moods were erratic. It made him feel better too, since every pack member feared his monstrous form.

Sliding my arms under Liliana, I hoisted her up. It was bliss having her against me, and I couldn't help but squeeze her tightly. Her arm fell to the side, swaying as I rushed her to the manor. Once I'd climbed the stairs, I went directly to Lore's room, the only room in the house that was neat. Mine, a level down, would have worked, but the bed wouldn't have fit both of us. Lore hated anyone in his room, but I was sure this was the exception. I shoved the door open and gently lay her on the mattress.

My palm pressed to her wound, and I felt around. She'd have a bruise and a slight goose egg, but she was well. Thank the Moon Goddess. The ball in my gut faded. She would be okay. I fetched a damp towel and cleaned the blood and dirt off her face. Then rubbed the drying blood off my shoulders. I rubbed my thumb over her little teeth marks. They'd be healed soon. I frowned, not liking that. I wanted to be marked by her in any way possible.

I settled next to her, hugging her tightly to me. Exhaling shakily, I blink the tears from my sight. I missed her so much. The knot in my throat continued expanding, and I inhaled deeply. The soft, subtle peaches made a shiver crest through my body.

The door slammed open, and I tensed, pulling her to me tighter.

Lincoln, Alex, Johnnie, and Veritas dragged Lore into the room with sweat beading on their foreheads and strain on their expression. The bed creaked and slanted under Lore's weight. Lily's limp body started rolling in his direction, so I gripped her tighter.

Their scents invaded the space. A growl ripped free from my throat and I clutched Lily closer to my body, huddling her like she was a piece of meat. They simultaneously released their breath and retreated, baring their necks as they backed up.

She was mine.

The door clicked shut. Knox was probably laying somewhere knocked out, since they wouldn't have chanced getting near him. They were all scared of him.

Lore groaned in his sleep, the guttural noise leaving his muzzle was threatening. His breathing became erratic, panting. The bed creaked as he tossed his heavy fur-covered arm near Liana.

A claw sliced into my arm as he fitted his grip against her and stilled.

Even in unconsciousness, he sought her out. I snarled, and

shoved his arm off. I needed her to myself tonight. He was lucky I wasn't tossing his big ass body from the bed.

I fixed my eyes on her slightly parted lips, and I kissed her cheek.

Warmth bloomed in my chest as I wrapped my hand behind her neck. My thumb caressed her soft lips, and a shiver crested over my skin and peace settled my ravaged soul.

I knew she was alive.

Liana

A RIGID DICK PRODDED MY BACK, AND I GROANED, wiggling my ass into it. It twitched at my movement.

Had I brought Clay home?... I tensed. No, I hadn't. I sucked in a breath.

Where was I?

A crisp scent that only ever came from the pack I grew up in, filled my nostrils and nostalgia squeezed my heart. My eyes popped open, but I remained still. A big wolfman sprawled at my side, his head turned toward me. The faint lighting coming from the window fell over the fur tickling my arm.

Each breath became shorter and shallower as I stifled a groan.

I scooted and the arm around my waist tightened and the leg thrown over mine weighed me down.

The cocoon made me feel protected.

The fur-less arm stretched over my stomach, and I bit my lip to stop the moan.

Their pheromones were corrupting me. My pussy clenched

with need while my heart fluttered. *My mates. I missed their scent—No! Snap out of it.*

Heat flushed up my flesh, burning my skin.

It didn't help that I was naked.

Puffing out my cheeks, I breathed shallowly.

This... this was dangerous. I needed to get out of here.

Declan snored as he clasped me close to him, and I wanted to smack him away. I wiggled, and the snoring cut off at my ear. I'd woken him up. He was about to speak, but I kicked out to free my pinned legs and wiggled my toes to relieve the sensation of blood rushing back to them as I scooted down the bed.

Miraculously, Lore didn't move an inch.

Declan's fingers wrapped around my upper arm and I slashed out a hand and narrowed my eyes warningly. Wrapping my arms around my breasts to cover them, I popped off the bed.

I gripped the black shirt on the chaise beside the bed, knocking over the lamp on the nightstand.

Tensing, I scrambled to pull on the shirt that fell below my knees. Lore's familiar, heart-wrenching smell filled my nostrils, and I breathed shallowly, biting back the whimper of pleasure. No, I couldn't enjoy the smell clinging onto the material and permeating the rest of the bedroom. The bed took up the entirety of this wall. I had to walk to the door fifteen feet diagonal to where I stood. Where was I?

The dark shades decorating the room were unlike any I'd seen, and I'd seen most every room in the manor after Clara ordered me to clean every single one. Even the ones with the single wolves that lived on the second floor. The only room I wasn't allowed in was Lore's main bedroom, the one that wasn't his fuck pad. That conclusion mixed with the scent of everything could only mean we were in *his* bedroom.

But that was impossible. He hated when people were in his space and he never allowed anyone in. The bed creaked as if someone was lifting off it, but I ignored it. I didn't want to look at Declan.

My feet padded over the thin carpet covering the wooden floor, and I paused near the door where my jimmies were haphazardly tossed in the corner, dirt-stained and crusty. I flattened my lips tightly. *Shit.* My poor babies had cost me too much for this to have been their fate.

"Lily," Declan said, his low voice rough and grainy. I quickened my stride. I needed to get out of here.

Shoving out of the room in a rush, I stumbled to a stop when I recognized the familiar top level. I sneered at Lore's sex room near the stairs, jealousy rousing in my chest. My wolf writhed. The hair rose on my arms as memories of all the beauties he'd taken in that room filled my brain.

Nausea churned my stomach while my wolf snarled, making a growl slip from my mouth. I snapped my lips shut and stumbled back a few steps until my back pressed into the wall and I slid down.

What was I doing?

I had no way to get home without help, and I doubted anyone in the pack would help me.

Randy must be worried sick, so I needed to find a way to contact her. I wiggled my bottom on the hard surface of the floor. It was pretty hot in here. Fanning my face, I frowned. The air conditioner was on. Why was it so hot? Not only that, but Lore kept the place much... nicer than what it was right now.

The door creaked, and I didn't look up until jean-clad legs were standing before me. An inch-long beard covered Declan's face, and he pushed back his messy, dark hair.

I turned my head away from him and scrambled to my feet when he reached for me. I slapped his hand away. There was nothing I wanted to do with him. He could stay away. "Don't touch me." He sucked in a sharp breath between his teeth, the sound hiss-like.

Declan dropped to his knees and bared his throat. My lips parted on a gasp, shoulders tensing as I fixed my gaze on the throbbing vein at the side of his neck. The top of his head hovered at breast level since he was so tall.

I hugged my suddenly clenching stomach. My wolf was going crazy, and she wanted out. Declan fixed his eyes on my lips, not looking anywhere else.

I rubbed my sweaty palms against my thigh, furrowing my brows.

I was already shaking my head. In my entire time here, I'd never seen Declan defer to someone, *never*.

Even when he spoke to Lore, he was never submissive. The knot in my throat thickened and my back flattened against the wall.

His hand clasped my leg, encompassing my upper thigh with his palm. I licked my lips and tried tugging out of his hold reflexively, but he didn't budge.

It never failed—in the history of womanly history—that when a woman decided to move on, for the men that destroyed her to come back like a tornado. The collar of the shirt I tugged on wasn't tight, but it felt suffocating.

My lip trembled, and I bit back frustrated tears. I ached to fall into his arms.

"Stop," I rasped. "Get up."

"Lily…"

I sucked in a breath and I couldn't hold back the tears

anymore. Angling my head, I fixed my gaze over his shoulders. His fingers gingerly touched the droplets sliding down my face, and his breathing became ragged.

His palm cupped my cheek, and he lifted to his feet as I squeezed my eyelids tightly. I needed the warmth, biologically speaking. My mind didn't necessarily want it, but my encroaching heat made me crave it. It was the same as every other heat, which was why I had tons of blankets I burrowed under during this time. Declan cupped the back of my head and pressed my wet face against his chest.

Relief weakened my shoulders, and I slumped against him.

This had nothing on blankets, though.

I was so invested in sniffing the hell out of him when another body pressed into my side. Declan let out a rumble but quickly settled. The delicious scents of citrus and sex filled my nose and my toes curled. I pushed my ass back into the hard cock resting against my spine while simultaneously pulling Declan closer to my front. I needed them to press me more tightly between them.

Lore's furred body tickled my arms, but I loved how it felt against my skin. I loved how *they* felt. I'd missed them so much.

I whimpered. Their pheromones were spurring on my heat. They smelled so good I wanted to drown myself in them. I was reaching the point where there could be a pile of jimmies burning to a crisp, and I wouldn't bat an eye. The horror.

Lore groaned, the sound a cross between a growl and a moan.

"Little One," he started and trailed off. His words sounded broken up and rough with him in the wolfman form.

"This means nothing. I-I'm going into heat."

Their hands simultaneously clasped me tighter. And they

were going into a rut as soon as I was full on in heat-mode. Luckily, I knew what was about to happen, but they didn't know how it felt to fall into a rut.

Declan's head dipped and buried into my neck, and he moaned against my throat.

They were about to be a heck of a lot more touchy.

LIANA

"I NEED MY NEST," I MURMURED TIGHTLY AS I trembled between them. The heat on my neck was a dead giveaway. Soon, my body would become hypersensitive. Every graze and touch would make me rub up against things and it didn't matter what kind of things.

I'd learned that the hard way.

Before my and Randy's heats synced, I'd rubbed myself over a human delivery man. According to Randy, the poor guy had cum on his jeans from my rabid rubbing all over him.

She managed to pull me off him with some silly excuse involving a crisis and alcohol.

My face still warmed at the recollection.

What sucked worse was when my reason came back to the forefront. I'd been mortified. I'd hidden under my blankets for a week.

Then there was that time I wrapped my legs around the guy a year younger than me and pinned him as I dry humped his thigh at the entrance of my apartment. The encounter was seared inside my eyelids. At that moment, a part of me knew what was happening, but I had no control over my body. I just did what I wanted, and he rubbed against me just as hard, which didn't help.

Like I said, instinct.

I likened it to when I was a wolf. She took over, and I took the backseat, often blending into a subconsciousness. Yet, I was an observer as she took the reins in my brain.

It was exactly like that.

When the human's cum scented the air, I'd started dragging him to my nest to fuck him and that's when Randy intervened. She'd known I was too hurt to embark on anything intimate. It had been a whole conversation a week before when I told her about my deadbeat mates.

The good thing was I had a handle on dealing with the blinding need, but it sucked that it was hitting me *here*.

At least when I was at home, in the comfort of my bed. Where I had everything I needed to feel comfortable. The blankets... I shivered with pleasure.

I'd be unable to control myself. I would shamelessly throw myself at them like a starved madwoman.

It always started with an incessant warmth that would prod me into preparing my nest—the current stage I was in. Yet, this one felt different, more enhanced and there wasn't a doubt in my mind it was because of their proximity.

"I need a room," I spat out rushed, the words desperate.

Lore wrapped his claw-tipped furred hand around my arm and pulled me. I stumbled after him, shaking my head to help clear my mind. A door creaked and he forced me into the room.

"Yours," he half-growled in a gruff tone. "Do what you want with it."

I exhaled, and a growl slipped free. The fuck pad. I

narrowed my eyes and slit them toward him, but he wasn't looking at me.

He wanted me to nest in here. The lack of consideration ravaged my heart. It shouldn't have surprised me.

"What's wrong?" Declan murmured near my ear.

I swallowed hard and shook my head.

"What is it?" Lore rumbled.

I took a step back. "Nothing," I muttered belligerently and surveyed the area to see what I needed to tackle.

Declan scrubbed his face and stretched his neck from side to side. We were all on edge. My gaze trailed down to his naked *warm* chest, caressing the indent of hard pecks and muscles. I licked my lips and yanked my eyes away from him.

Dragging my nails against my arms to relieve some of the tingles, I paced the bedroom. It was pretty much the same as before except for the sheen of dust on every surface.

I needed it clean in here. A frown tugged at my lips. It wasn't like I hadn't cleaned this place before. I couldn't help the bitter curl of my lip.

"Can you get me cleaning supplies?"

I side-eyed Declan who hesitated before turning on his heels and disappearing. I paced around the bed. Hating the sight of it, but stopped and gripped the sheets, jerking them off angrily.

"Get rid of these," I muttered at Lore, tossing them in his face. I sucked in a breath and looked away from him. I hadn't meant to be so snappy, but I couldn't help it during my heats. Every emotion heightened and my attitude tended to simmer.

The sheets dropped to his feet, and my eyes followed them, catching on his huge cock. My face warmed and my chest rose and fell sharply.

I whined and forced myself back to the pillows.

Last time I was in here I'd sniffed them just to catch a whiff of Lore, but I didn't bother this time. Cloth scraped the floor as Lore dragged the sheets to the entrance of the room and tossed them the rest of the way out.

Steps pounded up the stairs and Declan entered, dropping a bucket.

I reached to grab it, but he caught my wrist.

"I'll clean," he said gruffly and tugged me until I smacked into his chest and kissed my forehead. I stilled, stunned. Butterfly wings fluttered in my stomach, and my face heated. I squeezed my thighs together as my breathing elevated.

Lore leaned against the wall, his expression smooth, yet darkness slithered through his eyes.

I worked to swallow as I shivered.

He still intimidated me, but that expression was never directed at me. I kept hold of his eyes, frowning.

A howl rang outside and my head swung toward the window at the stroke of agony that squeezed my stomach.

I tugged free of Declan's hold as a gray wolf padded into the room. He growled around whatever he had in his mouth and stopped directly at my feet, dropping the *thing* on the ground.

I gawked at the carcass piece of what I was pretty sure was part of a deer. My stomach roiled, and I swallowed hard as Knox pressed into my side, rounding me as he sniffed me.

He stuck his nose in my crotch, and I smacked him away.

"What are you doing, Knox?" I knew without a doubt it was him, but there lacked a human aspect to his eyes.

Knox's wolf's side nipped my thigh and rounded me again before stopping and lifting his hind leg.

"No!" I shouted as the spray hit my leg in slow motion. I

froze as the bottom of the shirt I'd tossed on plastered to me and piss trickled down my legs.

He dropped the paw and clicked his teeth at Declan, showing his fangs.

I tipped my head back and groaned.

"Turn back," I snapped, gritting my teeth.

"He's been like that since you disappeared." My eyes rounded at Declan's words. I blinked quickly. That didn't make sense. Retreating into our wolves posed a danger, since we could stay like that forever, becoming wolves in truth. "When he thought you died... this happened."

My hands trembled, and I fisted them. No, I couldn't soften toward him.

"Go shower. Lore and I will finish in here."

I nodded distractedly. "I need more blankets, clean blankets, Declan." I licked my lips as I looked at the bare mattress. I scratched at the itchiness of my arms and a whimper escaped. I should be doing that. It was the only way to get rid of my antsiness, but...

I sighed and shook my head at the wet material sticking to my leg. It was just as uncomfortable and I needed to be able to slip into my nest completely clean, so I exited the room to rush to the bathroom. There was one in here, but I didn't want to use it. Plus, there was a little dent in there that I knew well was from one of Lore's sexcapades.

I shivered and wrinkled my nose, sucking down the nausea that encroached. Knox's wolf followed me, nudging so close that I tripped multiple times. I shoved at him to give me space, but the animal had no concept of it.

Moving down the hall, I went directly to the room I'd woken up in. Lore's room.

Turning the spout of the bathroom with onyx fixtures, I ran my hand under it, waiting for it to turn warm. A wet nose grazed my leg, and I glared down at Knox.

The spray fell over my face and I hummed at the heat, letting it wash over my entire body. When the clothing was plastered to my body, I peeled them off my skin and tossed it to the corner.

The steam made the mint of the shampoo fill the space and my shoulders relaxed as my clit throbbed. My pussy was swollen and hollow. I needed to be filled. I *hungered* for it. The jets of water hit my nipples and I moaned, tilting my head back. I bit my lip and my fingers slid over my breasts and down to the apex of my thighs. I dipped my fingers into my slit with a breathy exhale.

Knox whimpered, clawing at the tiles as his head shook back and forth.

My finger pressed on my clit and I cried out. I slammed my palm against the shower as I tugged at the glass trapping me and Knox in the shower. I needed to get to Lore or Declan.

I would take from them, but I wouldn't accept their mating bite.

Knox

The sweet scent of peaches reached into the recess of my soul. I wanted more. I needed it.

It was heaven, and I wanted it back. *Her back.*

My wolf snarled. Angry at me as I was at myself for putting her in danger, but instead of drowning in the guilt as I had been, I followed the peach scent, pushing back the instinct to hide. It was the first time I'd scented it and I pined to roll in it.

I opened my eyes and water dripped into them, blinding me.

Straightening from my hunch, I froze, eyes devouring what was in front of me, not believing it.

"Baby?" I rasped, staggering back. "Y-you're not dead."

My cock hardened to a painful extent at the sweet peaches filling my nose, and my head tilted back as I groaned.

I didn't know how or why she was here, but I needed to claim her. Lunging forward, I grasped her arms and tugged her up as I bent to kiss her.

My mouth devoured hers. I kissed her so roughly my teeth sliced her lip. The metal taste coated my tongue, and I sucked on the little wound. *Liana was alive*. The thought rounded my head over and over. The tip of my cock nudged the soft swell of her belly and I groaned.

Her tongue swiped across my lower lip as she pushed against my dick, wrapping her hand around the length to push me against her.

I gripped her silky ass cheeks and hoisted her. She wrapped her thighs around my sides, pressing her heel into my spine.

Thank the Moon Goddess for this gift. My baby wasn't angry with me. She wanted me and I would show her how sorry I was for playing with her life by worshiping her. A purr started up in my chest, vibrating against her.

Liliana sucked in a deep breath and frantically gripped me, moving to spear herself on me. I moved just as feverishly, thrusting up until I was buried to the hilt.

Her pussy was so wet it drenched my cock. I wanted to feel her warmth dripping off me and instead it washed down the drain. I couldn't wait to cover my face with her juices. My stomach tightened, body twitching as a painful sensation stretched my flesh. Her channel gripped me hard and pinpricks tingled over my flesh. I snarled and swiped to turn off the shower. A growl erupted from my throat and my head fell back as my limbs burned and elongated. What the fuck was happening? My groan turned into a snarl and Liliana sliced her little nails into my arms, leaving behind ribbons of blood. I groaned, cock squeezing.

It was a wonder that I was still conscious with the luscious feel of her. I never wanted to move and if I died here, my life would be complete.

My gums burned, and I howled as my wolf rushed forward and collided with my human side. Fur grew from every inch of my body at an alarming rate until I was covered. The shower pressed into my sides, restricting my movements. It burned in the best way imaginable.

My vision blurred, and I shook my head as I helplessly rammed into her, unable to help the need for her slick all over my cock. She must be claimed. Mine.

I nudged my snout against her neck, grazing my teeth against her neck.

She tucked her chin down, denying me. The wolf didn't like that, but he couldn't force it. Neither of us could force her to accept my mating bite. Even if we did bite her, it would heal just like any other wound and because of her lack of acceptance there would be no brand.

My purr started up again. *I could get her to accept me.* I ground my teeth, and she whined in a low-pitched tone, but then she sank her human teeth into my chest. The act made my cock spasm and my balls draw up, thickening as I thrust deep until I was to the hilt. A shiver coasted up to my navel, and I flexed my claws, digging them into her skin. Her silky core gripped me hard, and I whimpered. The full sensation at the base of my cock kept expanding and I could no longer move. The resistance as I tried to retract kept me in place.

I knotted in her.

My knot spurred her release on and she clawed her fingers into my chest, tugging my fur as she whined and thrashed. I roared as my dick jerked in her pussy, filling her with my claim. A shiver crested over my body and my chest stopped moving as all the air was sucked from my lungs.

Liliana didn't stop grinding against me. She was sopping wet with her release and my knot lessened an inch, allowing me to pull back enough to feed my dick into her. I bit back a moan at the onslaught of the delectable sensation.

Her lips parted, and she looked up at me with half-lidded eyes.

"I-I need my nest," she whimpered. Her fingers curled in my fur and she gripped tightly as she lifted herself, rubbing her breasts against me. She liked the feel if the clenching of her channel was any indication. She pulled herself so high that I slipped out. My lids fluttered.

Fuck.

My cock was so fucking hard it rested straight up against my stomach. Liliana grappled to keep her grip, so I pressed my palm to her spine, making sure to take care with my claws as I steadied my precious cargo. With me holding her, she braced her legs at my waist as she wrapped her fingers around my cock and speared herself on me.

I staggered as I exited the bathroom, whimpering as I thrust up helplessly.

She was a needy little thing.

"My nest," she insisted again, rising and dropping on my cock again.

I continued my painful steps forward as she fucked me. My eyes were crossing with how fucking good she felt.

Her juices and mine combined and dripped down my dick, wetting the fur at my thighs.

I needed to lick her Omega slick up until she couldn't give me anymore. I stumbled to the side of the hallway, panting. I was close to the room she pointed to, but I didn't think I could walk anymore.

My knot at the base of my cock thickened again, readying to swell to lock me in place

I came hard as I entered the threshold of the bedroom and dropped to my knees, making sure to keep a tight hold on her.

She whined and writhed against my dick, clawing at my shoulders.

My cock was drained as fuck, but she wanted more. Each of her little movements made me twitch painfully.

Liana

I climbed off a panting Knox who knelt on the ground and crawled to where Declan stood near the edge of the mattress, his cock tenting his dark jeans.

I no longer cared about shyness. I was filled with pure want, and I demanded my due.

Setting my hands on his waist, I tugged the button free until his cock was out and I sucked him into my mouth. Declan gasped. I loved that sound. It sent another gush trickling down my thighs.

My jaw stretched with an unfamiliar pinch at the hinge. I moaned against him and met his eyes. His taste was lovely. The silky skin was slightly salty and yet the beading cum added sweetness. His lips parted and his brow furrowed as he reached down and gripped my hair in his fist, tugging at it roughly. The sharp sting made my pussy throb, and I squeezed my thighs together.

Hands wrapped around my waist. Big, clawed wolfman hands that engulfed my waist. Lore lifted me so I rested on my knees and I arched my back, presenting my ass to him. I needed him to fuck me. I could feel his growl to my core and he reached around me and brought over a bunch of soft blankets, bunching them under my knees. The position elevated me only slightly. Lore growled and his claws pricked my skin as he lifted me. I scrambled to grab hold of Declan's waist and to keep my lips around his distended cock, but there was no need to worry. One of Lore's large hands braced under my stomach as his other held my hip.

He didn't waste any more time and his thick cock slipped into my slick pussy. At first entrance he was gentle, but I shoved back, spearing myself on him.

I cried out on Declan's dick, who groaned and erupted in my mouth with harsh tugs, filling my mouth with cum. I swallowed it down, licking him until every bit of him was in me. Declan panted, staggering back a step. My hands flattened on the ground as Lore kept hold of my hips and fed himself into me at an angle.

Lore growled, and I bit my lower lip as he mindlessly rammed into me. Giving me exactly what I needed. Heat spread in my belly and sharp tingles starburst out from my clit. I shook against him, but he relentlessly kept up his pace as he fucked me deep and hard.

Pushing my ass against him, I tossed my head back, and he gripped my hair, making my arch more pronounced. Declan fell to his knees and cupped my neck, kissing me deeply as Lore fucked me. A wave of release crashed into me and I squeezed my eyes tightly as I came. Lore's knot stretched me, and he filled me with cum.

My eyelids twitched as the wave washed through me, and my body relaxed. I was blissed out, and an exquisite heat spread in my chest. Declan caught me as I fell forward and he pulled me into his lap as Lore pulled out. I whimpered, wanting more of that fullness.

Pushing to my knees and hands unsteadily, I turned to a furred Lore who stood at the end of the bed. I was most mad at him. My wolf and I hated him. I narrowed my eyes and growled, pouncing on him and forcing Lore flat. I had no doubt he'd allowed me to take him down, but I wouldn't ruminate on that because it just angered me more.

I wanted to fuck all the memories of the other she-wolves out of him. Another growl slipped free, and I sank onto his engorged cock. My head fell back as the fullness sucked the oxygen from my lungs.

"I hate you," I spat at him feverishly grinding on him. Lore's jaw tightened, sharp canine teeth flashing as his eyes narrowed. He lifted his head, his long wolf-like tongue lashing across my mouth. I gritted my teeth. I told him I hated him and he kissed me?

His palms flattened at my waist and he lifted me slightly as he prodded the tip of his engorged wolfman dick into my pussy, teasing me.

Declan's palm flattened against my back, caressing down my sweaty spine until his fingers dipped between the swell of my ass and he prodded the tight entrance. *Oh, that felt much nicer than I'd thought it would.* I helplessly curved toward him as he dragged his tip over my slick pussy near Lore's dick. There was pressure at my slit where Declan rubbed, dipping the tip in lightly. I sucked in a breath at the tightness, but before I could go cross-eyed from the tension, he pulled it free and trailed the juices to my rim. My legs shook, knees wobbling in the mattress, but I lifted my ass and wiggled, presenting to him.

There was a low, rumbling chuckle. Declan slowly dragged his tip back to my core.

"Mine," he grunted and simultaneously fed into my pussy with Lore. I keened and my sight blurred.

Moon Goddess, it was so *full*, so good.

I whimpered and writhed on their cocks. I loved how they were sharing me, and I wiggled my hips to get more of them inside me. My entrance stretched deliciously, the sharp pinch fading away as I adjusted.

"Still," Declan growled, fingers digging into my spine. I submitted to the dominance and froze. His hand trailed up to my neck. "Such a good girl."

My pussy throbbed around them at his encouraging words. I liked hearing the pleased tone. Lore lifted me as Declan thrust deep, seating himself deep inside me along with the tip of Lore's engorged werewolf cock.

A growl ripped from Declan's throat and his cock bulged and thickened inside me. I screamed.

I was being torn in two.

Declan's heavy clawed fingers landed on the mattress as he curved over me and black fur melted out of his skin. He thrust twice, in conjunction with Lore's thrusts. With this angle and with how full I was, the start of Lore's knot prodded my clit with every shallow thrust.

"Watch us fuck you," Lore ordered. I craned my neck down enough to see Lore and Declan's monstrous cocks wrapped in my pussy. I was so wet that my slick trickled down their cocks and trailed on Lore's belly.

Lore reached down and ran the back of his claw over the juices and licked them clean.

"Deeper," I growled, and they filled me until my pussy

throbbed around their building knots. The pressure was so intense that blinding orbs burst in my eyesight and it took me many beats to realize I was screeching like I was being murdered.

Declan's claws hooked into the mattress, tearing into it as effectively as he was tearing my pussy up.

Fire bloomed across my skin and I screamed as the blaze burnt me to ash and all senses stopped holding meaning. My pussy fluttered around their knots helplessly. I couldn't breathe. I was dead—I was sure of it.

I panted and rested my cheek on Lore's lower chest; the fur tickling my cheek. Knox rubbed his glistening cock as his feverish eyes remained on me. Angling to the side, I reached out, needing him in me, too. Lore's long tongue flicked out and laved my nipple. I cried out as my pussy clenched around their cocks.

Lore and Declan simultaneously moaned.

Knox gripped the back of my neck and guided his distended shaft to my lips. I wasn't going to be able to take all of that in my mouth. With my lips wrapped around the tip, I swirled my tongue and dragged it down the long shaft until I reached the thick knot swelled with his impending release.

Knox dropped to his knees, cock still twitching, and buried his nose into the side of my neck while Lore mimicked it on the other side. My heart raced.

I loved this—No! I reject. I reject.

Their teeth clamped into my flesh. The sharp sting at the sides of my neck and the one at my shoulder, burning like a blazing fire.

I shook with a silent cry as my body tightened, every muscle twitching as I came twice in a row. My channel milked Lore and

Declan into me, covering them with my juices. I exhaled sharply when reason filtered back in as my legs twitched. Declan caressed my thigh, teeth extracting from my shoulder.

Being with them was better than I'd ever imagined. All my lonely heats were worth suffering through now that I had experienced having my mates.

I dropped limply on top of Lore, and Declan's weight fell over me, so I was sandwiched between them. My heart thundered in my ears and searing need continued to throb between my legs. I'd been without them for two years. For nine heats.

"More," I whimpered.

LIANA

SEVEN DAYS. WE SPENT SEVEN DAYS HERE.

My stomach cramped, and I whimpered. How had I survived that?

Even though I knew the Moon Goddess created my body for my mates, I was mind blown that I wasn't torn to pieces.

I wiggled my feet and stifled my groan. The last thing I wanted to do was wake them up, although they hadn't budged with all my movements. My lids fluttered open, and I flexed the arm Lore pinned to his chest, hugging it like it was some sort of stuffed animal.

It didn't help that they were all in wolfman form, which meant they were incredibly heavy.

My fingers were too numb for this. And my legs weren't faring any better with Knox's head pillowed by my stomach. He particularly enjoyed licking me out. He'd spend a long time just going at it. I bit my lower lip at the sensuous memories. Got no complaints from me, but my heat was over. The reality was back, and I needed space.

Declan's palm gripped my breast, claws perilously close to the nipple he wasn't covering.

I blew the foam from the mattress off my arm. It had not boded well under their claws during all the fucking.

Good.

I never wanted to see that mattress again or this room because of the memory it brought.

My teeth clicked together.

That didn't matter to me, I wasn't with them.

So what if Lore had fucked many she-wolves on it?

My stomach soured, and I wiggled my fingers free and pushed off their limbs.

Lore was the only one that groaned and reached out, but fortunately, didn't open his eyes.

I tiptoed out of the room and headed to Lore's bedroom to shower and steal some of his clothing.

When I shuffled into the bathroom, my eyes widened at the destruction. It was in much worse shape than I remembered it being in. I turned the spout and water sputtered out easily. It still worked, good. It was mostly the walls that sustained damage and gouges in the tile. As I rinsed, I made sure to scrub gently because of the soreness and twinges all over my limbs. It especially stung when the soap ran over my neck and shoulders.

I tenderly touched the raw area that barely had a start of a scab over the wounds. The last week was so much. My heart throbbed and my nose stung. That was the longest heat I'd ever experienced. Being with them rocked my foundation, but this week was all that I would allow myself with them. Tears trickled out from the corner of my eyes at the influx of release. My body was spent and exhausted.

If I had accepted their claim, I would have woken up with

them healed, but since I hadn't, they were open, gaping wounds.

What was Declan even thinking? It would never be possible for him to claim me since he had a mate.

My stomach soured, and I swallowed hard.

He shouldn't have buried his filthy fangs in me or his cock.

I shook off the thoughts as I removed the soap and limped out of the bathroom, heading directly to the drawers. I tugged them all out until I found a long dress shirt that could fall below my knees and buttoned it up.

Of course, he had no underwear or boxers, but I knew who could help me out.

The slap of my feet echoed in the manor.

Why was it so quiet? Around this time, everyone was shooting the shit or hanging out in the living room. Something I'd never been allowed to join in on.

It had never been this eerily quiet.

I stuttered to a stop when I saw the sheets gracing every surface of the house. It looked like it hadn't been used in years and smelled like it too. I pressed the back of my hand to my nose at the ticklish sensation. The living room used to be where the Beta enforcers spent a majority of their free time, but there was no sign of them. I reached out with a fingertip and trailed it over the surface. A gray layer filmed over it.

Nose wrinkling, I shook my head, confused.

A tickle on my calf made me suck in a breath and something big rubbed on me.

Squealing, I jumped forward.

My heart was thundering in my ears.

"Knox." Even though I said the word low, it still echoed around me, too loud in the abandoned home.

He was too quiet.

My teeth clicked together, and I turned my back on him. Maybe if I ignored him, he'd go away.

I brushed the dust off my finger and sneezed when it traveled to my nose. At my dramatic sneeze, I bumped into the couch and the sheet slipped off.

My eyebrows arched.

What happened to the couch?

It was in pieces, slashes and claw marks gracing the surface.

Arguing filtered down from upstairs. Lore yelled my name. My eyes widened. It was loud if it drifted to the lowest level.

Something crashed, and I turned on my heel toward the door. I almost gave in to the desire to go through the side entrance.

I licked my lips. Never again. This place had too many negative memories attached.

Fisting my hands, I slammed the front door behind me.

Knox, being on my ass right now, and the behavior of all three of my *mates* last night, told me they had some notions about me. I scoffed.

They were nuts if they thought I was showing them my belly. I may be weak physically, but my mind was my own... unless I was in heat. But that was something else completely. It was some instinctual part of me that I couldn't control.

At least only *one* of them followed me.

I glared at Knox, but he dipped his head pressing into my side, tongue lolling out.

Gritting my teeth, I nudged him back, but it was no good since he was a beast with his ears hovering around my breast. I huffed and dragged my gaze over the quiet pack lands. I inhaled deeply and the dawn air filled my nose. There should be some sort of movement by now.

I needed to get a hold of a phone and call Randy to pick me up. No. I'd have her meet me an hour out. I couldn't put her in the path of this stupid pack. I'd call an Uber and meet her.

Janice would let me use her cell and while I was at it, I'd steal a pair of shorts or panties from her. My toes curled on the cement as I tried ignoring the feel of the loose rocks digging into my heels. I was already out of the manor. Hopefully she still lived in the unit at the edge of the woods.

I'd missed her these last two years. Wringing my hands, I quickened my pace, passing various homes as I wove through the community.

Goosebumps pebbled my arms, and I rubbed them as I puffed out my cheeks. I must get back *now*, because the scent suppressant was bound to run out of its effectiveness. There hadn't been a day that passed that I didn't take both at six in the morning everyday on the dot. What was probably saving me right now was that I'd doubled up before my date with Clay. The droplets lasted a week, each day, the affects faded, but overall held relatively strong. Even so, Randy and I took them daily. After the reaction of the men that had taken me, we hadn't been willing to risk it.

The narrowing of their eyes, the flaring of their nostrils... no thanks.

Bringing my knuckles down on the slat of the door, I waited, holding my breath.

After some muffled shuffling, the door swung wide to a lanky pre-teen. My eyes widened.

"Jamie?"

He squinted, and then his mouth dropped.

"Liana?"

My throat tightened. A familiar face was a nice thing to see when I was feeling so tense.

"What are you, eleven now?"

"Twelve." He grinned and swept forward. Knox released a rumble and snapped his teeth as he stepped between us, blocking him. Jamie gasped and stumbled away from the wolf.

I dug my knee into Knox's flank, and he showed his teeth at me.

Shaking my head, I watched as Jamie's eyes widened. "Mom."

There was a clang of dishes, and a beat later Janice was framed by the entrance. Her mouth dropped and her eyes watered.

"I thought you were dead," she whispered, trembling.

Sniffling, I stepped forward, but Knox blocked my progress, not letting me hug my only friend. Resentment swirled in my chest and I shoved him, but he didn't even budge. A growl built in my throat as I looked down at him.

His lips peeled back, and he dipped his head, ears flicking with obvious irritation. I uselessly shoved him again, but he remained in place. When I lifted my head, Janice's eyes were tearful as she eyed me, her arm corralling Jamie back as her gaze flicked to Knox.

"Be careful," she mouthed to me. Why was she worried about me?

She'd angled her body in front of Jamie's like she was protecting him from Knox.

"He won't do anything," I reassured her, but she shook her

head, blinking at me as she curved her arm around Jamie, pushing him back. He huffed, but he did as she bade and waved at me before disappearing.

"He's killed five pack members in the last two years," she said so low it was difficult for me to hear. She wearily flicked her attention to Knox and then away.

My mouth opened and closed.

"For no reason other than stepping too close to him."

He'd seemed like a jerk when I left him, but that had been his only offense, not killing needlessly.

I palmed my head. This wasn't my problem.

Anxiety prickled my skin, and I licked my lips. Burying myself in bed, beneath all of my pretty blankets sounded so perfect right now.

Janice's eyebrows lowered, and she waved me in. This time, Knox didn't stop me, but he still padded inside.

I frowned at him. He seemed less on edge, the fur at the back of his neck wasn't raised anymore. Wait a minute... my eyes widened. It was because Jamie was male.

I narrowed my eyes at him, but he was too busy prowling the living room. I hoped it wasn't that, but I wouldn't put the territorial stuff past him after he peed on me.

I sank into the brown couch beside Janice and bit back a groan. Oh, my ass hurt bad. I glared at Knox as he sat near my feet, ears pointed up as he watched everything.

Janice's nose flared, and she licked her lips. "There's something that smells really good, but it..." She shook her head, but suddenly straightened when Knox growled.

The scent suppressant was fading.

"You smell faintly like wolf," Janice said, frowning.

That was why our scent must be disguised. We smelled good to wolves, so much so that sometimes they liked to rub up on Omegas. Our scent was the only indicator that one was an Omega other than the ability to Call, which was why it was so important to hide our smell. It was a survival thing for Omegas. They were constantly killed off by jealous she-wolves, or trapped by covetous males.

Multiple mates protected their Omega, which was the tradeoff.

"I'm a wolf—"

"How is that possible? You didn't shift when you turned eighteen?" Janice's brows furrowed.

"I'm an Omega," I admitted, mouth drying with fear. I was so used to hiding it that airing it out felt weird.

Janice blinked at me. Her mouth opened and then closed before she sucked in a breath and she sniffled.

"Do you know what that means?" She gripped my hands. Knox growled, but she was completely focused on me, her eyes watering. I dug my knee into his side, and his growl cut off with a chuff. "You're hope, Liliana. Do you know what you can do?"

My eyes widened at her fervor. "You're not going to mention how they're extinct?"

"Liliana, I know you pretty well by now. You don't lie about anything." She licked her lips, a grin spreading across her mouth. "Now there could be more werewolves with you around. You can change *everything*."

I didn't want to admit in front of Knox that I wasn't going to stay so there wasn't a need to learn about calling forward dormant wolves.

"No wonder you didn't shift at eighteen. You had to tug it

out yourself and in the situation you were living in. Malnourished, beaten, unsafe," she cut off and Knox pushed to his paws, the hair on his back standing.

"Stop," I muttered at him, but he ignored me, and his fur spread along with his body as he shifted into his wolfman form. He towered over us, cock out and everything. My face heated, and I spread out my palm over his dick to block Janice from seeing it, but it was pretty pointless since it was drastically larger than both of my hands spread out together.

"Who hurt her?" he snarled, a rumble started up at his chest.

"Knox," I murmured, head dipping low. He shook his head from side to side and fur receded until he was fully human.

"No, baby." He knelt in front of me and pinched my chin, his purplish eyes flashing. "I remember how I found you. It feels just like yesterday that I lost you since I sank into my wolf, so it's clear as fuck in my head. You were bruised and malnourished, and I want you to tell me who did it."

My lips tightened, and I fixed my eyes over his shoulders.

"Clara. Declan's mate," Janice offered. I sighed and my lids slid shut. Knox's breathing elevated and a low, engine-like growl vibrated through the room. "I don't know why you're hiding who she is. She hurt you, Liliana."

Knox's nose flared, and he tugged my chin until I looked at him. "Declan has a mate?"

I swallowed hard at the intense look in his eyes, and mine shied away.

My stomach rumbled, cramping with hunger. I hooked my arm over my belly.

"Let's go get you some breakfast," Janice interjected into our staring contest. I hopped to my feet, nodding quickly.

A pissed-off Knox trailed after me. It wasn't over, but I'd held the argument off for a little while. I didn't bother asking Janice for the things I initially sought her out for. I didn't want Knox to overhear my conversation with Randy. He'd chain me up.

Liana

"Lore passed administration of Eastland Enterprises over to Lincoln. He hasn't been off pack lands for the last two years."

I frowned. "That's not like him." When I was here, he would spend days at a time away. So much so that it sometimes seemed as if he was staying away purposefully.

"Declan has been gone too much since you died. He hasn't remained longer than a day or two before he heads off. The rumor going around is he's fallen out of sorts with Alpha."

I swallowed with difficulty. What had happened while I was gone?

Other than their possessiveness, they'd been acting so normal, that I never considered how they'd spent these last years. After the way they behaved, I expected they'd been happy living their life without me in the picture since they'd acted like I was such a hindrance.

"Some also left the pack because they couldn't take how Lore changed. Everyone walks on eggshells around here now." She continued chattering at me, filling me in on everything that had happened in the last two years. There were a *lot of* changes, including that pack meals were no longer a thing. The years I slaved over making sure food was made on time flickered in my memory. If only Lore had gotten rid of them while I was in charge of them.

I winced when an especially sharp bit of broken cement stabbed my toe on the way to the manor. An arm slipped under my legs and tugged me off balance. Knox caught me as I fell backward and cradled me to him with my ear against his furry chest. He'd returned to his wolfman form as soon as we'd stepped outside. It seemed he liked it best. The chest that my ear pressed against vibrated as he released a short revving purr.

Eyes fluttering shut, I exhaled as the tension in my shoulders faded away. His purr was heaven.

"What is this?"

The voice invaded my peace, and I cringed into Knox at the memories. My chest rose sharply as my heart raced.

Clara stared at me, her mouth parted and her eyes widened. She blinked hard.

"I have to be imagining this," she snapped and moved forward. Knox was quick to growl, and she stopped in her tracks.

"Clara," I murmured, pushing the name from my throat.

"It is you," she sneered, eyes slitting. "I thought you were dead."

My lips parted and I couldn't tear my eyes away from the torn flesh on her arm. The jagged scars extended from where her arm peeked out at her bicep, and went down to her fingers to where half her hand was missing. The healed area left her with three fingers nearest to her pinky.

"W-what happened?" I rasped, not looking away from the

scars. To create scars that deeply on a wolf, the damage had to be severe.

"You're asking *me* what happened? When you have that hideous scar across your face?" she said, venom practically spitting from her mouth. I angled my head forward so my hair fell to hide my scar.

Knox's fingers flexed into my side and his chest rose sharply.

"My mate scarred me because of you," she said low and hateful, stepping forward.

Teeth clicked, and I was jostled in Knox's arms as he vibrated with rage. I hooked my arms around his neck and curled my fingers into his fur. If I released him, he'd kill her. The intention was clear in his predatory eyes.

"What are you doing on pack lands, you were banished," Janice shouted, shoving her back a step. The low revving of Knox's growl shook my entire body, and I squeezed the tuffs harder. "If you hadn't managed to hide away when Lore and Declan lost it, you'd be dead now. Why are you back?" I'd never seen Janice so fierce other than when she spoke of her son.

"I've lived the last two years fearing for my life, unable to leave my own home, but as soon as I received the message that this bitch was back, I needed to see." Her maddened eyes turned to me. Insanity glinted in them. Her attention flickered to Knox and her eyes widened as she scrambled back a step, clutching her ripped up arm.

"I'll finish what your mate began," Knox snapped, baring his teeth in some type of smile that sent chills up my spine. And it wasn't even directed at me. He jostled me, attempting to set me down, but I wasn't letting go.

She panted and moved back even more, dragging her

attention to me. Steps pounded in our direction and Declan was suddenly in front of me, blocking her from my sight.

"Clara. You were warned." The snarl sent chills down my back. His neck popped and then the rest of his body as black fur spread over his arms and bled onto the rest of him. His muzzle lifted into a snarl.

"Declan. Don't touch her." The jealous words slipped free unbidden and my face heated. That was not the point right now. I couldn't believe that slipped out of my mouth. It could have gone worse if Declan hadn't arrived and Knox managed to shake me off. "Never mind, ignore that."

Declan's furred humanoid feet stepped forward, crushing the stones under him. The black talons raked against the ground.

"My Lily," he murmured, reaching to graze my cheek with his sharp claw. "Turn away."

"I hope it hurts that he'll never be fully yours because of this." She jabbed a finger to where her mark peeked near her shoulder.

Tears sprang to my eyes, and I gritted my teeth.

"Enough!" Declan shouted and rounded so quickly he was a blur. His talons slashed out, and she screamed, the piercing sound shooting through my ears. She slammed against the ground, whimpering as she clutched her bleeding neck. Blood seeped between her fingers and she scrambled back, eyes wide and tear-filled as she looked up at him. The gashes were jagged and painful looking. Her movements turned sluggish, and within seconds she lay flat on the foliage, her chest moving shallowly. Declan strode forward, his head lowered and aggression in his every step. There was no need for him to continue slicing his claws into her.

"Declan," I shouted. His furred shoulders lifted raggedly. "Declan!"

He slowly turned his snarling muzzle in my direction. I licked my lips. There wasn't a way to deny that relief as I watched her struggle breathing. Soon she'd be dead.

"Enough," I whispered. He shook his head hard, panting.

Knox growled and dropped my legs, nudging me to the side, then smashed the side of his fist into Declan's temple who didn't bother blocking the hit. His head whipped to the side and blood spurt from his forehead where Knox's claw had sliced him.

"You allowed our mate to be mistreated while she was under your nose." Knox's words were garbled and savage. I licked my lips, stepping in front of him. I had to crane my neck from down here, so much so that it pinched. I put up my hands as a barrier.

"No more. I'm hungry," I said in a warbling tone. I didn't want bloodshed. I just wanted to leave.

Knox still didn't drag his attention from Declan, his sharp dangerous teeth on display. I stepped forward, ignoring the tremble to my hands and sank them into his belly fur. I could feel the indent of his abs. Combing my fingers through the dark gray fur, I scratched Knox's belly, and he blinked, attention fixed on me. I applied some more pressure, reaching deep into the tuffs, and he groaned, leg trembling. I gasped when it started to thump.

I pressed my lips together, holding in a laugh. Knox backed up until I wasn't touching him, and his body morphed back to normal. He scowled down at me, and I pressed my lips together in a thin line. Red crested his cheeks and I couldn't hold in the giggle that escaped. *Shoot.* I sucked in a breath. I shouldn't be laughing while Clara sputtered for life.

Knox glowered and turned on his heel, storming back to the manor and I followed on his heels. I peeked at Janice cowering in the corner and waved at her as she gaped. My gaze lifted to Declan, and he watched me with his sad brown eyes.

All humor fled. Was he upset about Clara? I hated thinking that. I hated that possibility, so I shoved the thought away. *I shouldn't care.* Now that he was in his human form, the gash at his forehead dripped down his face instead of matting fur.

They'd been too quick to fight each other.

They hadn't wanted me before, so why did they behave this way? Was it only because I was an Omega and they figured I could be useful?

I swallowed hard, nauseous. *They didn't want me before...*

My stomach soured, and I hugged my midsection as I made my way to the kitchen so I could find something to eat, and call Randy.

Lore

The time my Little One spent organizing the bedroom I gifted her, was ingrained in my brain. The memory seared into me. I couldn't move my gaze from her as she strutted around the bedroom and tossed blankets around along with orders.

It was so fucking hot that my dick hardened at the memory.

The feel of her curvy body rubbing against me the last few nights... a shiver coasted up my spine, and I groaned.

My cock tented my gray sweats, poking the stove.

Fuck.

With my free hand, I rubbed the front of my cock and tucked it into the waistband of my sweats, studying the prominent bulge. Not much of a difference.

The pan hissed, and I sighed low as I returned my attention to the stove where a mountain of sausage sizzled. I stirred the scrambled eggs, making sure I got all sides.

Now that I'd made it so there were no pack meals, usually Lincoln made my meals. Or was it Alex?

I couldn't stand the idea of that oversized kitchen, or the

fact that I'd been eating my mate's food for years without a thought. And the fact that she'd seen me with so many others... My stomach soured and I shoved the thought away. That was in the past and I would make up for it from today and on. She would never have to suffer or feel pain in any way, I would make sure of it.

My throat felt uncomfortably tight, and I tugged at the collar of my shirt.

The delicious scent of peaches filled my nose, and the tension in my shoulders loosened. I didn't think my cock could harden more.

"The heat is on too high," my Little One said in a soft voice, in that tone she tended to speak in. She hunched into herself and her eyes flicked to the side.

I ground my teeth, not liking the leeriness when she looked at me. She should be rubbing up on me, but she kept her distance, avoiding touching me. Control. My exhale hissed between my teeth, and I set the spatula down, crowding her against the counter by corralling her with my arms. I lifted my hand, cupping her cheek. A shiver coasted down my spine and I bit back a moan. My entire existence used to be the pack, and I'd always put them first, but I knew without a doubt that they would never come first again and they hadn't... for the last two years since I'd found and lost her. The words prodded at my lips, but I held them back. I needed to show her I would provide for her. I was never a werewolf of empty promises, so first I had to show her, prove it to her. The first step was closing the deed on the house I purchased for her away from here. But while she was here, I needed her to have everything she desired.

"You can decorate the bedroom however you choose," I said

gruffly, dipping my head to meet her eyes. "Go on whichever website you want and get everything you need."

This should get me some points.

She could have the entirety of the house if that's what she desired, but I gave her the room purposefully. I wanted her to know that my days fucking anyone were long behind me and she was the only one I'd allowed to breathe in my direction for the last two, almost three years since I'd last had her. That tension in my chest that had always been around? *Now* I understood what it was. Love. A concept so foreign to me, since I'd never experienced that emotion, but one that overpowered everything.

Dipping my head, I buried my nose into her neck, inhaling deeply, and growled against her when she shivered.

My cock throbbed, and I shook my head desperately when my vision blurred. My wolf wanted to claim, and I was holding on by a thread.

I would gain her trust enough for her to accept my bite.

Her stomach rumbled, and I groaned, moving back to the stove.

"I need to get some food in you."

As soon as I stepped away, she scrambled back a step, putting distance between us. I hated it. Footsteps pounded into the kitchen, one set angry and clipped while the other was slower.

Knox leaned against the counter, attention fixed on Liliana while Declan stood at the threshold of the kitchen, a tight expression on his face.

I grabbed a plate and scooped some of the browned eggs onto it and frowned at the crunch. Shaking my head, I tipped it into the trash and piled her plate with sausages. At least those were only semi-crisp.

Pulling out the bar stool, I tilted my head for my Little One to sit. She stared at me for a beat, side-eyed Knox, and stiffly made her way to the seat.

She slid in and plucked one of the sausages from the plate, nibbling the tip as her eyes bounced around the room. When she caught my gaze on her, she tipped her head forward, hiding her beautiful features.

Frowning, I fixed my eyes on her lips. "I have a gift for you."

I had to do with the best I could find around here. There was no way I'd be able to rip myself away from Liliana any time soon, but I wanted her to have something from me. It was my first step at showing her that it wouldn't be like before. That I treasured her.

I'd scavenged through the house and finally found a box of jewelry I was pretty sure belonged to the prior Alpha's mate. I scooted the blue gift bag I'd found from the closet toward her.

Her eyes brightened the most I'd ever seen them, and a smile stretched on my lips. I would move any dimension to keep that expression on her beautifully rounded face. She shyly peeked at me and reached inside, pulling out the wooden box. Her brows lowered, and she blinked quickly as she propped the lid open. Various jewels, from diamonds to rubies glinted in the light coming through the large window.

A strange look undulated across her expression.

"Why would you give this to me?" My stomach hollowed out.

"I—" I paused, not knowing what to say. I wanted to make her happy... I wanted to surprise her.

"Do you know how much this hurts?" she said choked.

Tears sprang to her eyes and my gaze dropped to her wobbling hand as she set the box on the counter. My heart rate picked up, and I licked my lips. I didn't like that look on her face. Why was she so upset? Panic tightened my body.

Clenching my fists, I squeezed so hard my entire hand went numb.

What had I done to my mate?

LIANA

"I thought you might like it. Women enjoy jewelry—"

"*You* would know what women like," I muttered bitterly, fixing my gaze on my bare toes. I wiggled them and they blurred in my sight.

Humiliation burned my face, and I got to my feet and gently pushed the chair in. Lore moved in my direction and I put my hand up to stay him.

"What do you mean, Little One?"

It was now or never. I needed to speak my piece and make my stance clear. I puffed out my cheeks, mustering up the courage. Tilting my head up, I stared directly into his face. His features blurred from my tears.

"Do you know what I went through here?" A rough half-sob, half-laugh slipped free. "I had to clean your bedroom every single time you had women over. Every. Time." Lore raked his hand through his hair then reached for me, forcing me to stumble back so the counter dug into the small of my back. "Then you have the audacity to give me the same bedroom I slaved over *and* the collection of jewelry the women you slept with left behind?"

"Liliana, I was trying to please you," Lore murmured, shaking his head. "I didn't think..."

The words were practically spilling from my mouth as fast as the tears in my eyes. My pulse sped up as they closed in on me.

"No, you didn't think. You're a self-absorbed asshole!" His shoulders jerked back as if I'd struck him. "That wasn't even the worst of it. I was forced to cook for the pack that looked down on me on top of Clara beating me daily."

"I didn't..."

I couldn't see any of their expressions with my blurred eyes.

"You thought you were such an amazing Alpha, but you never took care to make sure there was no abuse. I know I'm weak and useless in your eyes—"

Lore growled.

"Lily..." I ignored the broken way Declan rasped my name.

"You never truly looked at me, Lore. I was nothing to you, even after you found out I was your mate." My lip trembled, and I sucked in a ragged breath. "I didn't even know how to properly read and it wasn't until I left your stupid pack did I find out how easily I was cast aside and undervalued. Now that you know that I'm an Omega, you want me?" Tears wet my face and my breathing hiccupped.

Knox gripped my arm, and I yanked it away. "You're no better." He flinched at my spat out words. "You gave me away. Traded me to a disgusting abusive pack who locked me up. Do you have any idea what they planned to do with me? Do you?" My words rasped from my throat, pouring from me. Declan's lips pressed tightly together, his jaw muscles bunching as his expression darkened. "They were keeping me prisoner so they could rape me whenever they felt like it. So you have no say right now. And you." Declan's lips tightened as my voice cracked. "You rejected me and if that wasn't bad enough you have a mate you claimed. I remember the day she did this to me." My fingers trailed over the wetness of my cheek, touching the ridges of the scar.

"You're wrong, Little One—"

"I don't want to hear your excuses or your reasons, which I'm sure you will make sound incredibly convincing." I swiped at the wetness on my face. "Just because we fucked, you can't think that I'll accept you," I said in a warbling tone, stiffening my spine.

Lore was shaking his head, his head drawn back like I was speaking in tongues.

Another beat and they'd be all around me, surrounding me with their scents and warmth.

"Don't get near me," I cried, putting up my hands. "None of you."

They weren't going to listen to me.

Gritting my teeth, I swiped a kitchen knife from the set on the counter to my left.

I turned it to my neck, tapping the cool blade against my throat. Lore's lips tightened.

I winced at the sting. Shoot, that was harder than I meant.

"What are you doing? Put that down," Lore said with a growl.

"Give me my space."

"Lily," Declan said haltingly.

"You three can't be with me at all seconds of the day." Knox's teeth clicked together, and he backed up.

Declan grabbed Lore's shoulder, shoving him away from me forcefully. Grinding my teeth, I inched away, heart thundering against my ribcage.

Knox moved toward me when I made my way past him, and I tightened the blade to my neck. The sting made me hiss, and he dropped his hand. I grimaced at the trickle of blood dripping down my neck.

"Don't follow me."

My footsteps echoed to my ears as I fled the house. As soon as I was next to Lore's truck, I tossed the knife to the ground and hopped inside.

Thank the Moon Goddess that Lore tended to leave his keys in the ignition. Of course he did. There was no way anyone would mess with the Alpha. I revved the truck, and the wheels spun, kicking up gravel as I tore the truck out of there.

I didn't bother looking in the rearview mirror as I screeched around the corner to get onto the road leading off pack lands. There wasn't a doubt in my mind that they'd be right on my heels, but I just needed space, my home, and Randy.

LORE

Every breath sawed from my throat. My insides blistered as if a hot poker had been slammed through my mouth and into my gut. Her tears... the hurt marring her face...

The gnawing agony in my chest was unbearable.

I raked my fingers through my hair, gripping so tightly that strands ripped from my scalp.

"You're an idiot," Declan hissed.

My wolf mauled my insides, his agreement conveyed in the

rabid way he writhed. If I shifted, I'd tear the vehicle apart and I needed it working so we could keep on Little One's ass.

I felt flayed open. As if Lilian had slammed that knife in her hand into my stomach, dragged it up my sternum and with the wound open, grabbed my beating heart and taken it with her.

"You need to fucking think things through, Lore." Declan's voice grated across my skin, deepening the agony thrashing in my chest.

She left me. *Again.*

No, I'd pushed her to leave.

My body quaked.

"Lore," Declan snapped, his voice far away as a ringing in my ears almost deafened me. I pounded my fists into the dash and the entire thing collapsed in on itself. Plastic bits cracked off and littered the car floor.

"It fucking hurts," I roared, unable to hold back the words. The only noise was my ragged breathing. "What if she doesn't forgive me?"

Declan went eerily still and he exhaled sharply.

Liliana had turned me into a needy pup and I didn't fucking care. Pressure burned my nose and my sight blurred as a whine crawled up my throat.

"That isn't an option. Get a hold of yourself, Lore," he said quietly.

He was right, I needed to regain control. *I couldn't crumble.* I needed to show her she was mine. I could shout from every rooftop that I loved her, but my actions were what mattered. Where it really counted. It was all I could do since my previous actions were what hurt her in the first place.

I sighed shakily and refocused on the only aspect that calmed my whirling thoughts. We were tracking her position through the phone I'd left in the glove compartment of my truck.

An hour ticked by as I fidgeted, my only remaining thread of sanity connected to the little dot on Declan's cell that symbolized Liliana's location. She was less than a mile ahead of us. We were just far enough away that she wouldn't catch on to us following her.

"She won't want to see you anytime soon."

My lip lifted and I growled at Declan.

I did know that, and she deserved her space, but him saying it didn't make it any easier to swallow.

The stretch between her dot and our location lengthened into two miles. We were falling behind her too much. My heart rate accelerated.

"Fucking step on it," I gritted out between my teeth.

"I'm driving as fast as I can without blowing out the engine," Declan growled.

It still wasn't fast enough. It would never be fast enough until we caught up with her.

LIANA

THE TRUCK SCREECHED AS I PULLED INTO MY PARKING spot and turned the key. Blessed silence. The last four-hour drive was grueling, and I'd been nodding off toward the end.

My shoulders dropped, and I exhaled sharply, wishing away the painful throb in my chest. I slammed open the truck door and hopped out, smoothing the shirt over my legs.

The hair lifted on the back of my neck halfway to the entrance and I froze, looking over my shoulder. My heart rate picked up, and I licked my lips. I was on edge.

Quickening my pace, I hightailed it directly to the elevator. The button practically popped out with how many times I jammed it.

I tapped my fingers on my thigh as the elevator ascended. When it creaked to a stop for someone to hop on, I groaned. The older man did a double take at my clothing and tsked. I wiggled my bare toes. How terribly awkward. Fixing my gaze on the numbers as we continued going up, I exhaled sharply when we reached my level.

I brought my knuckles down in quick raps, and the door was jerked wide open.

"Randy," I cried, and threw my arms around her shoulders. Her arms squeezed my waist and there was a thump as she released the phone.

"Where have you been? I've been looking everywhere for you." Randy smoothed her palm on the back of my head. "You reek of male wolf."

Her voice trembled, and I straightened, shaking my head. "It's not what you think. Clay's brother took me and handed me over to Lore—one of my mates."

Randy gasped and looked over my shoulder at the shut door.

"He's not with me," I quickly added.

"How did you get away from him?"

"I'm sure it won't be long until he comes knocking. But I needed to get away. It was too much."

"Of course, it's too much," she said indignantly. "Do those mates of yours understand how much they hurt you?"

"I think they know now." I rubbed my forehead.

"You look exhausted and your smell... you need to take a dosage."

A little voice buzzed through the room and my eyes dropped to the cellphone she'd had to her ear before she dropped it.

"I filed a missing person report," she swept it up and put it to her ear. "I apologize for any inconveniences, my sister returned...," she continued making up a story about my disappearance.

My eyes watered, and I sniffled. Her arms wrapped around my shoulders as she spoke, and we squeezed each other again.

Extricating myself, I went to our bathroom, turned the spout of the shower, and shucked my shirt off.

"Liliana!" The shout sent me running out to the living room, heart pounding. "There's a naked man at the door for you."

I careened to a stop and met Knox's eyes. Storming up to the door, I slammed it in his face. I'd expected to have more time.

Randy peeked through the peephole. "Which one is this one?"

"Knox." The bitterness to my response wasn't lost on her.

"Ah, the one that gave you away so he could get information about his family's death."

The corner of my lips tilted down. When you put it that way...

I shook my head and went back to the bathroom, removing the rest of my clothes. I was scrubbing my body hard, trying to get their scent off my skin, and avoiding the deep bites, when Randy entered.

"I had to let your naked mate in. The neighbors were calling, and they were gonna call the cops."

"Randy!" I jerked the shower curtain to the side to glare at her and she made a sheepish expression. I grunted and straightened the curtain. She definitely felt bad, and if the cops were about to be involved... I sighed. We didn't draw attention to ourselves, but if cops arrived to drag Knox away, the existence of werewolves wouldn't remain hidden. "Inform him to stay away from me."

This was not a good idea. Knox wouldn't listen to her. I rubbed my face and angled it under the waterfall.

The door creaked, and there was a slide and a thump. The

steam filling the room brought Knox's scent to my nose, and I bit my lip to stop the whimper.

"Keep being angry with me. I deserve it." He paused, and I madly scrubbed at my hair. "I want to explain myself a little more and why I was desperate to get the names of my family's killer."

I speared my fingers into my strands and tugged. The sharp sting raised goosebumps on my arms.

"It doesn't matter," I rasped. Silence. I lowered onto the ground as water cascaded over me.

"My pack wasn't the biggest or the strongest, but we were close knit and kept an eye on each other. My father, the Alpha, made sure there was mutual respect, and it was peaceful. But one day another pack invaded ours and killed everyone and set our community on fire. I wanted to know who did that to the pack I wasn't able to protect as future Alpha."

The visual of a blaze filled my memory, and I sucked in a breath. It seared my brain and screams echoed through my mind. Fear lifted the hair on my arm and I scrubbed them.

"That's awful," I finally croaked.

"I know it's difficult to believe me, but I wasn't going to leave you with them."

The regret in his tone pounded against me and tears squeezed out of the corner of my eyes at his words. Surfacing some of the faint memories I'd stifled from my last pack. The flashes were brief. Blistering flesh... dead bodies. My father's torn-out stomach. My mother running. My friend...

I exhaled shakily and finished my shower, sleep pounding on my temples. My heart was a mess and the knots in my stomach were tightening with every second as I worked through the discovery that our pasts intertwined. The pack my mom and

I had run from as it was being torn apart was the same pack Knox belonged to. I'd known Knox when I was a child, but there was nothing concrete in the fluid memories weaving through my mind. Trauma had stamped them out.

I WIGGLED my hips in bed at the heavy pressure of my clit. My hand slid down and I pressed my palm onto it. A soft growl worsened the throb, and I whimpered. Fingers wrapped into my shorts and tugged my panties down along with them. I canted my hips for Knox and squeezed my eyes shut.

A wet tongue flattened on my core and he lazily licked from the knot of my ass up to my pussy. His purr loosened the tightness lining my shoulders, and I moaned, rubbing myself on his mouth.

Fisting the sheets, my lips opened with a silent cry. A flattened *human* tongue delved into my core, deep and prodding. He caressed my clit with gentle nudges, flaming the need to life until I was wiggling my hips, needing more.

"Knox," I moaned. At my voice, he growled and stilled, arms trembling. There was a silent beat and then his body rippled, fur bursting from his skin and ears popping up. He shook his head and peered up at me with his purplish eyes in his wolfman form and then buried his snout into my pussy.

Oh... *Oh.*

In this monster form, his tongue reached deep inside my core. I panted, head thrashing from side to side as he thrust his tongue inside me and pressed the flat of it to my clit. He growled, and the vibration set off my orgasm. Sparks burst behind my shut eyelids and my stomach tensed up as throbs pulsated from my sex.

His tongue was magical.

He slowed his rapid pace, and his tongue brushed the inside of my slit, dipping it into my sheath. My pussy clasped at the tongue curving up, tilting and reaching deep with the long appendage.

Knox flicked the tip of his tongue and I screamed, arching my body as he found my G-spot. He prodded roughly and the oxygen was sucked out of my lungs. A deafening wave crashed over my senses and it felt like I was floating out of my body as my pussy spasmed with his every flick. Claws dug into my ass cheeks and the sharp sting subsided under the movement of his muzzle.

My body flattened on the bed and my panting was loud, even over the ringing in my ears. That was... wow. I could barely formulate thoughts with the floating sensation falling over me.

His arms wrapped around my waist and he lay his head on the swell of my belly with a satisfied groan. My fingers curled into the fur at his head as it slowly melted away and was replaced with his untamed hair. When had Knox snuck into my room?

I didn't even have the energy to be angry that he hadn't stayed in the living room. I lulled in satisfaction, my blinks coming slower and slower.

"Was your younger sister's name Chloe?"

Knox's grip on my thighs tightened, and he lifted his head.

"Yes," he responded cautiously.

"Your pack... was my pack and that attack you mentioned happening was the day my dad was murdered. When you explained what happened, the images flooded forward. You put words to something that's always been elusive in my memory." I exhaled sharply. "They were searching for an Omega." I'd made the connection earlier and I tried shying away from it, but it was the only thing that made sense. They'd been obsessed with Omegas. I recalled the painting we'd burned and the death of the girl they had captured. I couldn't imagine what would have happened if they had caught me. "That's why everyone died, because they were searching for me. It was because of me." Verbalizing it squeezed my chest viscerally.

"Baby. It's not your fault." The staunch denial made my nose sting.

My throat was uncomfortably tight, and tears spilled from the corner of my eyes. Yes, it was my fault for existing.

"You don't hate me for causing your family's death?"

"It's not your fault," he repeated and crawled up my body, curving himself around me as his purr rumbled against my body.

"Did you find who did it?" The tightness in my chest made it difficult to speak.

"That day I thought you died." He paused, and his swallow was audible. "It ceased mattering."

I shuddered and curled closer to Knox and let myself take comfort in him.

Liana

I POPPED MY BIRTH CONTROL PILL AND TIPPED MY suppressant drink back, gulping quickly before Knox realized what I was chugging. He sneezed and rubbed his nose, frowning. He caught on when I was not even a third through the drink.

"No," Knox snatched the cup from my hand and I frowned at him.

"Give it back."

"No."

I narrowed my eyes. "Knox," I dragged his name out warningly. In answer, he strode to the sink and dumped it.

Knox snarled, glaring at me. I crossed my arms and glared right back as Randy rounded into the kitchen and took in our stare down.

"Shut it, mate-that-gave-her-up."

His lips tightened, jaw working hard. Guilt glinted in his deep eyes, and I sighed.

"I need to go to work and I can't be smelling like Omega."

"Work?" He was already shaking his head. "You're not going to work."

I scoffed. "I need to make a living somehow."

"My money is yours," he responded so matter-of-factly.

I blinked at him and just shook my head and collected the truck keys. He dogged my steps as I moved to the front door.

"What are you doing?" I pressed my hand to his naked chest. "You're staying here."

"I'll just follow you there."

I didn't doubt it one bit. I blinked at the towel around his waist, then at Randy and she sighed, nodding. She returned moments later with a pile of clothing and shoved them at Knox. His nose scrunched.

"Why do these smell like a male?"

His eyes narrowed on me.

"I'm running late," I huffed, and my heels clicked loudly as I made my way to the door. He cursed and there was shuffling. I pulled the door open and peeked back. My hand flattened over my mouth, but a giggle escaped at the tight clothing.

You could see every dent of his abs. My eyes trailed lower and my face heated. Everyone would be able to tell he was crazily endowed.

I huffed and pushed the door open for him.

"You should be fine for your shift, but take a full dose as soon as you're back home," Randy called out, completely ignoring Knox's glare.

He could have his way on that part, just because I was running late, and I didn't have time to argue about it.

"Love you!"

"Love you too," she responded.

The door clicked, and the heavy weight of his gaze fixed on

my shoulders. I ignored it until we were in the elevator. "What?"

"Why does she get a 'love you'?" The frown marring his mouth was pretty cute. "Tell me you love me." My face heated at his direct statement, and I tilted my head back.

The elevator dinged to a stop only a floor down Clay's floor. *Oh, Moon Goddess, you weren't about to test us like this, were you?*

At the ding, the doors opened and Clay's eyes fell on mine. His mouth parted. The paleness to his features indicated lack of sleep.

"Liliana," he said, half sighing as he stepped into my space. "You're okay. Randy and I have been searching everywhere for you." He reached for my hand and I tensed up. This was not going to be good.

Knox's arm lashed across my chest, and I teetered on my heels, unbalanced, as he yanked me against him.

"Hey man, be careful," Clay growled back, meeting Knox's eyes. Clay's quickly lowered since he wasn't dominant and I heard him cuss under his breath.

"You will not tell me what to do with my mate." Knox's words sucked the breath out of my lungs and I groaned, rubbing my face.

If I fought his statement, it was just going to be worse for Clay and I didn't want to put him in any danger. True mates that hadn't mated were more prone to getting murder-y.

So I settled for mouthing 'sorry' at Clay. He frowned and shook his head. He'd always been such a good guy. I couldn't believe he had the type of brother he had.

"Is your brother gone...?" I chose the words carefully, since I wasn't sure if he knew I'd been taken.

Clay snorted. "He disappeared like he always does. I'm sure

he'll show up in a few years, needing a couch to crash on." That reaction told me everything I needed to know. He was blissfully in the dark about what his deadbeat brother had done. I hummed and Knox tightened his grip, growling in my ear warningly. The elevator jerked unsteadily to a stop.

"Take care, Liliana," he murmured, not looking directly at me, the corner of his lips tilting down. "I'm glad you were just holing up with your mate." I waved tightly at him and Knox gripped my wrist, stopping it.

I huffed and yanked at my arm in his hold as I watched Clay retreat quickly.

"You're going to need to let me go so we can get to the car," I muttered. Knox slowly unclasped me, but gripped my hand in his.

My face warmed, and I fought a smile all the way to the truck. Firing it on, I lowered the volume of the radio and then put the vehicle in reverse.

Knox lowered the window and hung his arm out the side while the other went to my seat, tapping his fingers near my car.

I wetted my lower lip, mustering up the courage to ask him something I'd been curious about since we'd last seen each other.

"So," I cleared my throat. "That woman at the diner you took me to. How long was she your lover for?"

His tapping stopped, and the silence rang louder than his fidgeting. He tugged at the collar of his too-tight shirt.

"About five years," he finally responded tersely. "It was purely, uh, a physical thing."

My foot came down a little harder on the break than I meant, but Knox caught himself before he slammed face first into the glove compartment.

"You should put your seatbelt on," I muttered, face hot.

"I... I apologize for putting you in that situation."

I nodded jerkily, unable to say anything with the knot in my throat.

Buildings flashed by as I sped through downtown.

"How did you get here by the way?"

He smiled secretively. "I rode in the trunk."

My mouth popped open. Of course, he rode in the trunk. I was shaking my head as I pulled into the parking structure.

Unbelievable.

KNOX

"What is she doing here?" Declan snapped, walking up to where I sprawled within the vantage point of Liana's job.

I ignored him. Liana was mad at him, so he was fucked if he thought I'd speak to him.

I was intrigued by watching her work. Running around back and forth as she hunted shoes down for customers in those sexy little heels. The smile she offered them was brilliant and hollowed my stomach out. I wanted it directed at me.

The only way she'd convinced me to sit out here was because the large entrance of the store she worked in allowed me a clear view inside. All except for when she went to the back, which put me on edge, but she never failed to pop back out within fifteen seconds, so I was managing.

A kick on my leg jerked me out of my head and I scowled at Declan who glared at me.

"Why haven't you both approached her?" They'd been right on her heels when she'd taken off, but unlike me, they'd remained in the car for the night. Their loss.

I'd hoped they hadn't followed us to her work, but look at them now.

I craned my head to take in the supposed great Alpha, gazing at her with longing.

"I'm going to get changed and buy her something," Lore announced. "Don't take your eyes off her."

I scoffed at the order he directed at me before he strode away. Fucking dick.

I set my gaze back on my baby, absorbing her with my eyes. At one point, a woman approached me, lust clear in her eyes. I scowled and turned my eyes away from her as she talked. After realizing I was actively ignoring her, she huffed and stormed away.

Lore and Declan eventually returned. Declan in a fresh pair of dark jeans and a shirt that hugged his shoulders and Lore in a crisp suit.

"Why the suit?"

"Women prefer a put together mate." Lore glowered, raking his gaze over the too tight clothing she'd given me.

"Yeah, use that generalizing phrase with her again." I smirked tauntingly. That was what set her off in the first place. I was all for her being angry with them. "I want to see her reaction to it for the second time."

Lore glared, a tick in his jaw. "That's not what I mean."

My gaze dropped to the fancy bag from a jewelry store he clasped in his grip. "Did you purchase the entire store?"

"You're insufferable. How does she stand you?" Declan growled, rubbing the back of his neck.

"She stands me a helluva lot better than you two fucking idiots." I lifted a brow. "The suave ladies' man and the mated one."

This was the first real conversation we were having with each other. It was... interesting to say the least. We were all intrinsically tied to each other because of one woman.

Their scent didn't piss me off when they were near Liana. My wolf had gotten used to them in the last years he'd been at the forefront. He recognized them as more protection for his mate. A fact I begrudgingly accepted.

"She repeatedly wanted me to change the sheets because she didn't want to be in that room, so I want to get her something nice, especially after the jewelry box situation."

His fucking idiocy put me in danger of losing my mate. I lifted my lip in a sneer. "And you think buying her something will make her feel better?"

"It doesn't hurt to try."

I raked my hand through my hair. Whatever.

"So, did you make sure that bitch that hurt her was dead?" I leaned forward, lacing my fingers together, staring directly at Lore.

"We didn't have time to look at the body." Declan was the one who responded. "But I didn't hold back when I attacked."

I didn't bother asking Declan his thoughts. If the cold look in his eyes was any indication, he didn't give a fuck.

"What is that woman saying to her?" Lore said, a growl vibrating in his words. I shot straight up and focused. Liana wrung her hands before waving them widely while the woman glared at her.

In unison, we all moved forward.

As I crossed the threshold, Liana's low, sweet voice blanketed me, but her tone was off. Her voice strained as she explained why the woman's order hadn't arrived.

Liana's stress filled my nose, and my teeth clenched. Before I could tear off in her direction, Lore slapped a hand on my chest.

"Remember, they're humans."

I breathed hard and shook him off, but the moment offered me enough time to relax.

My long stride slowed, and I popped my knuckles.

A smile spread over Lore's lips and he met the woman's eyes with a sharp look.

"Is there a problem?" Lore directed his full attention on the woman. Her eyes widened, and they quickly dropped to the ground. Holding an Alpha's stare wasn't easy and though she was human, she felt the effect of his dominance. "Then I'll steal my wife from you."

Lore gripped Liana's arm and shuffled her to the side, while the woman was left gaping. I narrowed my eyes on her and she lifted her eyes to mine. They widened, and her heels clicked as she rushed away.

"Wife?" Liana hissed under her breath. "Lore, stop, I'm working."

"Let's go."

"No," she muttered. "I'm working." Her eyes flicked back to the other worker looking in her direction, and the woman started to make her way over.

"Is there some sort of issue, Liliana?"

Liana yanked her arm out of Lore's grip and licked her lips, brushing her hair behind her ear. "Not at all, ma'am."

The woman's eyes narrowed disbelievingly as her gaze bounced over all three of us.

I lifted a brow, and Declan crossed his arms. Her mouth thinned, and she cleared her throat.

Lore directed his attention to her and the corner of his lips lifted. Liana sighed as if she knew what was about to happen.

"It's his business smile," Declan muttered, and I snorted. "Pisses me off."

I could see why. It was almost mocking.

"What size are you," Lore asked Liana.

She frowned and shook her head. "You don't need to—"

She cut off on a squeak as Declan lowered and gripped her ankle, lifting it back so he could see the bottom of the heel. Liana wavered, and he gripped her hip, holding her in place. Her fingers sank into his shoulders and she scowled when Declan mouthed the number at Lore.

"Miss," Lore said, the polite tone edged with an order that the woman subconsciously felt from an Alpha if her backing up was any indication. "Get me all the heels on that table." Lore waved at the display where all the high-end shoes were placed. "And that table in eights."

"Lore, those are ridiculously expensive," Liana hissed.

Lore pinned her with a warning glare and her mouth snapped shut.

"I didn't know you were married to such a man Liliana," the woman tittered.

"I'm not," she responded weakly, but the woman was already radioing the man at the counter as she walked away.

Lore walked to the counter and reached into his pocket.

Liana tried to follow after him, but Declan gripped her arm and tugged her close to him.

"Declan, let me go."

"No."

Liana huffed and glared up at him. He leaned forward and pressed his lips to her nose. I shook my head, folding my arms across my chest. Liana's cheeks flushed bright red, and she blinked, stunned to silence.

So nose kisses and purring calmed her down.

I grinned. Lore finished his business and made his way back. "I'm having them delivered, Little One."

Her face reddened even more, and she licked her lips.

"Liliana." Lore gripped her chin. "You being an Omega isn't the reason I want you." She blinked up at him, face reddening. Her lip trembled, and I moved forward to snatch her away.

"I'm taking my break," she exclaimed high-pitched and grabbed my arm and Lore's tugging us behind her.

"No problem, Liliana," the woman responded, waving enthusiastically.

Liana

"Why are you guys so determined to get me stuff?" I mumbled.

Lore suddenly stopped and approached me. I licked my lips at the determined stride. His brow furrowed, and he caught my jaw. The grip was gentle, but I couldn't help quaking like a leaf.

"So tense." The hand at my face slid over my neck and then he circled his hands around it until it collared me. The bag hooked on his arm brushed against my elbow. His fingertips dug into the muscles, digging the tension out. Despite myself, I relaxed, enjoying his ministrations. He bent to whisper in my ear, "I want to spoil my mate."

I would be lying if I said I didn't like stuff. I adored gifts, but I'd had to save up to treat myself to things since I lived paycheck to paycheck. I roughed it most months, but it wasn't a bad life. "I got you this." He lifted the heavy bag from one of the jewelry shops. "But I'll give it to you at home." He smiled secretively, and I sucked in the urge to snatch it from him.

His eyes crinkled at the corner like he knew what I was thinking. Lore released me, turning on his heel, and I frowned at the back of his head. I cleared my throat and focused on speed walking. My toe pinched with how quickly I had to walk to keep up with their stride. They were lucky I was well versed in heels.

I peeked at Lore's slight smile. I appreciated the way he handled those women, but I'd rather die than admit to the butterflies fluttering in my stomach at watching him defend me.

Declan was walking so close to my ass that his arm grazed against me a few times.

I wasn't surprised when I saw them come in my direction earlier. I'd caught sight of them with Knox, so I'd had a moment to freak out about their presence. Fortunately, they'd headed off, and it had allowed me time to wrap my head around their arrival.

I wasn't exactly sure how I felt about them, but I felt better now that I'd let out all my pent-up emotions. I needed that release and I needed them to hear me out, and they had. Yesterday, the pressure combined with all those memories overwhelmed me. It was too much.

My shoulders were looser than they'd ever been. I was able to actually relax in public for once. Usually, the fear of coming into contact with werewolves kept me on edge, so I never enjoyed being outside of the apartment.

"Let's go in here, Little One," Lore announced, striding forward purposefully. The endearment melted my insides, and I had the strongest urge to stamp my foot. Despite my determination to keep my hatred, Lore was making me soften, and those looks he kept shooting me... I licked my lips. I liked them—a lot. They were soft and lust filled, and *loving*.

Declan pressed his palm into my back, nudging me toward the home goods store, and Knox gripped my hand, engulfing mine. The contrast in size was startling, and I stifled the pleased smile.

Grr, I liked the attention too much.

I'd been at this store before to window shop. Most everything in my bedroom came from here. They had the *best* blanket selection. They were to die for.

My gaze automatically settled on them.

"She wants blankets," Knox announced. "Her room is full of them."

"No, stop," I said, raising my tone. All three turned to face me and my face heated. "You don't need to get me anything..."

Lore was already perusing the section with his arms crossed and eyes narrowed, completely ignoring me.

Declan pressed against my back, urging me forward to follow the other two. The long line of his body flattened against mine, his cock nudging through his jeans. *This was not the time, Declan.*

I pressed my lips together, trying to contain my rapid breathing. Declan dragged his palm down my arms, soothing me. I leaned back into him, absorbing the comfort and calm he radiated. He leaned down and pecked my cheek and I hummed happily.

"I'm sorry about what Clara did," he murmured in my ear. My neck tightened, and he clasped my shoulders, rubbing his thumb into the stiff muscle. "Janice explained some to Lore and me." He growled softly in my ear. "I didn't protect you as I should have, and I will make it up to you. You have my word. She isn't a problem any longer. If you don't want to return to the pack, then we'll be away from all of that, anyway."

"I'm sorry—"

"Don't apologize," he ordered softly. "We were never good in our relationship, and it had nothing to do with you."

"Oh," I whispered and frowned, absorbing his words. "What do you mean that *we'll* be away from the pack?"

"Lily, I'm not leaving your side." He said it so simply, so matter of fact that my mouth dried and I wrung my hands together.

"Oh." My face was hot, and I forced my eyes away. He'd stay with me in the city if I decided not to go back. I looked over to where Knox and Lore were discussing and got the sense that Knox would do the same, but as for Lore... I could never be too sure about him.

I wasn't sure what to say, but I didn't think words were necessary. He was trying to comfort me and bring resolution to my pain. Clara was out of the picture. I couldn't bring myself to feel happy or bad about her. Her actions caught up to her.

"Are you okay?"

Declan gripped my hands, pulling me out of my thoughts.

"Yeah, just... looking at that pretty pillow." It was actually incredibly comfortable looking. The oval cream pillow was plush, and I ached to squish it.

Declan plucked the pillow I was eyeing and I lifted my hands, preparing a spiel that I quickly sucked back in.

"I feel like I can't look at anything without you guys grabbing it."

"You're starting to understand," Declan murmured near my ear and nipped it. My lips parted, and I squeezed my thighs together at the tingles that struck my pussy.

I gawked at him dumbfounded as he moved to join the other two. Shaking my head, I rushed to catch up.

"She likes those light colors." Knox waved his hand at the section. "Like that."

"Pastels? You idiot?" Lore muttered.

"Do you like this, baby?" Knox asked, waving a soft yellow blanket at me. He strode to where I stood and held it up for me to feel.

Sinking my fingers into the blanket, I hummed. This would feel amazing against my skin.

"I didn't bring my cards. Lore, I'm going to need to use yours."

Lore glared at Knox, but his expression softened when his gaze settled on me and he grunted.

I crossed my arms and heat flooded my face when the shopkeepers behind the counter gawked at the men and then me.

My eyes snagged on a circular chair that looked like it was made of feathers. The pink of the fur looked to die for.

"I saw her eyeing that chair," Declan announced, striding directly to the round seat.

"Declan!"

I palmed my forehead. That time my eyes *just* wandered.

Knox went back to digging through the blankets and piled three more in his arms.

My cell vibrated, and I took a few steps back, hovering near a different aisle. I smiled down at the caller ID. Randy. "What's up?"

"Come alone or I kill her on the spot." My heart dropped to the ground and my lungs spasmed.

The line went dead and then my phone vibrated against my cheek. An address flashed across the screen and I pressed my palm against my mouth.

Shit. They're going to know I'm scared. I needed to leave. Now.

"I'm going to get you guys a cart," I called. "I saw something I liked at the front of the store."

"Hurry up," Knox warned, without looking up as he picked through some trinkets. Thank the Moon Goddess.

I needed to leave now before they looked at me too closely. My face wouldn't be able to hide anything and tears were building already.

They would be angry with me, but I couldn't leave Randy alone.

LIANA

THERE WAS NO WAY THEY WOULDN'T KEEP US BOTH. Breathing with short bursts, I calmed my brain enough to think properly. They wanted me to be alone because they weren't going to release me. Two Omegas? There wasn't a chance they'd release me, and I couldn't have that.

After all, they said I had to arrive alone, not *stay* alone.

As I pulled on the highway, I plucked my phone out. I didn't know Lore's number. I rubbed my sweaty forehead with the back of my hand.

But I had Janice's memorized. Hopefully, it'd remained the same in the last few years.

I typed in her number, dividing my attention between the road and the phone.

A vehicle honked at me, and I hunched low in the car, straightening the truck.

Not my brightest moment, but I was desperate.

The line rang, and she answered.

"Janice. Text Lore's number on this phone."

"Liana? What are you doing—"

"Please Janice, quickly."

"Okay, okay. Sent!"

I hung up on her and clicked on the number in the text, quickly saving it. Opening his contact information, I clicked on the voice memo button to record myself.

If I called him, he would convince me to wait for them and who knew that they would do to Randy in all that time?

"Lore. Someone has Randy, and they want me to come to them." I recited the address I'd memorized. "Please come."

It wasn't long after that he was blowing up my phone. After sending him directly to voicemail twice, he sent me a voice message.

"Stop the car, Liana. We'll go get your friend, but don't think of putting yourself in danger." His words were half growled and I could feel the wildness of his tone. He wasn't happy.

"Sorry," I muttered back to him in response.

"Liliana!"

I winced at my shouted name, vibrating my speaker phone.

I pulled the truck off the exit and revved the engine as the wheels bumped on the uneven drive. The further I drove the fewer hints of life there were until even the 'road' was questionable. Following the map's directives, I took a sharp turn through some foliage and broke through a winding road curving up. Something caught my eye and a wolf's eyes glinted back at me from the lowering sun.

A sharp howl rent the air, lifting the hair on my arms. My wolf wasn't happy. She was antsy, and it was making me more nervous. I ignored the wolf tailing the truck and stepped on the engine.

"Turn left," the phone ordered suddenly. I jerked the wheel

to the side so quickly the tires spun out, forcing me to stomp on the brakes. The house was maybe twenty feet away and there were werewolves in their wolf and human forms pacing the front as they stared at me.

I swallowed hard as I put the car into park.

My door was jerked open harshly, and I gasped as my arm was gripped roughly. It was a good thing I had taken off my heels when I got in the truck to drive. I winced and scrambled to catch my footing as I was dragged in the direction of the house. My hip slammed into the edge of the stair as he dragged me up them. I couldn't contain the cry that tore free from my throat. A wolf we passed sniffed at me and whimpered, but the guy dragging me ignored them.

The front door opened as he stepped onto the porch and with a violent toss, I went flying. My hip stung on landing and I winced. Pressing my palm to the ground, I leveled myself up with a wobbling arm as I scanned the area.

Two men stood to the side of the room, their heads bent together. A different man walked into the house, steps vibrating the baseboards, a huge rifle in his hands.

Where was she?

My heart raced in my ears, but I wasn't prepared to drown in my pain. I needed to find Randy.

My wolf writhed in my chest from fear and fury. She was as angry and scared as I was, but at least she had claws to defend herself, and a better nose to find Randy with.

"No shifting," he barked the order out. I ignored him, pushing my wolf forward. Then a man I hadn't seen in the room with his eye missing grasped my chin, and squeezed so hard my jaw creaked. I winced and pushed the shift back.

"Lore has been hunting us for years because of you." He

crouched in front of me and I froze. "Do you know how many of my wolves he's killed?"

He paused as if he was waiting for a response. "N-no."

"Look around. It's all that's left now."

His palm flashed across my cheek and I screamed at the painful hit, falling to the side.

"Kelly." A woman rushed out from the kitchen with her head lowered at his shout. "Bring the binds."

"Let's see how Lore likes having his entire world defiled, beaten and ruined." His hand wrapped around my neck. "Maybe I'll add to that scar of yours." He traced the indent of my old wound and I gritted my teeth, not moving my eyes from his. As an Omega, I could feel his dominance, but I had a little more control over my reactions. When I bowed my head to Lore, it was mostly from the rioting emotions, not the fact that he was dominant.

He looked into my eyes, his lips quirking up in a rotten smile. "It was my pack who killed your father when he stood in our way to getting to you. Then your mother hid you, but she made a mistake when she decided to leave Eastland pack. I found you the day I snapped her neck, but I wouldn't make the same rash mistake, so I watched you, but *nothing happened*. It was only chance that your mate brought you right to us."

Those werewolves that had attacked on other occasions... the attack to Lore's pack the day I'd left, the ones that Knox had met because of his pack's destruction... they were all connected to this pack. To this Alpha. He'd stayed in the background as his people did the work.

I needed to know the cause for all this. Why had he targeted *me* even back then?

"How did you know I was an Omega?" I forced from my

dried throat, the confirmation of what I'd suspected he'd been behind giving me the strength to speak.

"My family line passed down this neat little book with names of Omegas and their information." They'd kept records of Omegas? Like—like a commodity? How *sick*. "They were especially interested in recording the existence of every known Omega. I tracked down each lead, but many on the list had been documented as dead. Yet, there were some that seemed to simply disappear without a trace. Like your great-great-grandmother. No record of her death. Simply gone. Eventually, I found your mother, but the gene skipped her. But when I saw her daughter..." His eyes glinted with avarice. "I kept tabs on you once I found you again, Liliana, watching and waiting for you to bring your Omega out. But you did nothing, not even turning on your eighteenth. That told me one of two things. Your Omega was hidden inside you or you were defective. I was tired of waiting for you to shift, so I came to retrieve you. One way or another you would have called your Omega wolf out for me, or you would have died as a pitiful defective." I wasn't the only one he'd found. He'd hunted Randy with the same determination.

As Kelly returned and lifted the brown frayed rope, I sat in disbelief. He just confirmed my worst fears. It really was me, I caused all of this. Me just being an Omega. I couldn't imagine how many others had called their Omega forward and had been taken by his pack as soon as they shifted. I would have had the same fate if I'd turned.

My fingers flexed against the floorboards.

"Get out of my sight," he snapped at the female werewolf hovering nearby.

"Yes, master." With that, she scurried away. A man groped her ass, but she did nothing more than wait until he was done to disappear. The man without the eye forced me to face down and yanked my hands forward. So, the Alpha was done enlightening me. The rope dug into my wrists, burning as he continued to tighten.

This was no good. I wouldn't be able to shift like this without the danger of breaking my limbs being there. There were some instances where the rope was too strong and too tight that they cracked the wolf's legs during the shift.

I'd heard of packs like this. The ones that lacked all respect for she-wolves—especially the low level ones that usually fell into the hierarchy as the pack whores. Old fashioned, and so deeply entrenched in blocking out all advancements to the point that they hindered themselves.

The subservience in the female wolf's eyes made my skin crawl. I wasn't sure if it was forced there or if the woman was brainwashed to that point, but it was sad.

Lore had tons of downsides, but he never acted like he was better than anyone else in the pack. He was respectful, prompt, and professional. And he'd never allowed pack whores.

Randy's familiar voice filtered over to me as she shouted obscenities, and I used my core strength to sit up, heart racing at her voice.

"You're the one that made her suffer aren't you, you fucking bitch!"

A hand clamped on my shoulder, fingers digging into my skin. I winced, but breathed through the pain.

Near the small kitchen section, a bedroom door creaked open and Clara dragged Randy out. My nostrils flared, and I pushed against the hold on me as pressure bubbled in my chest. Not her.

She was supposed to be dead. My heart pounded against my ribcage. She'd survived Declan's attack. I'd left quickly after that situation and she'd slipped my mind. I'd felt weightless after her death but here she was.

Clara stopped at the threshold of the living space entrance and her eyes narrowed on me, but I ignored her and raked my eyes over Randy. She seemed relatively okay other than the bruise blooming at her eye.

Help would come soon. I tried conveying it to her through my gaze, but the dark looming shadow moved forward and I was able to make out who it was.

"Jacob?" At first, I held a sense of hope. He would help me, right? He was part of my old pack... which was stupid considering Clara was too and look how that had turned out.

He reached down and grabbed my arm, pulling me up. His other hand clasped my chin and he bent and kissed me hard. I struggled to keep my lips tightly closed, but he managed to slip his tongue through, invading my mouth.

Tears flooded my eyes.

"I've always wanted you," he murmured, breath brushing my face as he ground his dick against me.

"You promised me I would have my time with her before you, Jacob." I clicked my teeth at Clara's petulant tone. Jacob squeezed my ass once more and palmed my breast before releasing me. I thumped on the ground.

Humiliation warmed my cheeks, and I swallowed hard to stop the vomit from rising.

The one-eyed man sank into a seat at the corner. "Just make sure you don't kill her. I want to use her once you two are done."

Clara inclined her head. "Thank you, master. I appreciate your leniency."

Clara dropped her hold on Randy and walked over to me. My gaze attached to the wrapped bandages around her neck.

I was so stupid. I'd let my squeamishness stop me from letting Declan end her. She must have crawled away while I was inside with the guys.

"I've been waiting for you to get everything you deserve since you dared touch what was mine," she hissed in my face. I shook my head frantically.

"You're insane."

Her brows arched.

"So you grew a backbone while you were gone?" Clara scoffed. "What, do you feel important now that you're an Omega?"

"I'd always had it. I just didn't want to draw out your bullshit." My limbs trembled so hard that my wrists rubbed against the rope.

Her hand slashed out, and I rocked on my knees, but remained sitting up. Lifting my chin, I met her eyes.

She didn't like that.

Her eyes narrowed, and she fisted her hand. I grunted at the impact and blood spurt from my nose.

Randy cried out.

"Shut the girl up," the Alpha barked, prompting one of the men to grip her hair and force his hand over her mouth. She fought, but he eventually pinned her to the ground.

Clara continued smashing her fist into my face, and alternated with slamming the tip of her shoe into my gut. This was all reminiscent of her beatings from before.

My ears rang, and I groaned, cheek to the floorboards.

I lay in a puddle of my blood. Panting as I struggled to breathe. Now that I had my wolf. I was able to take the beating more, but I knew I had to fake I was more broken than I was, or she would kill me.

My face throbbed with each pulse of my heart.

Clara pressed her hands to her knees, leaning over as she panted.

"I don't want her to pass out while I'm fucking her, Clara." My stomach roiled at Jacob's words. He inched closer and inhaled sharply. "Do you smell that?"

He moaned and fell to his knees, burying his nose in my hair. His meaty hand turned me onto my back, and I whimpered at the sharp tug at my shoulder. Since my hands were pinned between us, the angle hurt, especially with him invading my space.

I tensed up as he buried his nose in my neck, dragging his wet tongue up the side.

Jacob loomed over me, his eyes sinister in the lack of lighting. He unbuttoned his pants and his dick sprang out as he forced me down, forcing a kiss on me. I struggled to turn my head to the side, but he didn't allow me.

"She smells delicious. Hurry up, Jacob. I want my turn." No, not another one.

Fighting against his hold, I breathed hard. He quickly pinned me and brought his fist down on my chest, sucking the oxygen out of my lungs. I whimpered, and he was quick to smooth his hand over my heart, gently.

His reaction was a dichotomy. It was like he didn't want to hurt me or it pained him to hurt me.

Because I was an Omega, men tended to want to coddle us.

We were born to be cherished and he fought against those instincts.

I needed my mates. They had to come. Tears trickled out from the corner of my eyes.

"Knox, Declan, Lore," I cried out repeatedly, angering him.

"Shut the fuck up."

I ignored him and kept shouting my mates' names. So loud that my throat burned. My ears rang with my screaming.

Jacob's weight lifted off me and I snapped my mouth shut, scrambling backward as fast as I could with my legs. The Alpha was on his feet, shouting something. I shook my swirling head.

"We need everyone outside. Clara, Lyn, Brian, watch them."

Everyone but three people slipped out of the room, tearing out of their clothes and shifting.

A hand wrapped around my arm and I screamed, but I quickly cut it off when I met Randy's eyes. She tugged me behind the nook beneath the kitchen island. Her hands were stained with blood as she lifted them to my face and brushed the hair out of my eyes.

It took me a moment to process what she was asking.

"I'm okay, I'll just be sore tomorrow," I answered and roved my eyes over her, but she seemed fine, considering.

"Shit," she muttered. "You smell really good." She met my gaze. "No wonder that Jacob guy was acting weird. He got the full effect of your scent. You never took the full dose to suppress your Omega scent."

My eyes widened. Oh shit.

Howls and snarls erupted from outside and I huddled lower behind the island. The door ruptured as the familiar wolfman form of Declan tore through the door.

One of the men charged at him, but he tossed him aside,

lifting his nose as he inhaled and turned on Clara. She lifted her hands toward Declan. Pleading.

He showed his teeth.

"You have my mate's blood on you." The voice sent chills down my neck and within the next second he slashed his claws deep into her throat. Her neck burst open, hanging by a ligament and then her body thumped on the ground as five wolves poured into the house all attacking Declan.

There was no way she could survive a detached head.

I should feel something. Disgust. Happiness... But I couldn't. There was nothing but a void concerning my feelings toward Clara.

Declan turned and fought his way through the wolves as he backed toward where I hid. A fissure in the wall ruptured and Knox broke through the slab of the drywall as he tossed wolves around ruthlessly. From the sounds of screaming outside, I was sure Lore was out there.

A musky scent wafted to my nose, and I moaned, biting my lower lip. It smelled like home and safety. Heat flushed over my skin and my nipples hardened.

Panting, I lowered my tied wrists and curled my fingers on Randy's arm. "What's happening to me?" I whimpered. "It feels like my heat."

She peered into my eyes and then looked over at my fighting bloodthirsty mates over the counter.

"They're going into a rut," she said grimly. I gasped and my widened eyes pinned her. "They probably can't determine the difference right now while they're fighting."

"I thought that was only during my heat!" I whisper-yelled. "I already went into heat around them."

"Well, I don't fucking know. It's like there's some sort of

delayed reaction since you had taken such a large dose while you were with them. They haven't gotten a full blast of your scent. I think their rut is inciting your heat too," she grimaced.

"Not another one," I whimpered. I huddled closer to Randy.

She grunted and lifted her arm around me, squeezing me tightly.

Declan

A WOLF BARRELED INTO ME AND I LASHED MY CLAWS out, taking advantage of my range in this form. I snarled at him and gripped his hind and foreleg, pulling in two different directions.

Guts and shit littered the ground. I panted, snarling, as another two wolves buried their teeth into me.

I roared and lashed out, hooking my claws across their bodies. I needed to check on Lily. I'd slowly been inching my way to her, but these wolves kept multiplying. On one hand, it was good because I needed something to take my rage, especially after hearing her call for us. I needed to claim her over and over again to prove to her that she was mine and in being mine she would never have to fear.

The way she screamed would forever be ingrained in my memory. I never wanted to hear her so terrified.

Knox fought a handful of wolves as I neared my mate, where she hid behind the counter with her friend.

"Lily," I snarled.

"Declan." She poked her head over the lip of the counter so the island was the only thing between us.

Her scent slammed into me like a tidal wave, and I staggered. My cock suddenly hardened, readying to take her—breed her. I wanted to fuck her so long and hard that she was brimming with my cum.

My spine bowed, and I howled sharp and loud. She curled closer to the other female and her round eyes widened more than I thought possible.

"Run," I snarled, and she took off at a dead sprint.

Falling to my knees, the overwhelming scent of peaches filled my nose, and I inhaled every bit of it. The further she got the more faint the scent. It was so potent that my mouth watered.

My muscles twitched, and I dragged my claws across the wood, leaving behind deep burrows. I couldn't take it anymore.

My cock needed to be in her *now*.

All that pounded through me was the desire to get to Lily. My need for her surpassed everything I'd ever desired or cared for. She was everything to me, and I ached for the ability to show her.

The surroundings faded and my sight focused on what was ahead of me as I tore through the woods, inhaling her peach scent deep into my lungs.

I hunted her meticulously. Breathing her in with every step and savoring her smell.

There she was.

She tripped over a branch and fell to her knees, catching herself before her face slammed into the ground. Then I was on her.

My furred palm pressed her down when she tried to stand, and she screamed. I leaned over and nipped her shoulder with a growl. She automatically softened.

"Declan," she whimpered as she said my name and my cock throbbed, cum beading at the tip.

Her voice worked to rip some sanity to the forefront. Breaths sawed from my throat as the scent of her blood reached my senses.

"You're hurt." My claws twitched as I struggled to regain a semblance of control. "I can't... control myself... Love." Need blistered through my gut. An unquenchable ache pumping through me. "I don't want... to hurt you. Run." I snarled and a growl vibrated my diaphragm.

"I want you." A small whimper escaped her lips, and she curved her body into my talons. My restraint snapped.

I clawed through the side of her clothes and they slid off; the remnants clinging to her as she arched her back, presenting her ass to me. My cock twitched.

I buried my snout in her pussy and growled. She tensed and groaned as her slick drenched her thighs, preparing for me.

Licking her sweet juices, I dipped my tongue deep into her cunt and lapped the walls of her pussy as they constricted around my tongue. She continued leaking for me, her wetness drenching my muzzle.

On my knees, I inched close and gripped her hips, pulling her with my clawed grip and slammed her onto my cock. She keened, her head falling forward as my thick cock burrowed within her channel. She ground against me; her round ass in the air.

I moaned, shivering.

Mine. *Mine.*

"My mate loves my knot, doesn't she?" The words growled from my throat. It wasn't as big as it would be right before I exploded, leaking my cum into her. "Take all of me. I need to fill you with my cum until it's leaking out of you."

She was the fucking air I breathed. I lived for her. Hammering into her with an incessant rhythm. The base of my cock ballooned painfully with my encroaching release. I fed the base into her and her shiver every time the ridge slipped into her pussy wasn't lost on me.

Her slick drenched me—she liked me talking to her, and I rubbed closer, needing her essence all over me.

I leaned over her and nipped her ear, burying so deep she sucked in a ragged breath.

"Accept me, Lily, my love."

Her fingers speared into the dirt and she shook, wiggling against me, wanting more.

"Let me touch you," she whimpered, making my knot swell painfully, draw up tight to my cock. I loved her like this. Wild. Begging. *Mine.*

"Stop tugging at your wrists."

She quickly did as I ordered, and her frantic movements against the rope at her wrists ceased. I smoothed my claws down her ass. "Good girl."

Her slick pussy throbbed at my words, squeezing me tightly as she came again.

My knot swelled to an excruciating point, locking me into her pussy as the first wave slammed into me. Fire blazed through my stomach and poured into her in a jerking release that convulsed my body. Then the next and the next... Unable to help it, I sank my teeth into her neck, where her pulse fluttered

—claiming her as mine—finally. Her pussy squeezed me so tight that I shot off harder than the last three times and my roar rocked the trees, and birds scattered into the sky.

I continued spasming inside her, jerking so hard that it sent her into another release. Her arms wobbled as she fell to her elbows.

LIANA

MY ENTIRE BODY SHOOK AS DECLAN PULLED OUT OF me. The slick cock slipped out, and the insides of my thighs tickled from his cum dripping from me. His claws pressed into my hips and he turned me on my ass, so I stared up at him, panting hard.

I couldn't move my gaze from the thick member pointed up, still ready for me.

A rumble vibrated from his chest as he stared down at my pussy. I followed his gaze and whined, staring at the mix of our release drenching my thighs.

His claw slipped down and he brushed the back against my sensitive flesh, bringing it up to my mouth.

"Lick it."

My clit throbbed at the order and I leaned forward, tonguing his claw as I made sure to lick the mix of cum and slick on the fur of his hand.

A growl came from behind and another from the side, sending spasms down my body. My nipples tingled, and I lifted my bound arms, rubbing the rough rope against one of my breasts.

The scrape wrenched a moan from my throat and I met Lore's eyes as he shoved through branches, prowling closer. His gaze dropped to my spread legs where the moonlight glinted off cum and slick. His teeth showed and my eyes dropped to his hard, extended cock.

I spread my legs wider, slipped my hands down, and buried my fingers into my pussy, drenching them in moments.

My nose twitched as I sucked in Knox's delicious scent as he widened my knees more and his head dipped, his tongue dipping into my slit, lapping up my essence until I trembled. My eyes slid to find Declan palming his hard cock, and I orgasmed, twitching as he met my eyes.

Knox moved to my right thigh, opening his maw and clamped down on the meat of my thigh, teeth close to the soft point where my leg bent. His claiming bite.

A warm gush from my pussy squirted from my folds, drenching him as I dropped to my back, spine arching. I screamed, neck straining from the climax. My eyes crossed and my sight became fuzzy.

Before I was done riding out the wave, he gripped my hips and forced me onto my knees. Pressing my fists into the ground, I jerked at the ties again. Knox's furred, warm body bent over me and he sliced a sharp talon through the material, freeing my hands. I barely just managed to slap them into the ground when he slammed into me from behind. I cried out, tears slipping from the corner of my eyes. Lore gripped my hair and pulled my head back, forcing my neck into an arch.

Lore slammed his dick into my mouth, thrusting shallowly. My mouth stretched painfully for him to feed his cock into my mouth, and even then it was only a fifth of his cock—mainly the tip. Knox kept his punishing pace, pushing me toward Lore and vice versa as they fucked my pussy and mouth as if they were trying to drill a hole through me. I swirled my tongue and Lore pushed in harder, making my jaw creak. He was so big it pushed my tongue back and I gagged.

Lore groaned, head tipping back as the knot at his base swelled and he erupted in my mouth. Filling me so much, I coughed with my lips wrapped around him. His cum dripped off my chin as he pulled out, as he still shot streams of cum from the tip. Declan stepped beside Lore, jerking in his palm as he aimed his cum on my face. The wet seed trickled down my brow and cheek, dripping off my chin. Lore held my neck, stilling me as his spunk joined Declan's.

I licked my lips, lapping up the salty taste and wanting more.

Claws gripped me, but without being able to see, I didn't know whose. I was lifted and my legs automatically curved around thick furry thighs.

"I want you swelled with my cum," Knox growled, nipping my cheek.

I wanted that too.

My head fell forward on his shoulder and I was able to clear my eyes by rubbing them on his fur. I blinked just as another big body pressed against my back and a cock nudged the bud of my ass.

Declan growled and pressed against my side, closer to Knox, and gripped one of my hooked legs and lifted it so it bent up, exposing me more. My knee pressed into Knox's chest as Declan pushed forward and they hoisted me higher as he prodded his thick cock beside Knox's until his tip slipped into my sheath. My pussy throbbed, clasping at him, full to the point of agony.

Lore bucked his hips, working the ridge of his tip past the rim of my ass. I whimpered, surrounded by fur.

All three of them filled me.

Declan stilled, letting Knox move me on their cocks. Lore's teeth sank into the indent where my neck and shoulder met, as the base of his cock swelled at my asshole. I screamed, writhing in their arms.

Claimed. I was claimed, and I wanted it. Heat suffused the area and spread, warming me.

My scream was cut off by Declan's lips as he kissed me deep and needy.

My body was a cooked noodle. Overdone. As soon as I came with all of their cocks, my body slumped against theirs.

Since then, I'd been trying to catch my breath with my head pillowed against Declan's thigh while Knox left to find clothing. Declan dragged his fingertips over his claiming on my neck, sending delightful shivers through my limbs. My eyelids were too heavy to open, so I didn't bother opening them when grass crunched. An accompanying heat warmed my belly, spreading from the bite marks and I sensed another of my mates near me. A light touch at my chin had me slitting my lids to find a clothed Knox with an armful of clothing.

He set it on his lap and lifted a damp cloth to my face, wiping me gently. I watched his concentrated expression and warmth spread in my chest. His eyes lifted, and he leaned down to press his lips to mine. Warmth pulsated from the bite at my thigh and I shivered.

Knox's head rose and Declan's thigh tightened as steps approached.

"The vehicle is fine."

Lore was back.

Declan curled his arms under my body and curved me close to him. "Let's get you home," he said roughly, and kissed my forehead. He set me on my unsteady legs and swiftly got dressed before pulling me back into his arms.

I swayed in his arms and let my eyes fall closed, lulled by the quiet only broken by the sounds of the night.

Sighing, I blinked up at the moon, basking in the shine cast across my skin. The tingle around my neck and inner thigh squeezed my belly and warmth tipped the corner of my lips.

A rustling moved within the bushes and Declan's arms tensed around my body. He peered into the swishing leaves and he clutched me tightly. I couldn't see anything other than shadows and the outline of greenery. Knox's bright eyes slitted and a snarl broke the silence as something flew in our direction.

My scream caught in my throat and I jerked in Declan's arms. Knox lurched forward and captured a small pale gray wolf. He wrestled with it as it wiggled and struggled in his hold.

"I'll do a quick sweep to make sure there aren't more hiding around," Lore half growled as he stalked off, melting into the surrounding trees.

The wolf released a choking cry. Knox was squeezing her neck. If he didn't stop, he was going to pop its head off.

"Don't kill it," I cried out. There was enough murdering. Maybe the wolf would be willing to work with us. Maybe it needed help.

"Turn," Knox ordered. His fingers tightened around the tuff around its neck, and it whimpered. Her body started jerking and stretching with her shift until a woman sat naked and panting. Her hair fell around her sweaty face. It was the girl from earlier. I saw how they treated her. We could offer her a place in the pack.

"Let me go," she hissed, practically spitting with anger. Knox gripped her hair.

"Wait," I shouted, and she tensed. "It doesn't have to be like this. Why don't you come with—"

"You killed them all," she hissed. They'd treated her like a second class, and she still wanted to defend them? "You killed *my* pack."

She suddenly shifted and pounced. I sucked in a breath as claws extended in my direction. I jerked back against Declan and his biceps flexed. Knox wrapped his hands around her neck and a snap bounced off tree trunks. Birds scattered from the trees and silence settled.

Vomit rose up my esophagus, but I swallowed a few times until the nausea passed.

Knox released the she-wolf and her body thudded onto the ground. He met my eyes and grimaced.

I forced a small smile. I understood why he had to do that.

She wasn't going to listen.

I wasn't sure if it was brainwashing or if they enjoyed the subjection. Either way, I couldn't help but feel sad for her.

There were more of these abusive packs out there, with women who willingly stayed and maybe some that were stuck. I couldn't tear my gaze away from the too still body.

Declan turned to continue the direction we'd been going and I curved tighter to him. I could have helped her if she'd let me.

I sighed, rubbing my palms against my eyes.

"Some people are better left in their own bitterness, Lily."

I remained quiet. There wasn't much I could do, anyway. I had to let it go.

I wiggled my toes and soreness radiated up my thighs. The madness of the last moments couldn't take away from the bliss coating my body and the little reminders from the twinges between my thighs.

"That was a much shorter amount of time than last time I went into heat." Much, *much* shorter.

"Mates need to be able to provide and care for their mate when they're in heat. Ruts don't last as long as heats." My eyes widened at Declan.

"I researched," he said shyly. "I want to be able to care for you in all ways."

A shy smile trembled on my lips.

"You guys came in time."

"Before you messaged Lore, we were already looking for you. We thought someone took you."

"Either way. Thank you."

"Always, Lily. You'll never be alone again."

I sniffled and curled closer to him, wrapping my arms around his neck.

Swallowing hard, I mustered up the courage to bring up the elephant in the room.

"About Clara..."

His palm smoothed down my hair, and he remained quiet, waiting patiently.

"Are you..." I paused. "Did you..."

Words failed me and for the life of me, I couldn't figure out what I wanted to say. My top teeth sank into my bottom lip.

"I will always answer your questions, Lily. Take your time."

I nodded jerkily, nestling my nose at his neck, inhaling his minty scent deep into me. He shivered as I tried sucking in all the calm and warmth he instilled in my heart.

"If you're asking if I'm upset. No. There was never love between us. Our entire situation was a mistake. I'm more apologetic to you for putting you in a situation where your true mate was connected to your abuser."

I swallowed hard. I couldn't say it was okay because it frankly hurt. The ever present draw to him was something I never understood, subtle and encompassing. I always figured it was the haven he symbolized. "You were always kind to me."

"Even when I didn't know it. You were everything to me." He exhaled shakily and loosened his chokehold on me and tucked me into the car. "Put this on." He handed me the robe Knox found and I pulled it on as I took in the front of the house littered with bodies.

"Randy!" I waved at her madly, peeking through the cracked door. Declan's shoulders tightened, and he slammed the door in my face, standing in front of it vigilantly.

What was going on?

My eyes tracked Knox as he ran in the direction of Randy. A scream crawled up my throat. What were my mates doing?

I yanked at the lever of the door, but it wouldn't budge with Declan's hand pressed to keep it shut. A man tumbled to his feet, swaying as he aimed the gun at Randy. As if in slow motion, the gun sparked and the echo of the shot vibrated my eardrums. Knox barreled into him, slamming his fist into his face repeatedly before snatching the gun and turning it on him. Lore checked Randy over, lips moving quickly as he checked the wound. He shook his head hard and scooped her up.

I slammed my palm on the window repeatedly, tears streaming down my face.

Lore ran toward the other side of the truck and I scooted to shove the door open. He slipped her in head first and I inched over to make room for him to lay her on the seat.

"Help her, please Lore, help her," I choked through my tight throat as blood seeped through her shirt, leaking from her stomach.

Her head thumped onto my thigh.

"Sh, Little One. We'll do everything we can." Lore tore his shirt off and bundled it, forcing it into my hand. "I need you to press this to her wound, okay?"

I nodded frantically, hands trembling as I applied pressure to her stomach. Lore bent her knees, resting her legs against the seat to shut the door and jumped into the driver's seat.

Knox opened the door on my side and squeezed in next to me, wrapping his arm around my belly.

"Is there a hospital around here?"

Declan popped the glove compartment in front of the passenger seat and pulled a cell phone out at Lore's question. "You need to drive out so I can get cell reception."

Lore didn't waste any time. The truck jerked, and he took off over the uneven road. Knox kept his grip on me, steadying me as I gripped Randy.

Her head lolled on my thigh and she met my gaze with a pain-filled one of her own.

"I'm losing too much blood."

I pressed down harder on her wound at her words, and she grimaced.

"Don't be like that. You're already being all negative," I snapped.

"My, my, Liana, I think that's the snappiest you've ever sounded."

"You can joke right now?"

Randy smiled, and the scent of blood filled my nose.

The bumping of the truck finally evened out, and Declan's phone dinged as reception came back.

"The hospital is sixty-seven miles out." His grim words hollowed my stomach.

That was so long. I fixed my gaze on the blood drenched shirt on her stomach.

"I want you to be happy." Randy paused, lips tightening as sweat beaded on her forehead. No. No. She was starting to say goodbye. "If they make you happy, stay with them. Plus, it'll make me feel better knowing you're protected." She attempted to smile, but it looked more like a macabre grimace.

"Randy..." I wanted her to stop talking, to press my palms over my ears and bury my head in the sand.

"That doesn't mean you shouldn't give them hell. You've come a long way from being a doormat, and stop holding your emotions in," she ordered.

She blinked hard, each one coming slower and more weighted.

Lore pulled the car to the side of the road and the car doors slammed, but I didn't move my eyes from hers to see who it was.

Declan opened the door near Randy's legs and straightened them. His palm flattened near her wound.

"It hit her kidney." Declan shook his head, grimacing.

"Thank you for saving me that time. Without you—" I cut off, my body shaking so hard. "I should have come—"

"Don't go blaming yourself. What happened, happened," she said roughly, mustering a glare.

My lip trembled, and I held her gaze as her blue eyes glazed over, unseeing.

A fissure opened in my chest. A wrenching ache slashed across my body and bloomed outward. The world spun and my entire body went numb. I couldn't feel anything but the agony clouding my brain.

A keening cry echoed in my ears. It was me, but it felt so separate from me.

"Let go, baby," someone said in my ear, prying my bloody hands away from the rag. I was tugged back and pulled out of the truck, but my legs wouldn't hold me.

I fell to my knees crying, palms pressing to my eye sockets.

A hard line of bodies pressed into my side, huddling me between them. Hands smoothed down my sides, petting every side they could. A purr reached deep into my soul, wrenching some sanity and calming my heart rate. Knox... and Lore were holding me while Declan rifled through the truck and lifted a tarp. Knox forced my face to his chest as Declan gently set her on the gray material. My hand balled in Knox's shirt and Lore petted my hair.

Almost three years with her. Such a short time in the grand scheme of things, but even so, Randy was family. Tears continued pouring down my face, my entire body shaking.

"Little One, you're going to make yourself vomit if you keep crying this hard." Lore smoothed his hand over my hair repeatedly. "There's a motel nearby. Let's get her some rest before we continue."

My body swayed and time blurred as I was lifted again. All I could think about was the happy times I'd had with Randy. She'd had so much she wanted to do. She wanted to find a way to help other Omega's with the scent suppressant that her family passed down.

She would never get the opportunity.

Eventually I cried myself into exhaustion and woke to a lulling pace of being carried.

My back sank into a mattress as tears continued wetting my cheeks. Knox settled over me, his face burrowing into my belly as he peered up at me. Lore buried his nose in my hair and Declan at my neck.

My crying eventually tapered off, and I was left hiccupping as my body shut down.

I fell asleep, enveloped by warm bodies.

The ride back to the pack was silent. I stoically stared out into the woods. My emotions were on lockdown, and I'd spaced out for the last two hours.

I shrugged Lore's hand from my shoulder. Since I'd slept in their arms for two nights straight, they figured everything was under the bridge and while I was on the way to forgiving—but not forgetting—I wasn't one hundred percent there.

"Just because you saved me... and then claimed me. It doesn't mean I accept you," I muttered and hugged my chest. My heart squeezed, and I closed my eyes tightly. My tumultuous relationships with my mates weren't the priority right now. I mourned Randy, and all I could feel right now was numb.

My stomach had ached all day, and it was slowly turning into a burning. I slipped my hands under my thighs and tensed. Oh no, I knew this feeling.

A gush between my legs forced me to tip my head back and squeeze my thighs together. This was not the time.

"I smell blood," Lore snapped. His fingers dug into my shoulders as he forced me to face him. He gripped my hand and lifted it to his face, and then searched the rest of my body. "Are you injured?"

It made sense that he was confused since he'd bathed me at the hotel when I wouldn't stop shivering. He'd warmed me up in any way he could, but the cold hadn't been why my body shook—it was loss.

"I-I need to stop at a convenience store."

Lore's brows furrowed.

"Liana, are you injured?" Lore's tone was sharp, and he speared his fingers into his blond hair, dragging it back. I slit my eyes at him.

Knox gripped the back of Declan's seat as he twisted his torso to look over at me with alarm. I met Declan's eyes from the front mirror. They were on the verge of freaking out.

"I'll pull over—"

"No." I interrupted Declan and cleared my throat. "I, uh, got my period."

On top of my heat, I had to deal with the menstrual cycles. The only difference was these were monthly. A sharp cramp speared my belly, and I gritted my teeth.

Awareness brightened Lore's eyes.

"Closest store, Declan."

The truck jolted as he stepped on the gas. I remained as still as possible.

"No touching," I snapped, sharper than I meant. Lore's hands fisted, and he rubbed his forehead.

"I'll give you your way for now, since you're visibly uncomfortable." He couldn't have sounded more irritable.

I remained on edge until the truck jolted to a halt. Lore and Declan were out of the vehicle as soon as it stopped. I huffed. Overbearing werewolves.

Knox reached back, and his hand palmed my cheek. I leaned into it slightly and sighed. "I don't know why they ran out of here like they were on fire. I need to go in there," I grumbled.

"Let's go, baby."

I scooted to the end of the car, tightly cinching my thighs together. My panties were going to be done for, but my first day was never terribly heavy. Knox held the door open for me, making it easy for me to get out and shuffle to the mart. The door wiggled when I pulled it open with Knox at my back.

They were down the second aisle, frowning at the feminine products.

Lore lifted a box toward Declan who scowled at it and scratched his forehead.

"I'm not sure. All of it seems like it'd be uncomfortable for her."

My heart squeezed, overriding the sadness that had numbed me.

I pressed my lips together, but when I focused on Lore's pursed lips, I couldn't help but giggle. Their attention snapped up as I approached and reached for the box of the organic cotton tampons. I headed directly for the restroom, figuring I could pay for them after.

"Take a picture of the brand she got so I can stock them," Lore ordered. "I left my phone in the truck."

I snorted and pushed the door open to the clean restroom and quickly did my business. I balled my undies and dropped them into the empty trash.

Knox waited right outside the door, so close my nose smushed against his chest. He peered down at me, and his head tilted and then he narrowed his eyes.

He slipped behind me and plucked the undies from the thankfully clean bin and pocketed them.

"What are you doing?!" I whispered. "There's blood on them."

"It's *my* scent."

I pinched my nose at his caveman behavior. There was no use arguing with him. He was going to do it despite my protests, and I didn't have the energy.

I laced my fingers around the box and headed toward the front.

"Stubborn, jerk," I muttered under my breath.

The cashier blinked at me owlishly and I flushed, thinking she'd witnessed what Knox had done. Or maybe it was the various bruises on my face in different stages of healing.

"Those guys paid," she muttered, pointing at Declan and Lore near the door. Oh, it was more likely she was blushing because of them. They did look rather intimidating... and hot. I tipped my head in thanks and scooted past them, moving directly to the car.

Lore slipped in after me and slammed the car door in Knox's face.

"Fuck you, Lore," Knox bellowed and moved to the passenger side.

Declan started the car, and we were on our way again.

I leaned against the door, my forehead resting on the window as I hugged my stomach.

Lore pressed his palm over my belly, and I tensed, but the warmth of his palm seeped into my flesh.

"You like the heat?" he murmured into my hair. I nodded jerkily. His body shook and fur sprouted from his arms as his clothes ripped. His neck bent and he lowered his head so he could fit in the back. I inched more to the side to give his big body room, but he guided me so I leaned against his furry body and his arm curved around my back. Heat surrounded me and I nuzzled my nose into his furry chest. His other claws raked through my hair, scratching against my skull, and I hummed in pleasure.

That was heavenly. I lolled against him, accepting the comfort.

Liana

I'D SPENT THE WEEK ALTERNATING BETWEEN numbness and agony. I was in mourning and I always would be. That was the thing with death. It left a mark, but it was the little things that brought me low. Like our nightly tea ritual... that I'd never have with her again.

Heat warmed the mark on the left side of my neck and spread outward. One of my mates was nearing and if I focused on the sensation of the heat, I would bask in it all day, so I made a point to block it out. When all three of them were near me, I was blissful. The heat that originated from their bites and fused me at their proximity was like the world's best hug times a billion.

"Open your eyes, Little One," Lore whispered in my ear. "I know you're awake."

I sighed, lids fluttering open. The guys never left me alone and the only time I managed to have privacy was when Janice was around the last few handfuls of times she'd visited. Out of the three, it was hardest to convince Knox to give me space, but he'd eventually had no choice when Declan forcefully dragged him away. Knox had been ready to fight, but one look at me and he sighed, going along with Declan.

"Get dressed, Lily." Lore placed a set of clothing near my bed and bent, pressing his lips to my forehead.

I groaned, pushing myself up.

"Where are we going?" I asked, tugging the sweater and sweats on. If I was to go off the clothing, it was outside.

"On a little walk."

My brows furrowed, and I shrugged, figuring I'd see soon enough. The steps creaked as we descended and I pressed my palm to my mouth to cover the yawn.

I was still half asleep, so I appreciated Lore's palm at my back, guiding me forward. I sniffed as we exited the manor. It was super weird exiting through the front door.

Cool air brushed my face, ruffling my hair, and I brushed it behind my ears.

The gravel crunched under our feet as we walked down the path through the entire town. Lore had some street lamps installed to illuminate the small town, but they were dimmed since it was past ten.

We passed a woman and her son near the schoolhouse, and I instinctively dipped my head, making the hair fall forward over my scar.

"Alpha," she murmured, hurrying her son past. Since I was staring at the ground, all I heard was the quickening of her steps. Lore captured my hand, squeezing it tightly.

I hadn't interacted with the pack since I'd arrived, considering I was in mourning and sequestered to the manor. I wasn't sure how I should feel about them. There were a lot of differing and conflicting emotions.

We'd passed every home in the pack and still, we were

continuing. I frowned. There wasn't much more left to see except for the cemetery. I hadn't visited in years, even when I was here, because I was too busy.

Lore guided me through a small path in the woods and shoved overgrown branches out of my way, pulling me forward to the sprawling clearing stretching miles long. If I focused, I could get a vague sense of heat at the bites on my thigh and the other side of my neck. We were nearing Knox and Declan.

Grave plates glinted from the moonlight and I turned toward the repetitive scrape and hiss that filled my ears. It was a shovel digging into the dirt.

My throat tightened as he lead me toward the flat stone where my mom's plate was. Knox and Declan were almost done digging the hole a few feet to the side of it. The top of their heads bobbed over the lip. Lore guided me closer, and I peeked in and found them dirt-covered and breathing hard.

They were diligently at work, so they didn't look up. A beat later Knox inhaled deeply and his head whipped up, eyes directly on mine.

I tried smiling, but it wobbled. Declan was watching me from the corner of his eye as he kept digging, a serious expression on his face.

I knelt at the side of the wooden coffin and placed my palm against it. There were engraved elegant flowers lining the side of it.

"Did you make this?" I met Declan's eyes, but he faded in my sight, blurring under tears so I was hardly able to see his nod.

He was great at craftsmanship. He loved making furniture in his off times, which he didn't have much of. He must have hurried to make this for Randy.

My throat was uncomfortably tight. "Thank you," I managed to choke out.

The harsh line of his lips softened. Declan and Knox pushed out of the grave and I inched back to give them room to grip the ropes looped beneath the coffin.

"Are you ready?" Declan asked me as they waited.

I tipped my chin down sharply, and they gave each other the signal, lifting simultaneously to inch the coffin over the hole. Lore's hands smoothed down my arms, and I leaned against him as Randy was lowered gently.

Knox strode over to me and lifted a shovel, tilting his head questioningly.

"She should—" Lore started, but he was cut off when my fingers wrapped around the handle. I joined Declan and Knox in shoving the dirt, dropping it into the hole, and covering my friend up little by little.

Tears streamed down my face silently as I worked and heaved, but nothing was said as we continued.

I'd found strength in my mates and in the memory of Randy. She wouldn't want me to be curled in the bed in her name. She would have smacked me to the moon if I'd dared. My arms were shaking halfway to the hole being full, but I didn't stop. Thick arms wrapped around me, setting themselves over mine, helping me shovel.

I panted within Lore's embrace as we finished. The dirt grains settled and all I could hear was my ragged breathing.

The weight on my shoulders loosened, and I exhaled hard, shuddering.

"They're installing the engraved plate tomorrow."

I nodded jerkily and pressed my lips to Lore's arm before extricating myself from his grip.

I crouched in front of mom's plot and traced her name with my fingertips.

Thanks, mom, now I understand how much you sacrificed. The crescent necklace was all I'd had of hers, but maybe it was best that it had been lost in the fire. There had always been negative thoughts attached to it, but now, I could truly admire the memory of my mom without negativity.

Puffing my cheeks out, I stood and started walking back to the manor.

At the threshold of the neighborhood where all the houses began, I mustered the energy to verbalize something I'd been meaning to tell Lore. It was best I spit it out now when no one was around.

"I want you to speak to Janice's mate. Before I left two years ago, he was beating her."

Both of Lore's eyebrows lifted. It might have seemed out of left field to him, but not me. Randy was my closest friend, right beside Janice. Before, I was in as much a bad position as Janice, if not worse. Now that I could somehow help, I wasn't standing by as she was hurt even though she said he wasn't hitting her ever since Lore went bonkers at my 'death'.

According to Janice, he was too overworked and tired to do anything after all the hunting, but who was to say he wouldn't hurt her now that Lore was better?

"Little One, I don't get involved in personal relationships. Especially if I'm not approached by one of the parties beforehand."

I narrowed my eyes and crossed my arms.

"That's not right. Someone in your pack is getting abused, and it's your job to maintain the safety of everyone."

I licked my lips. I could have nodded and accepted his

response, but Randy was right. I kept everything too close to the chest and always thought to deal with things myself. A second plan bloomed. I could ask Knox or Declan to get a hold of Janice's mate, but I needed Lore to understand that I wasn't going to keep it to myself. He would have pushback from me.

"She's right." Knox slid his arms around my shoulders.

Lore snorted.

"Ass kisser," Declan muttered, stabbing the shovel he carried into the ground.

"I-I will not be some figurehead, Lore. I will listen to you, but I expect the same. I can't be steamrolled if I am your partner. If you can't accept that, then we may not be fit as mates—"

He growled, cutting my words off.

"Don't threaten me with leaving me, ever again."

My mouth tightened, and my face heated at the order. I shuffled from foot to foot. I needed to keep going while I was on a roll.

I fisted my hands and tilted my chin up.

Lore scrubbed the back of his neck and smoothed his blond hair at the front, where it spiked.

"I see this is important to you. I will make sure to discuss his behavior with him."

My mouth snapped shut, and I exhaled, relieved.

"Thank you."

Lore smiled and stepped forward, gripping my chin hard. My eyes widened, and I stared into his nearing blue eyes as he claimed my mouth. My hands fluttered at his wide shoulders as butterflies erupted in my belly.

LIANA

"You feeling any better?" Janice crossed her arms. I nodded, a small smile spreading on my lips as I smoothed the tape on top of the cardboard box, sealing one of Lore's less attractive bed sheets. I didn't understand his need for dark colors. Fortunately for him, he'd told me I could decorate his room however I wanted. Honestly, I wasn't sure if he understood fully what that meant, but he was going to learn. A small, evil smile spread across my lips.

After standing up to him yesterday, I felt tons better doing what I wanted, and this new bedroom scheme was just the first of many.

"I've never seen that smile on your lips." Janice's voice held a level of laughter and I wrinkled my nose at her. "Do you want me to help you bring your bedsheets to the new room?"

I hated admitting it, but I didn't bring her into my bedroom because I hated her scent mingling with my mates'. It was stupid and illogical because I knew she wasn't like that. Even so, that was why we were currently in the room Lore had given me when I first arrived. *That* room. After I'd left, Lore ordered Janice to make it into storage, which meant she'd spent a lot of time shifting everything around.

"No, thank you," I responded, face warming. She smiled knowingly and giggled.

"I can't imagine having three mates, Liliana." She shook her head, a grin on her face.

I pressed my lips together. "It's great."

She squealed, laughing. "I never thought you'd be so dirty."

"By the way, thanks for getting me the birth control," I murmured low, peeking over my shoulder at the door. I wasn't sure how the guys would react especially after going on and on about stuffing me with their cum, but I wasn't arguing with them about it. I didn't want children anytime soon, or maybe at all.

"Anytime. By the way, I heard they took you to the cemetery." I lifted an eyebrow. "Gossip spreads like wildfire here," she answered the question in my eyes. "You guys strutted down the main road. *You bet* everyone was watching you guys behind their curtains."

My eyebrows lifted, and I shook my head. "I'm asking him about my business plan today." I wanted to honor Randy's dream by helping Omegas. "Are you still willing to help me?"

She bobbed her head.

"I never know what will happen with Isac, so I want to be able to provide for Jamie if anything goes bad."

I pressed my lips together, and her eyes fixed over my shoulder.

"Lore will always help you if you don't want to be with him." I offered gently. "So, I hope in the future, you feel safe enough to tell me."

"If he hadn't stopped when you disappeared, and

everything went to crap here, then maybe I would leave him, but..." She licked her lips. "I want to give my son the best shot with his dad."

That was her choice, and I couldn't do anything about it. Life wasn't rainbows and sunshine, it was tough and decisions had to be made that some wouldn't like. I was leery about her decision to stay with Isac, but I respected it. That didn't mean I wouldn't be keeping a close eye on the guy. If he lifted a harsh hand toward her or Jamie ever again, I was sicing my mates on him.

"I'm not afraid of raising him alone, but since we've been together so long, I should give it one more shot." She tacked on nervously, wringing her hands.

I pressed my hands over hers.

"I understand."

A shaky smile tilted up the corner of her lips. My Lore senses tingled. And by that, I meant my neck mark.

"Mate," Lore called, heavy steps nearing.

"That's my cue. See you later."

She rushed out of the room as Lore rounded the door, and she quickly tilted her head. Lore's eyes were set on mine and his lips spread into a smile.

Lore pulled me into his embrace, leaning down to set his chin on my head.

"You finally get everything out of the room?" I hummed my affirmative, nuzzling my nose into his shirt. "Have you ordered all the furniture you wanted?"

"Yes," I mumbled, lips pressed to the material at his chest.

"Good," he rumbled. Pulling me back by the shoulder, he looked around the room, lips turned down. "If you want, we can demolish the house and you can design it however you want."

My brow furrowed. "There's no need for that."

"Are you sure? The memories won't make you keep a part of you from me?" Anxiety seeped through his tone. He cupped my face and stared into my eyes.

Pressure made my nose hurt.

Sighing, he pressed his forehead into mine. "I regret all of my decisions involving how I treated you." He paused, words rough. "I fucking hate myself for it."

I blinked at his closed eyelids, fixating on his long blond lashes cresting his cheeks. His lids fluttered open and his eyes glinted with unshed tears.

I frowned, holding his eyes with ease. Fear flashed through them and his finger twitched on my face and I sank into him.

"No, it won't, Lore. You have all of me." He exhaled, his body shuddering. My chest ballooned with happiness and love and I rubbed my cheek on his chest.

"Er, I have a question," I started and pulled away. "Can I go get my stuff at the apartment?" I licked my lips, looking at my toes.

Lore tipped my chin up, and a purr started up. My eyes widened as the vibrations reached my body, relaxing my shoulders.

It was no fair—Knox told them about my weakness.

"Don't fear asking me anything, Little One. Everything will always be what you want in some way or another."

"It's a habit."

"Well, break the habit," he ordered in a playful growl, digging his fingers into my ribs. I snorted out a laugh, wiggling against him as he tickled me.

I wrapped my fingers around his forearms, forcing his grip away. Pushing to my toes, I smiled wide. "Help me, please?"

"Hm, I don't know. I don't think you're putting much enthusiasm into your request."

I growled, narrowing my eyes at him. Realizing my aggression, I sucked in a breath and tensed, but he smiled down at me. Lore swept me close to him and he purred again, forcing me to relax.

I moaned against him, blissful. Now that they knew about my weakness, I didn't doubt they'd exploit it.

Knox walked in and I rounded in Lore's arms and poked a finger at him. "You traitor!" I glared. "You told them about the purring."

He smirked unrepentantly.

"The delivery arrived, Lore."

I turned to Lore questioningly, but he gripped my shoulders and forced me out the door, guiding me downstairs.

Knox pulled the front door open and grinned at me. What were they up to?

Lore brought me to a stop in front of a light pink mini cooper.

"What...?"

"It's yours." The proud way he announced it forced me back a step. Mine? "Look in the back seat."

I mechanically opened it and released a squeal as I hopped on the balls of my feet. The box was packed with my stuff.

"You're happier about a pile of blankets?" He growled playfully.

I threw my arms around him. "Thank you."

"There's more in the trunk."

I couldn't help the excitement bubbling through me, or the

grin widening my mouth. Knox popped the trunk, and I gawked at the slim boxes. There were piles upon piles of heels neatly and compactly organized to save space. The name brands glinted off them.

"There are more that will be delivered." I gawked up at Lore.

"When we were at the store... how did you know I liked heels?"

"I paid attention to everything in your apartment." I turned to Knox. "Everything *I* ordered you will come in a week."

"I wasn't sure. It was a guess at the store when I saw the ones you were wearing and the ones you left here, but thank you for confirming it. Now I get to spoil you." I whipped back toward Lore.

"Do you like the car? I chose the color," Knox murmured near my ear. He moved fast.

"And I chose the model." Declan stepped up to where we were.

"We'll move all your stuff inside." Declan and Lore lifted boxes and started moving.

"One rule, you have to make sure one of us is with you at all times and you have to take that scent thing." His lip curled in a sneer. "Before you go out."

I gawked at the car and then at him. He was being serious.

Tears filled my eyes, as Lore stepped into my space, swiping them away with his thumbs. "Don't cry, Little One, you destroy me."

I swayed forward and pressed my cheek against his chest.

There was a gasp, and I whirled to see a pack member stumble as they watched us. I ducked my head, barely noticing the handful of people walking around.

"Don't hide your beautiful face," Lore murmured, kissing my ear, and then smacked my butt before leaning into the car to pull a box into his grip. "No helping, you just sit. I don't want you getting hurt," he said when I reached for another box.

I rolled my eyes and hugged it to my chest. He growled, dogging me as we made our way upstairs to the bedroom.

As soon as we strode into the room, I tipped the contents of my box onto the mattress.

Two of my smaller blankets rolled out, and I picked my way through the other boxes, tossing more blankets on the bed. I worked on folding them and organizing them by size as all of my boxes were brought in.

"Knox wasn't lying. You *really* love the pastel colors," Declan said, eyebrows lifted. "Blankets are practically all you own."

My face warmed.

"I couldn't afford much," I admitted, clearing my throat.

Declan's face became stricken, and he tugged me to his chest. "I'm sorry, Lily. That was stupid of me."

I giggled into his chest. "I'm not trying to make you pity me."

His chest rumbled with his laugh.

"I don't, but I hate thinking of you out there alone and fending for yourself." He shivered.

"It wasn't bad, plus I had Randy, so I wouldn't trade it for anything."

Declan sighed, pressing another kiss to my head.

"I'm going to finish bringing in those shoes of yours."

He left, and I sank onto the end of the bed, lifting my blankets to my nose and humming in pleasure. The room had to be perfect before my next heat. I had certain particularities when I was nesting, and what happened last time with the half-made nest couldn't happen again.

Lore shouldered through, crouching to drop the shoes.

"I want to try using my Omega Call."

Lore paused at the threshold. "No."

That was a swift response. I scowled, recognizing the stubborn turn of his mouth. He wasn't going to let me anytime soon. *If he knew about it.* I hid my smile.

Lore stepped over to me, looking down at me. I had to crane my head to look him in the eyes.

"We purchased a home in Mexico."

My eyes widened. I'd always wanted to go to Mexico. How had he known? My nose stung and a smile spread over my lips, hurting my cheeks. "Do you want to move there?"

I blinked and opened my mouth then closed it as I wrapped my head around the question.

"You want me to leave?"

"What! No." He knelt and even then I had to inch my head up to keep his eyes. His hands flattened near my thighs. "I wanted to know if you want to leave. Here. Declan, Knox, and I spoke about your comfort and history in this pack. If you want to leave, we will leave with you."

I kind of liked hearing that they were getting along. It was touch and go with their interactions, but I knew I had to take a step back and let them figure themselves out.

"But what would happen to the pack?"

"Lincoln would take over as Alpha."

I was speechless, utterly taken aback. It took me a few tries, but I eventually got the words out. "You're offering to leave your pride and joy?"

Lore squeezed my thigh. "You're my pride and joy. Nothing else matters as much as you."

My eyes flicked to the side before I forced myself to look him straight into his blue eyes. "Is it because you don't want me to be a weak Luna?"

His brows rose sharply.

"I didn't even think you may take it that way." He shook his head hard and my fingers curled into the sheets so I could stop myself from burying them in his soft hair. "No, if you want to stay, we will stay."

I licked my lips, staring at Lore's lap. Mexico had always been a far-off dream of mine. I'd wanted to visit, but never had the means, so I'd stuffed it away. My mom used to tell me stories of our culture and how she and dad met over there. I'd always wanted the connection.

"We should stay. I don't want them to lose an amazing Alpha, but... the Mexico home...," I muttered, eyes flashing up to his with a small smile. "Can we keep it? Like as a vacation home or something."

A throaty laugh exploded out of him. "Of course."

"Sir." I jumped at the sudden intrusion.

Lincoln's scent filled the space, and I sneezed, not liking it mingling with everything

Lore snarled, and Lincoln's eyes widened. I pressed my hand to the small of his back and he froze.

"I'll mention it later." Lincoln swallowed audibly and backed up, eyes fixed on the ground.

As soon as he was gone, Lore relaxed and pulled me to his chest.

"We'll stay, but I'm getting another house built for us with no memories attached. That way I can offer this house to the un-mated wolves. I don't want their scent anywhere with yours." Lore paused and looked down at me. "What do you think?"

I hummed and softened against him.

"That's a great idea."

"Since you want to stay, you're going to have to take responsibility as Luna."

I pressed my lips together, and I nodded against his sternum. I wasn't wimping out of that. He was putting it in my hands, trusting me. I wouldn't let him down.

"What if someone challenges me?"

"No one would dare, Lily," Declan said, entering the room.

"But you can't stop someone from an outside pack challenging me."

"Trust us to protect you," Lore murmured.

I exhaled hard.

"Okay."

There were different types of strong, not just physical, and I would prove that to my pack mates and my mates. I would provide and offer every other type of support, so what if I couldn't beat someone up? That wasn't really my jam, anyway.

"I have a business idea." My gaze bounced off every one of my guys. "If I work on figuring out Randy's scent suppressant droplets, will you help me get a product out?"

I didn't have to verbalize why I wanted it, they seemed to understand already. There *had* to be more Omegas out there, hiding or sequestered. If it was happening here with *one* pack, I had no doubt there were circumstances similar in other places. I wanted to help them in as small a way as I could and thanks to Randy's family formula I would.

"I'll help however you need, Little One."

Liana

I wrung my hands as Declan smoothed his palm down my back.

"Are you sure she'd be okay with meeting me?"

"Yes, Lily." He was verging on sounding exasperated, but I couldn't bring myself to care. I'd never met Declan's mom, sure I'd seen her around, but more often than not she'd been bedridden while I was here.

"You said she liked Clara."

Declan pressed his lips together. "If you don't want to meet her, you don't have to."

I puffed my cheeks out at his offer and flicked my eyes toward the door and back to his earnest brown eyes.

"No, I want to meet your mom." I tipped my chin up, determined. It was possible she wouldn't like me since she'd had a soft spot for Clara, but I had to meet the woman that meant so much to Declan.

The door was opened by a woman and she smiled at Declan, eyes practically glowing with happiness. My stomach soured, and I shuffled from foot to foot.

"Lou," he said lightly, happy to see her.

"Finally, you have time to come see us."

I didn't like the look in her eyes. I pressed closer to Declan, and he curled his arm tightly around me. She poked his shoulder, and he huffed, frowning.

A growl rumbled from my throat, and I didn't bite it back. Her eyes met mine, and I held hers. I'd seen her around. She had pale hair that fell down her back in waves and blue sparkling eyes. She was incredibly gorgeous and seemed nice. Her eyes dropped, settling on my lips.

"Sorry, Liliana, right?"

I said nothing and kept staring her down. My face was hot, and it was taking a bit of effort to not hide behind my hair. "She's so serious. Cute too." Declan growled at her and she tossed her head back, laughing.

"I'm more interested in a different type," she winked at me. She could be interested in whatever she preferred. I just didn't like her staring at my mate *like that*. She reached toward my shoulder but stopped short when she looked at Declan's face. "Nevvvver mind. See you around, Luna."

She inched past Declan's side, still laughing under her breath.

"She takes care of my mom."

My lips rounded in an O as heat flushed down my neck. Now that she was gone, my jealous reaction seemed a bit overboard.

"Sorry." I cleared my throat.

Declan chuckled, and his fingers at my waist tightened. "I love your possessiveness."

He guided me into the house and shut the door behind us.

We strode through a hallway and it led us out into the living room where his mom was reclined on a couch.

"Declan," she said, voice rough. Her eyes flicked to me and her smile widened.

"Mom." He moved to her and pressed a kiss to her weathered cheek. I awkwardly moved forward.

"Hello—"

"Liliana, it's so nice to meet you, *mija*. Take a seat." I blinked hard at the endearment. I hadn't heard that since my mom died. Warmth bloomed in my chest and I sucked oxygen into my lungs, trying to get a handle on my heightened emotions. She patted the spot next to her, and I dropped down gently beside her on the bed, making sure that I carefully avoided both her oxygen tank and the hose leading to her nose.

"I had Lou pull out the albums to show you some baby pictures of Declan."

"Mom," Declan growled, playfully.

She grinned up at him and patted the stack at her side. "I should have gotten rid of those," he groaned as his phone rang and he shut it off.

"I don't know—"

It went off again, and he sighed.

"Go answer it." Declan frowned. "I won't scare your mate," she tacked on exasperated.

His eyes narrowed at me, and I nodded, shooing him away. Turning on his heels, he disappeared around the hallway.

"I know he's nervous about leaving me alone with you, but he's being dramatic," she said. "He thinks I'm blind to everything just because I have a weak heart and lungs."

My teeth sank into my lower lip. "He's worried you're upset about Clara being gone," I admitted, ripping the bandage off. I didn't want to be on edge or dance around the topic. I left it at that. For one, Declan told me he didn't tell her about Clara's death, and I was keeping that tight to my chest.

Her eyes leveled on mine. "The girl was as sick as I was, but in a different way. In a worse way, I think." She shook her head. "I'd thought he'd loved her, so I accepted her outbursts, but the girl wasn't the kindest."

I frowned. "But I thought you were close to her?"

"We were, but as years passed, her temper peeked out increasingly. I didn't want to worry him, so I never mentioned it, but I should have. Then maybe he would have admitted to me that he didn't want to be in the relationship." She sighed. "He's always been a serious boy, Liliana, but I'd never seen him how he was these last three years. Even before that, he was apathetic, but when he thought you died, he was devastated. I know that if I wasn't around for him to take care of, he would have joined the Moon Goddess."

My eyes widened, and my hands fisted on my legs. "Then he got it in his head that you were alive and he was frantic with the need to find you. He told me about you, you know."

"He did? How?" My brows furrowed.

"Even before you knew you were mates, he mentioned you to me. He said you seemed sad. It was just a slip of a comment, but I should have known then. He never concerns himself with other people's emotions. After he thought you were alive, he told me everything else he'd noticed about you. Talking about you seemed to calm him." Her hand shook as she held it out. I quickly set mine in hers and gently squeezed it. "Either way, it feels like I finally have my son back after more than a decade. You bring him happiness."

Tears sheened my eyes, and I blinked quickly

"Now." She cleared her throat. "Let me show you his baby pictures. He was such a scowly little bundle. I have a few of the Alpha too," she whispered the last part, and I grinned.

They'd be pissed that I snuck out of the manor without them, but they were crazy if they thought I wouldn't try to do more now that I'd decided to stay. After Lore's reaction to my question, I knew I'd have to try it without them.

I'd begged Knox to drive into the closest town to get me ice cream and Declan? I'd asked him to build me a rocking chair in my bedroom.

Lore was in his office, getting a rundown from Lincoln about everything he missed for his business, so he wasn't going to be seeking me out any time soon. The perk was that I'd sense them if they came near, and if that happened, I'd take off and hide.

I made sure the door clicked quietly as I inched out of the manor.

Janice already found someone I could try my Omega Call on and if she'd done as we'd planned, she had him at her house right now.

I was there within moments because I was rushing. Time was of the essence after all.

A group of about eight stood in front of her house.

"She doesn't know what she's doing—"

"You're making everyone hopeful for nothing—"

I cleared my throat, lifting my chin.

"Liliana." Janice gripped my arm, pulling me forward and in front of a guy. I'd seen him around. He was shy and tended to keep to himself. "This is Archie. He was supposed to shift a year ago."

A small smile tilted the corner of my mouth and I inched my head forward on instinct, hiding my scar.

Archie inclined his head. No better time than the present to get started.

I licked my lips and looked into his eyes. The muttering around me intensified and the hair on my arms lifted.

I felt too closed in.

"Can I get some space?"

"Back up, you're crowding her!" Janice shouted.

"What's the point of this? She can't do this," a sharp tone exclaimed.

The buzz faded, and I focused on Archie's brown eyes. There was a pinprick in his eyes. So tiny, I could hardly see it. As soon as I focused on it, there was a tug on my gut.

Evening my breathing, I imagined yanking, and it was like unraveling yarn. I jerked so hard that my body twitched and I heaved, my hold on the string slipping. His hands gripped my arms to stop me from collapsing, and the connection heightened. I managed a better grip and pulled it with both hands. Archie's fingers dug into my arms and he gasped, head tipping back.

We both dropped to our knees, but I caught hold of his arms when his fingers went limp. I tugged the rest of the yarn until there was nothing else to pull, forcing the last knot past a tiny hole.

Archie suddenly convulsed, bones snapping. His body undulated, and fur erupted from his skin as his body reshaped itself.

I panted as a gray wolf writhed in front of me.

I did that. *I did.*

How could Omegas be hunted to extinction when they could do this? I'd been so fearful of trying for no reason. I was made for this. It was instinctual.

I blinked the tears from my eyes and lifted my head. The group of people stared down at me, eyes wide.

My face heated and the blush spread across my face at the attention. My body was sore and too warm, like an engine that had run for too long. Exhaustion made my movements sluggish, and I shook my head.

"My son, he's shifted," a woman cried, hands to her mouth. She rushed forward, gripping my shoulders. "Thank you, Luna."

She stood and tittered around her son as he wobbled to his feet. In a few steps, he was rubbing up against me, sniffing my neck. His cold nose huffed against my throat and he whined.

Uh oh. If he kept rubbing up on me, the guys were gonna have a fit.

"You're welcome." I patted his flank and inched back, mustering the strength to stand.

A hand gripped my arm, helping me up. I looked over at the man I was leaning against, his eyes were dilated as he stared at me.

"You smell good."

My eyes widened when one of the bites on my neck prickled. Oh… shit.

"Liliana."

The roar shook me to my bones, and I jerked away and scooted back a few steps. Janice saw my expression and she stepped in front of the man, creating another layer for Declan to have to go through. Fortunately, he was far away enough that it gave me a second to *think*.

My new car screeched and dust flew up as the wheels spun. Knox looked pretty funny shoving his big body out of my car.

Declan and now Knox were barreling in my direction, eyes tracking the pack mates I was with.

I nibbled on my lower lip. There was only one way I could distract the single-minded determination to commit the violence in their eyes.

I took off in a sprint, directly toward them. The ground spun, and I shook my head, but it was too late. My toe smashed into a pothole.

This was going to hurt. Putting my arm up to catch my fall, I skidded a few feet before coming to a stop. I groaned and spat dust from my mouth.

"Liliana," Declan shouted.

He was suddenly kneeling at my side, hands trembling as he ran them over my body. Knox clasped my face, and I peeked from the corner of my eyes as Janice shooed off the males that had rubbed against me.

"Why do you smell like others?" His canine fangs sprang out as the shift pulled at him. I balled the front of his shirt in my fist.

Gravel crunched as someone else ran in my direction.

I knew exactly who it was. I squeezed my lids tightly. My embarrassment was complete.

"Alpha, she's a miracle—"

"Alpha—she's done—"

Each and every compliment heated my face. I appreciated the kind words, but at the same time; I didn't. These were the same people that overlooked my presence. Only a handful of the pack were ever outwardly cruel to me, but I faded into the background for all the others.

Declan tugged me up to lean against his chest. "We can't leave you alone for one second," he snapped and inhaled sharply, rubbing his face against my neck.

"I'm fine," I muttered, disgruntled.

"I don't know who you smell like, but now I need to feed my dick into you and rub my cum all over your body."

Knox growled in agreement, grappling to gain control.

"Or I can just kill whoever it is," Knox added.

I bit his chin, and he growled.

"We will discuss later," Lore shouted and everyone quieted.

A throb started at my pussy and I pushed off Declan, pressing a palm to both their shoulders as I jumped to my feet.

"You guys will have to catch me first," I said throatily, taking off at a sprint, high-tailing it out of there.

Unlike earlier, I was more steady and with my wolf so close to the surface, I was able to navigate the woods easier.

The baying behind me spurred me on faster, and I grinned as I let my wolf take over my body.

They kept behind me, letting me take the lead as I ran.

My wolf pushed forward, and I sat back, letting her take the reins as she played and mated with her loves.

LIANA

RESTLESS ENERGY PRICKLED THROUGH ME, AND MY grip on Knox's arm tightened.

"We can leave if you want, Lily." Declan rubbed my other arm, squeezing my shoulder. "You have nothing to prove."

"I want to." I flattened my lips at my forceful tone. Lore sighed and pushed through the entrance. They'd already tried talking me out of it. Cajoling me, using sex, bargaining, but I didn't give in.

Chattering and laughing washed over me and the door swung shut. Glasses clinked and conversation flowed as Lore moved forward. My nose twitched from the alcohol permeating the air. Lore wove to the side between closely placed occupied tables. I trailed after him, releasing Knox's arm so I could squeeze between the sections. Inching around a barstool, it was a tight fit, so I accidentally grazed against the person seated there.

He turned too fast and tipped forward. I pressed my palms to his shoulders to keep him from falling on me.

His lips parted, and he inhaled deeply, glazed eyes fluttering.

Declan shoved him back.

"Sorry," he rasped, putting his hands up and scrambling back. "She smells good." His throat bobbed. The guy seemed innocent, and the embarrassed flush told me everything I needed to know. I clasped Declan's hand and tugged at him. It took a few tries, but he eventually followed, stiffly.

Fortunately, it was only him I had to drag away since Knox was busy studying the exits.

Lore led us to the corner closest the entrance and I was relieved that we didn't have to cross through the entire place, since the hair on the back of my neck lifted from scrutiny. The rounded booth was cushy, and I bounced on the surface as Declan settled next to me. I was corralled between Lore and him. Knox perched on the other side of Declan; legs wide as he balanced on the ledge.

We were drawing more attention. Heat flushed my face, and I automatically tilted my head forward so my hair fell across the side of my scar. It was a good thing their nearness warmed me. I focused on the heat radiating from the claiming bites and a blissful smile tipped up the corner of my lips.

An older waitress brought over a plate with appetizers. My stomach rumbled at the greasy scent. I swept my gaze across the room and settled on Brenda. Her mouth was open, and her gaze was attached to me. My hand flattened on Lore's thigh as my stomach dropped.

I hadn't wanted to see her ever again. My insecurities roared forward and my mouth dried up. *Don't panic, Liana.*

Lore's shoulders tightened and a firm frown tilted his lips down.

"I feel like I'm missing something," Knox murmured to

Declan. The rest of their conversation faded as I watched her pick her way around the tables, hips swaying.

Brenda pressed her palms to the table, leaning over so her breasts jutted out. I gritted my teeth.

"Leave." The snap in Lore's tone seethed with aggression.

Her nostrils flared and confusion flickered over her expression when she noted Lore's fingers digging into my shoulder. Awareness finally flicked over her expression. So late that it was embarrassing. Her gaze dropped to my throat where the mating bites hinted over the collar of my top. Was it that crazy for Lore to be mine?

An old man at the table to the side of us gasped.

"Omega," he rasped. The younger woman with him gripped his arm. "That's what you are. I've been wracking my brain since your scent filled my nose."

All three of my males narrowed their eyes. They weren't about to go all cave-wolf on an older man, were they? I nudged my knees into the two mates surrounding me. Declan huffed and crossed his arms, but Lore remained eerily still.

"A what?" Brenda sneered. "This girl is a weak human. No cause for concern."

"Have some respect." The feeble voice snapped harshly, and his bushy white brows lowered over milky eyes.

She sneered at the old man.

"She's not someone worthy of my respect." I dropped my gaze to the plate in front of me as humiliation flooded me.

Knox shoved to his feet, a growl rumbling from his chest. He was the one with the shortest temper, and that was saying something since they were all quick to bite. Lore and Declan became scarily still. They were about to pounce.

"What the fuck are you looking at?" she snapped at Knox.

A hot flush spread across my body, aggressive and blazing. I gritted my molars and fisted my hands.

Her words when I'd met her played in my memory. The rudeness. The haughtiness.

I gripped the plate as she scoffed, and she was evidently done with me as she turned her attention to Lore.

My lips tightened, and I tipped the plate of food over. It spilled onto the tabletop.

I didn't want to shame Lore. He hadn't wanted a weak mate. Yes, he told me that no longer mattered to him, but it mattered to me. I would show them there were more ways than just the physical of being strong, and this... this *bitch* right here wouldn't speak to my mate as if she could easily take him in front of me. Nor would she be rude to Knox.

I flattened my heel against the table and kicked against the bottom. Fortunately, it wasn't bolted to the ground or that would have been embarrassing as all hell. It skidded to the side, clattering. Silence fell over the bar as I popped onto my feet and swung the plate across Brenda's temple. Blood spurted across my arm as the plate shattered. She staggered as her eyes rolled to the back of her head. The thump of her body falling didn't sound pleasant.

Still, nothing was said, and the only noise was my panting breaths. I took in the mess I'd made and blushed.

I dipped to grip the end of the table I'd kicked and lifted it. Why weren't my mates helping me? I grunted, pulling it up, and when I brought my attention to them, I noted why. They gawked at me from their seats. A matching set of shock in the set of their brows. They'd also exploded into their wolfman forms.

Knox's ears teased the ceiling of the bar. He raked his claws through my hair as I neared him, his nose prodding my cheek. I bit my lip to hide my smile. It felt good standing up for myself. I'd never had the guts to do it in such an overt way, like I had today, and it was thrilling.

I cleared my throat and reclaimed my place beside Declan and Lore, which was now a much tighter fit. Blond and black fur tickled my skin.

"You didn't have to do that," Lore growled, licking the gash on my forehead. His long tongue lashed across half my face. His chest rumbled, the noise vibrating through me. I winced and bit back a whimper as he cleaned the stinging area. I'd felt the bit of plate slicing across my forehead when I'd slammed it across her, but it was easy to ignore.

A clearing throat dragged me out of the pleasure of him licking my face. I liked that way too much.

A large man watched us. His expression was tight and wary. My gaze skipped over him to the werewolves seated around the establishment. The music was a low hum, but other than that you could hear a pin drop. The expressions ranged in levels of terror, though some stared fascinatedly between my wolfmen and me.

"I apologize for my cousin."

I smiled slightly, but said nothing as he addressed Lore. Lore's muzzle lifted in answer, teeth slightly showing.

"Word spread that you have an Omega mate, and I see that's true." His tongue wetted his lower lip. "I'm the Silverback Pack Alpha," he stated directly to me, dipping his head. The respectful move made me automatically like him.

"Don't look at her," Knox growled, and the Alpha's lips thinned but he returned his gaze to Lore.

"Would you be willing to have her visit my pack to see defective—"

"Later," he retorted in his deep, monstrous growl, cutting the man off.

I buried my elbow into Lore's side, and he clicked his teeth near my cheek, but I pressed a kiss to his wet nose. Lore huffed in my face.

"It may be better if you bring your wolves to Lore's—our pack —then that may work better for now, but he'll reach out with a plan," I said, stifling a grin. The Silverback Pack Alpha inclined his head again, not looking at me.

"I'll keep in touch." The man's cheeks flushed, and I followed his gaze. I was so used to their naked forms that it hadn't struck me as weird, but everyone could see their cocks. Mostly Knox's since he was standing.

"You're naked," I whisper shouted, face flushed. He looked down at his hard cock and shrugged.

I rubbed my forehead. "I don't want anyone to see you."

The words ripped out of me. His head tipped to the side, ears twitching. He chuffed and shifted fully into a wolf.

My shoulders only slightly relaxed. Declan and Lore were covered by the lip of the table at least.

Lore leaned back and slipped his hand onto my thigh, his claws extended further than the width of my leg.

"Don't deserve you." His rumbling words wreaked havoc on my insides. "Go?"

"In a bit," I replied. I wanted the attention to get away from us for a second.

I dragged my fingers through the fur at Lore's thigh.
Thump.
I tugged the fur lightly.

Thump. Thump.

I lifted my gaze to Lore's wide ones. His *tail* was wagging. I pressed my lips together tightly.

Would Declan...?

I reached up, dragging my fingers at his neck. Declan groaned, tipping his head to the side. I stifled a giggle and pushed onto the seat so I could reach Declan's ears. The fur-tipped ears flicked as I rubbed behind them. He groaned and his leg twitched. As soon as I lifted my hands, he straightened, some sort of snarl on his lips. I was pretty sure that was a grimace.

Turning to Lore, I stretched to reach up and tugged at his ears. He grumbled, but it turned to a groan as I dug my digits into the tuffs below his ears. Lore was the shaggiest, so I had to burrow my fingers deep.

Thump. Thump. Thump.

The quick rhythm bounced against the cushion of the seat. He straightened and gripped his tail, stopping the wag.

"Not now, Little One," he rumbled gruffly, yet forcefully. I smirked at the disgruntlement in his eyes.

"I'm ready to go," I whispered, a low throb starting at my clit. Declan pulled me into his arms, hoisting me into their cradle.

Lore burst into his wolf form. Patrons scooted away from him so fast that they fell out of their seats.

Declan strode through the path Lore carved. Fresh air filled my nose. It was nice and breezy out. I cuddled into Declan's fur with a moan of happiness as he made his way to the truck parked in a private spot next to the bar.

"You like teasing us, Lily girl?" he rumbled, pressing me into the hood of the truck, hiking me higher onto the cool metal. He dipped low, nuzzling his snout beneath the hem of the dress. The wet nose felt cool, and I squealed, trying to back away, but his grip didn't let me. This must have been why he'd forced me to come without panties. His whole spiel about the panty line showing through the material must have been a load of crap.

"Declan," I moaned his name and reached up, raking my nails beneath his ears. His maw opened, and his top teeth grazed my mound. I sucked in a breath at the sharp fangs near my sensitive area.

His teeth rasped over the skin, and my legs trembled. He pressed his nose into my heat and purred. My body released tension, and I went lax. His tongue flicked out, lightly lapping my clit. The purring combined with the licking was shooting off every pleasure sensor I had. His purr kept me calm and lax while the tonguing put me on edge. Since the reactions were at different spectrums, it was short circuiting my thoughts.

"I'm almost there," I whimpered.

He growled, and it vibrated against my clit, and I cried out, thrusting against his muzzle. Just as my orgasm was about to hit, he pulled back, setting his snout on my mound. I panted as the peak slipped from my grip. Huffing, I glared at Declan.

"No fair, Declan!"

He lifted off me, and I gaped at him. Was he laughing at me right now?

The truck roared to life and Declan gripped my ass, dragging me close.

I shoved his shoulder, but he let out some cough-sounding chuff. He was definitely laughing at me. Lore was in the driver's seat, hunched into himself so he could fit with his massive body.

It was a good thing his truck was a beast. He shook his head as the fur receded and he morphed back into his human form.

My ass landed on the back seat and Knox squeezed past Declan and jumped in. Declan shook his head and went to the passenger's side. Knox's wolf body crowded me, and then his shoulders popped as he expanded until he was his wolfman form. It was a tight fit. I curved closer to the edge of the seats, since he could barely fit. His head bowed and the fur at his neck flattened on the car ceiling.

Knox forced me on my back and tipped my legs up so my knees rested against his furry chest. He pressed his palm to my spine to offer support. My dress slid down my thighs, baring me to my stomach. His head nuzzled into my heat, the fur of his face tickling slightly. I groaned as he prodded my entrance.

I was still wet and hot from Declan's ministration. My core clenched needily from the lack of relief. I wanted to come.

"Don't give it to her, Knox," Declan growled.

Knox thrust his tongue deep into my pussy in answer. My channel clutched him needily, and I arched as he lapped at the clit.

"Don't listen to him," I practically hissed, gripping the fur hard as my muscles tensed. I keened—reaching...

Knox pulled back.

Dammit! My body slumped—a panting, sweaty mess.

"I'll get you guys back." I threatened and cried out at the loss of another release. Evil, cruel, monsters.

Liana

Undoing all the folded blankets I'd pulled out of the closet, I piled them onto the huge mattress with a grin on my lips. This was my favorite part of every night.

I fell into my bed face first, nestling into the thick, soft pile of blankets.

The door creaked as I rubbed my cheek into the faux pink fur.

"Little One." There was a clatter. "Here. I have something for you."

I pushed up on the mattress and curved my legs under my butt. I zeroed in on the teacup in Lore's hand. It looked so tiny in his hold and it seemed like with one pinch it would shatter.

"Your friend told me when she got shot to make sure you always had your nightly tea." A huge knot appeared in my throat, making it difficult to swallow. "I was waiting for you to feel better."

My hand trembled when I lifted my hands. He set the small plate in my palm. I tipped it into my mouth and sipped. Honey and chamomile exploded on my tongue, heat blooming through my chest and belly. I squeezed my eyes, and a tear escaped.

I held it out for him to take, and he set it on the nightstand. Dashing my tears away, I sucked in a lungful of oxygen and flopped on my back, a smile lifting my lips.

Randy's memory filled me like tea. A warm, comforting hug that spread through my chest.

"This is how I like seeing you."

I lifted my head, eyebrow raised.

"Happy."

"Me too," I responded, sighing. The bed creaked as Lore climbed onto the mattress and hovered over me.

"I love you." My lips parted, and I blinked up at him. "I'm sorry for all the suffering I've put you through."

I lifted my hand, pressing it against his cheek, and he turned and kissed the inside of my wrists.

The door slammed against the wall.

"I'm not going to have my own bedroom," Knox snapped. "I want my stuff around hers, smelling like her. How are both of you okay with having a separate room?"

"We're thinking of *her* comfort. She's going to want to have her own space—"

"I don't want to hear it, Declan." Knox turned his attention to me, crawling up the bed to where I was. "You don't want me to be all sad and alone, do you, baby?"

His eyes widened, lips pursing.

A smile tugged at my lips, and I shook my head.

"If you ever need space like—" he sneered at Lore. "These two say, I'll give you your space."

Lore sighed and fell to the side, lying next to me and resting his head on his fist.

"We're going to fill this room with stuff for her. She's not going to have room for our stuff. And if my stuff can't be with hers, none of either of yours can either. It's only fair," Lore said.

"We're building a home for her. When I design the structure, we'll make a closet big enough for all four of our stuff. Easy as that."

My brows lifted. Knox was into architecture? That was news to me. I blinked. I would be learning much more about all of them. Everything I knew of them, I already adored, but the little moments in their life that I missed?

I couldn't wait to learn everything.

"That doesn't sound like a bad idea," Declan interjected, leaning against the wall with his arms crossed. Knox's hands burrowed under the blanket at my side and he frowned, pulling out a rattling object.

Shoot, shoot. Moon Goddess no! I forgot I'd left them in there after taking it this morning.

He lifted the bottle to his eyes and his nose flared as he sat on his haunches.

"What are they?" He squinted, reading as my heart fluttered like hummingbird wings. "Birth control."

"I'm not ready for kids." I scooted back until my back hit the headboard.

"What?" Lore growled, stilling so quickly that my heart froze. We'd been so good and I didn't want to fight with him. I licked my lips.

"I'm not willing to negotiate. I won't apologize for my decision, but if you can't accept me because of it, I-I understand, Lore—"

"Don't take him seriously, Lily," Declan called out. "He's

messing with you. None of us want to share you with anyone. Even our children."

Lore grinned, and I narrowed my eyes at him. I snatched a pillow up and smacked him across the face.

"Why are you always trying to leave me?" he muttered disgruntled.

"Because you make her feel the most insecure in your relationship." My eyes lifted to Declan at his observation. I hadn't even realized I was doing that, but... it was true.

Lore lifted off his lulling position and hovered over my face. "You're a fixture in my life, Liliana. Without you, I don't care what happens to anyone or anything. I'll make sure all your insecurities disappear soon enough."

I nodded frantically.

"You know it's whatever you want, baby." Knox grinned wide. "But I'm going to keep filling you with my cum like I'm breeding you."

I pressed my hands to my hot face and slumped into the pillows.

"Speaking of cum. I want yours all over me again," Knox shivered, a growl roughening his voice.

My face was scorching at this point. I still couldn't believe I'd come so hard I'd squirted. I blamed it on my heat and nothing more. But dear Moon Goddess, the way they fucked me was so good. I shivered, a throb starting at my pussy.

"Knox!" I yanked a pillow over my face.

"It was hot as fuck, baby."

Hands gripped my hips. I grunted when my back flattened on the mattress.

Lore gripped one of my wrists, and Declan gripped the

other. The pillow fell from my grip. Panting, I looked up at the ceiling and tugged at their hold.

"What are you guys doing?"

My heart thundered as they stretched me out, Knox pinning my hips. Lore's big rough hand slid under my shirt, pressing over my breast.

It was a good thing I liked being braless when I was in the house. He lifted the shirt more until my breasts were exposed. My chest heaved as he slowly leaned down and spread his lips over my brown nipple.

I bit back a whimper and wiggled at the tickle at my thighs. I peeked down as Knox's head tipped down, hovering so close to my throbbing clit that his hair fluttered over my thighs.

Declan captured my lips, sucking my tongue into his mouth. I groaned as he thrust his tongue into my mouth, switching the sensation.

"I want to touch you," I murmured against his mouth.

"No."

I pulled back, squeezing my eyes at the overload of sensation.

Lore nibbled my nipple and then smoothed his tongue over it to soothe it while Knox finally pressed his mouth to my clit, sucking it hard.

"I'm close," I whispered huskily.

At my words, Knox pulled back, gently trailing his lips over my wet folds, not applying pressure.

"Knox," I moaned. Not the teasing again. When they last did this, I was a puddle of need, begging for them. Fortunately, Knox had given in before I'd gone mad.

Knox pressed down on my clit again, licking and tonguing.

My toes curled, and I pushed up against his mouth.

Almost there…

Knox pulled back, grinning up at me, lips wet with my slick.

I whimpered and tried kicking out at him, but his hold didn't loosen. His grin widened and fur sprouted from his face, seeping out on the rest of his body as his face became wolfish in his transformation to the beast. His gray ears flicked, and his purple eyes glinted with his laughter.

"Stop messing with me," I whimpered.

My nipples were hyper-sensitive from Lore and Declan playing with them.

I turned my head to Lore. "Make me cum."

He grinned, head dipping back to cover the tip of my breast.

My teeth clenched tightly, and I tried Declan but had as much success there as I did with the other two. Just as I thought. Declan seemed to particularly enjoy keeping me on edge.

By the eighth time they'd brought me to the edge, tears leaked out of my eyes.

Knox nipped my sensitive flesh and my back bowed off the bed, a wave crashing into my body and dragging me under. My ears rang and my lids fluttered as my eyes rolled to the back of my head.

Each spark behind my eyelids was a jerk through my body. I came to with my toes curled, panting so raggedly my throat hurt.

Knox's fur was drenched and glistening, his wolfish grin, toothy.

"That was so fucking hot." Declan released my arm and palmed the ridge of his cock jutting against me. He growled. I struggled to catch my breath as fur tickled my skin. Declan and Lore had shifted at some point while I'd come.

Lore nipped my ear and licked the shell, then his raspy tongue dipped into my mouth. I moaned, licking him back.

I tugged at their hold, but none of them budged.

"We're not done with you," Lore rumbled in my ear as Declan switched positions with Knox.

Knox buried his head into my neck, sucking and nibbling at the flesh. Declan's head dipped, and he swirled his tongue around my clit, dipping down and burying it into me. My pussy clenched around his tongue.

They were going to make me pass out.

A smile tilted the corner of my mouth. That didn't sound too bad. And I knew, without a doubt, they'd be there to catch me. Forever.

☾

ACKNOWLEDGMENTS

I was in urgent search of a beta reader and Rachel James came through for me. Her feedback was everything I needed. Thank you, Rachel. Nicole and CE Kingsley, thanks for listening to my rambles, reading my blurbs, and just always being willing to listen, I appreciate you guys. Gina Cortez thank you for brainstorming with me, and for being so damn patient with explaining writing stuff to me. You are an indispensable friend.

Thank you to literally every single Advanced Copy reader. You guys were so amazing, I wish I could meet you all just to give you a hug. There were *so* many people that gave me wonderful feedback and I am just so very thankful.

Araceli a.k.a Chely, I'm so glad I got you into monster smut. I finally have someone I know IRL to fan girl over it. Marissa, I appreciate you more than I can express and I send you nothing but positive, happy vibes. Claud, thank you for listening to my obsession with monster... stuff. Aaron, thank you for putting up with my book obsessions.

Gracias a mis papas y a mi familia.

About the Author

Allie obsessively reads books featuring sexy, possessive heroes and headstrong heroines. So, it's no wonder characters just like that bustle to escape her imagination.

When she's not working away at her keyboard, she can be found in bed with a good book or bingeing Netflix.